To Ha

I give that you fall in ~~love~~
I did. Thanks.
Breanna [signature]

I'll Always Be With You

I'll Always Be With You

A NOVEL

BRIANNA MITCHELL

A Division of WINEPRESS PUBLISHING

© 2007 by Brianna Mitchell. All rights reserved.

Pleasant Word (a division of WinePress Publishing, PO Box 428, Enumclaw, WA 98022) functions only as book publisher. As such, the ultimate design, content, editorial accuracy, and views expressed or implied in this work are those of the author.

No part of this publication may be reproduced, stored in a retrieval system or transmitted in any way by any means—electronic, mechanical, photocopy, recording or otherwise—without the prior permission of the copyright holder, except as provided by USA copyright law.

Unless otherwise noted, all Scriptures are taken from the Holy Bible, New International Version, Copyright © 1973, 1978, 1984 by the International Bible Society. Used by permission of Zondervan Publishing House. The "NIV" and "New International Version" trademarks are registered in the United States Patent and Trademark Office by International Bible Society.

Scripture references marked KJV are taken from the King James Version of the Bible.

Scripture references marked NASB are taken from the New American Standard Bible, © 1960, 1963, 1968, 1971, 1972, 1973, 1975, 1977 by The Lockman Foundation. Used by permission.

ISBN 1-4141-0796-X
Library of Congress Catalog Card Number: 2006907386

Dedication

*To Tessie: Thanks to you,
I found out my writing
was good enough for others' ears.*

Table of Contents

Prologue..ix

Chapter One 17
Chapter Two 26
Chapter Three 37
Chapter Four...46
Chapter Five..54
Chapter Six 62
Chapter Seven 71
Chapter Eight 81
Chapter Nine 93
Chapter Ten 104
Chapter Eleven..114
Chapter Twelve 126
Chapter Thirteen...135
Chapter Fourteen 145
Chapter Fifteen 160

Chapter Sixteen	171
Chapter Seventeen	185
Chapter Eighteen	196
Chapter Nineteen	206
Chapter Twenty	226
Chapter Twenty-One	249
Chapter Twenty-Two	260
Chapter Twenty-Three	274
Chapter Twenty-Four	290
Chapter Twenty-Five	295
Chapter Twenty-Six	308
Chapter Twenty-Seven	322
Chapter Twenty-Eight	336
Chapter Twenty-Nine	349
Chapter Thirty	362
Chapter Thirty-One	374

Prologue

In my life I've learned many things. I have learned that if you fight for what you want, anything is possible. My life has taught me that things can get hard, but you still have to find the good in it. I know that no matter how you feel, there is always someone who will listen to you, even when it seems they are gone. I learned all of this because of what I went through as a child and what I overcame. I will not tell you this for pity. I do not need it and do not want it. Anyone can do whatever they set their mind to if they are willing to work for it.

To explain what I mean, I'll have to start from the beginning—before I was even born—when my family's problem began.

My family was blamed for betraying our dear Frindeline to Lanski generations before I was born. That's when it all started. To this day, giving valuable information over to the enemy is considered one of the worst crimes you can commit. We were in the middle of a war. No one remembers why anymore; it was much too long ago.

Somehow, Lanski knew our every maneuver. The only answer was betrayal, for that was the only way they could have received the information. These messages were the reason for Frindeline's loss.

When King Jasper found out what had taken place, he was furious. Through his various networks he found his suspects: Count Stuart McCarthy and Duke Fredrick Jonestone. Both seemed to be the most unlikely people to have committed such a crime. These two men were the two most trusted and closest lords to the king. It was common knowledge that Count McCarthy did many things behind His Majesty's back, not that it could be proven. It was also known that these two men despised each other.

It so happened that my ancestor, Fredrick Jonestone's son, was betrothed to Her Highness, Princess Gittel of Frindeline. This arrangement was made when Duke Jonestone saved the king's life a few days after his daughter was born. The king's wife had no say in the man's prize and wanted her daughter to be married to a prince. She greatly disapproved of the arrangement. It was known by even the common folk that she would do almost anything to stop the betrothal from becoming a reality.

The queen's solution to the problem was that if no evidence could be found or nothing could be proven, the blame would simply fall to the Jonestones and the betrothal would be no more. From what I have heard, she persuaded the men who were searching not to look too carefully; she even paid them a little extra in secret, just to make sure. After months of searching and finding no evidence, the king went along with his wife's idea. How could he not? His people wanted justice and were becoming restless. So, he took away Duke Jonestone's land and everything he owned, stripped from him his knightship, and made him a servant, assigning him and his family to another family to work under. A decree went out to the people saying not to trust the Jonestones, and that my family was no good, and the princess's betrothal no longer existed.

No one would ever have the idea of going against his king. Those who thought King Jasper must be wrong kept it to themselves and joined in happily in the jeering and name calling. All the people in Drell, the capital of Frindeline, tried to stay away from my family, for they had gone from the top to the bottom. The only way out was for the Jonestones to prove they did not commit the crime they were accused of.

Time went by and many people tried to free my family. Three generations before I was born, Lynton Jonestone tried to prove the family's innocence, but the McCarthys interfered. My great-grandfather tried also, but once again the McCarthys stopped Great Grandpa by threatening to send his children to work in Hopeville, halfway across the country.

People in the towns in which the Jonestones worked soon forgot what they had done. Even more wondered why that family seemed to get assigned a home to work in, instead of applying, as most people did. No one cared or really wanted to know the reason for this peculiarity.

I'm sure all Jonestones felt trapped, just as I did growing up.

No one took the time those days to sort out other people's problems. They had bigger issues to worry about. Lanski was not happy with their king and was in the middle of a civil war when I was growing up. The king of Lanski was a weak-minded man and didn't have the mental ability to take care of a kingdom. He made one mistake after another, and this pushed Lanski into civil war. It ended finally when he was advised to do as the people asked. This king had a son who was only about four years older than me, named Yasir. He was too much like his father. But where his father would admit his shortcomings, Yasir never would. When his parents realized this, they betrothed him to a countess who came from a very prominent family. This girl was clever and understood politics to their fullest. Yasir's mother hoped that both of these things would rub off on her son.

When my father was born, my family was still guilty according to the law, so when my father turned five, he went to work for the Somners. At first he was excited;

his older siblings seemed to like it. This all changed, however, when he entered the house full of girls ranging in age from four to thirteen.

Annette, the eldest, didn't bother him much; she practically ignored him, thinking that thirteen was much too old to be associating with servants. Susan, Elizabeth, and Samantha were usually doing their own things or with Annette somewhere, which always seemed to be where he wasn't. That left only Grace, who was five and a half, and Rosemarie, four. They drove my papa, John, mad.

For John, it seemed normal to be ignored by the older four sisters and be bothered by the younger two. This was more than normal, and he simply just got used to it.

One day about ten years later, Grace and Rosemarie simply stopped following and bothering Papa while he worked. He wasn't sure why, but he missed that they weren't there to follow him. The more he thought about it, the more he realized it wasn't Grace he missed, but Rose.

The more he thought of this, the more he found himself trying to bump into Rose or watch her when he needed to trim the hedges. At first he didn't realize why, but after awhile he knew it was because he felt he needed to be around her all the time. Papa found himself thinking of her constantly. When he realized he loved her, he didn't know what to do.

XIV I'll Always Be With You

"Grace, Rose, I know you like to follow that John around, but it has to stop. You're now fifteen and fourteen years old. I'm sorry, but that is too old for two young ladies to be following a young servant boy around." Their mother's lips became thin as she informed them of the news.

"But, Mother, it doesn't do any harm. All we do is tease him. Please, tell me what trouble can come of that?" Rose pleaded with her mother.

"Rose, you know Mother is right. It is quite unseemly to go around practically flirting with a servant." Grace spoke great reason, and Rose knew it was true.

Rose knew exactly why she wanted to follow John Jonestone around; she also knew it was forbidden.

One day Rosemarie noticed something. John was staring at her from the other side of the courtyard. The way he looked at her made her tingle. Rose no longer cared what she was supposed to do, but she did know what she wanted. Rose wanted to talk to John, and she did.

"Hi," was the first thing to come out of her mouth.

"He—Hello, Miss…Somner," John stammered. He had never been more nervous, and he continued to try to say something as he inched closer and closer until their lips touched, but then he drew back quickly.

"Sorry, Miss. I didn't mean…"

She silenced him quickly. "Really, John, it's all right. Please call me Rose."

That was the end of it; they were never apart. Both of them knew they were in love. Even if Lord Somner would allow it, it was against the law for them to ever wed.

A few years passed, and John desperately wanted to marry Rose, who was now eighteen.

"My Lordship, I hope this doesn't come as a shock, but your daughter Rose and I would like to marry—only if you'd allow it, of course. Although there is one problem, my family…" Papa started to explain to Mama's father.

"I knew this question would someday come. I have known you loved my daughter for some time, so I've looked at your family's record and the punishment. John, I give you permission take Rose to Dimple, Aldreen. I have a house there. Stay in Dimple for six months, and then come back to Drell and free your family of this mess."

They left and were married on April 12, 1121. They stayed in Dimple much longer than planned, because they had a daughter ten months after being married. On February 19, 1122, Amythist Amelia Grace Jonestone was born. I have always hated the timing of my birth. If only I had been born a year or two later, all would have been well.

Chapter One

The beginning was probably the least worrisome part of my life. I had both parents and no idea of the situation I was born into. The earliest I can remember is my third birthday; it was a peaceful day, warm for the middle of February, and quite bright.

"Mama, Papa, hurry up! My birthday lunch will be cold soon," I yelled. I laughed as my father smiled and tickled me.

I have my father's smile, or so my parents told me. I also seemed to inherit his eyes, skin, ears, and build, and for the longest time I thought myself his girl version. Most people seemed to think I had my mother's beauty. I certainly didn't see it and find myself looking for it to this day. I could tell from a young age that my nose was neither of theirs, but a mixture. My mother had the most beautiful blonde, curly hair, and my father had untidy, very dark, straight hair. I ended up with brown, wavy hair, much to my displeasure.

Mama also laughed as she watched me try to squirm from my papa's tickling grasps. It was a blissful day that we all enjoyed in the fields of Aldreen.

To this day, I can remember my mother and how she looked. Even at that young age I wished I was as pretty as my mother, Rose. I envied her so much, from her perfect nose, which wasn't too pointy or too blunt, to her blue eyes. She had gorgeous blonde hair that curled all the way down to her waist. Most of the time these curls were kept in a tight bun, but birthdays were special. She'd let her hair down, allowing the wind to carry it wherever it wished. Mama had the sweetest smile anyone could ever see. It made me think of all things little girls held dear. Most importantly, when my mama smiled I knew I was, and always would be, loved.

As perfect as that might seem, I still had questions. All my friends seemed to have aunts and uncles, grandmas, grandpas, and cousins. I wanted that more than anything else. I wanted to be able to say, "I'm going to see Grandma today," just as my friends did. I talked to my parents often about this.

Every time I asked, they looked at me with sad eyes and said something like, "Amy, someday you'll see them. I promise." Never saying when or how. I could tell they hated to talk about it. They never told me why we lived in Aldreen; it was almost as if they didn't want me to know.

That night I fell asleep listening to my mother's angelic voice as she sang to me. Once I appeared too tired to listen any longer, she would kiss me on the forehead as she got up to leave the room. Just as she closed the door, I heard the slight whisper of, "Good night, precious."

My parents paid lots of attention to me, and it might have been because I was their world. They told me stories about my aunts and uncles. Like most boys and girls, though, my favorite was the story of the maiden. No matter what the story, however, I listened contentedly, usually wanting more.

Papa played many instruments, but the only one I could listen to without covering my ears was the flute. My papa tried so hard to play the piano, but it was awful. His violin was much too scratchy, and if you could believe it, his harp playing was loud. The strange thing was, he knew all the notes; he just didn't play them correctly. No matter what he played, I would laugh, and he'd stop to see what was so funny.

I know this sounds perfect, but I still felt as if I were missing something. I wanted my relatives. *If only I could meet them*, was the thought that started everything. Then it turned into, *if only I could live in the same neighborhood*, and my obsession seemed to get worse.

At four, I didn't quite understand what Aldreen was. I didn't realize how far away Frindeline actually was, either. You see, I couldn't imagine anywhere so far away that it could take weeks to get there. Not understanding made me wish what I thought would solve all my problems. "I wish I lived near my family, so I could know them," was my wish one night as I looked at the stars.

My life went on normally after that—until the middle of June, when the Aldreenian captain from Dimple came to the Somner mansion and asked to speak to John.

"Hello, I'm Captain Montour, and we recently discovered that Lord Paul Somner promised to give back this house about two months ago. We need you out by July fifteenth, or we'll force you out." The captain frowned, shook, turned, and left.

My parents had no chance to complain or say a single word to the captain. They just stood there, jaws wide opened.

After that, my parents weren't the same. My mama cried and wrote letters to an assortment of people. Papa was angry and frustrated at all hours of the day. They both seemed to avoid looking at me, as if ashamed. They were very distant. I didn't understand what was going on.

Everything had changed in a matter of minutes. I'd never seen my parents so flustered and out of control. It seemed that they had completely forgotten about me, their every thought and moment, their Amykins, their daughter and only child. I remember feeling unwanted.

A few weeks went by, and we still lived in my grandfather's mansion. In fact, my parents didn't plan on leaving. They had written to my grandfather, Paul Somner, who told them to stay as long as their food would allow, while he negotiated for a longer contract that would allow us to stay a few months more.

King Basil told my grandfather flatly, "No," so my parents tried to hold onto it for as long as possible.

On July 10, the captain returned to the mansion to remind my parents that they had five days to leave.

"Once again, I'm sorry to disturb you, Mr. Jonestone, but we are curious to know when you plan on leaving, since you need to be out in five days' time." The captain seemed sorry, but then again, I was four. Maybe he wasn't.

"Well, Captain, my wife and I have decided not to go anywhere. We have our reasons, and if you knew our situation, you wouldn't leave, either." Papa hugged Mama. She smiled at him proudly.

"Well, sir, I certainly don't know your situation, but isn't this a bit unreasonable?" The captain looked at my parents as if they were insane. Just then, I decided to step in front of my mother, and Papa picked me up.

"You see, Captain, if we were to leave, it would make things difficult for us," my papa told the man. I began to giggle and squirm as he tickled me.

"Mrs. Jonestone, your daughter is what...four? I'm sure she won't even remember the place." The captain seemed very confused, and since it seemed as if my father knew nothing, he turned toward my mother. She didn't reassure him any better than Papa had.

"Well, Captain," Mother said, looking very upset, "Something I think you don't understand is it wouldn't be just the move, but much more. Our daughter may never see her father again if we leave here. So, it wouldn't be awful only for her, but for me as well. I couldn't take it if Amy never knew her father or didn't see him again." She tried to make him understand, while suppressing the welling tears behind her eyes.

"Madame, I'm not sure I understand. I feel regretful about the whole thing, but I have no control over the situation. Duke Lintel told me that after a few years, Count Somner was supposed to give the—"

He was interrupted by Papa, who put me down. I ran and listened from the stairs. I hadn't understood a word they'd said, and I sensed they didn't want me to know, so I fled.

Shortly after that, Mama, Papa, and I were held prisoners in our own home. Finally, on August 10, Mama's birthday, Papa surrendered. It was the only thing he could do, I now realize. I used to find myself wishing he would do something so we could stay there just long enough that I could understand the situation I was born into. I didn't wish this then. I wanted him to surrender, and I wanted to move near those I'd dreamed of living close to. I knew this wasn't easy for Papa, I could tell; his hair was messier than usual. We began to run out of necessary items, and he had no choice but to surrender.

We left our home in Dimple, Aldreen, and headed for Drell, the capital of Frindeline. I couldn't have been happier. My dream was coming true—more than half my family was in Drell. We stopped in Hopeville on the way, just so I could meet my family who lived there, even though it was out of the way. Everything seemed perfect. The only thing I failed to realize was how much strain a little wish could cause.

I had so much to look forward to. We were going to live with my grandfather and grandmere. I had never met them before, but from what my parents had told me, they sounded wonderful.

In Hopeville, I met Grandma and Grandpa, who gave me cookies that tasted wonderful.

"Thank you," I told them politely, my lips covered with cookie crumbs.

"She's so sweet, John. You and Rose have done a wonderful job with little Amy!" my grandma, Margaret, told her son as she smiled Papa's corny smile.

"Thanks, Mama. We hoped we were doing a good job." Papa picked me up and sat me on his lap. Everyone in the room smiled.

"John, Amy looks exactly like you," Mama's older sister, Annette, said.

"I agree," Papa's brother, Matthew, added with a nod. Martha, his sister, just smiled in assent.

Grandpa was speechless. I found later that it was because he was in awe of me. I looked around the room as everyone smiled at me; I was unsure as to what I should do or what anyone would do if a room full of people were staring at you. I didn't think anyone would have known how to handle this, so I just continued to smile blankly and eat my cookies.

The journey seemed sad and endless. I was as happy as ever, but Mama and Papa seemed disappointed, as if they were walking straight into a trap. One day I decided I needed to know why.

"Papa, why is Mama so upset? Is Drell a scary place?" I stared at my father, more questions forming in my head.

"Well, Amykins, Drell isn't a scary place. Why?" He looked at me as if unnerved that at four I could come up with such a question.

"Because you and Mama have been sad the whole time, and we're moving closer to family. That's a good thing, right?" I wanted answers and I wanted them now. Papa didn't help much.

"It's not sad sweetheart…you'll understand when you're older." This was such an inadequate answer that I just couldn't respond.

Nothing seemed right. Mama was worried about something more than what my parents were telling me. I couldn't see how missing your old home could make you cry so much. It seemed like they were hiding something from me. Every time I asked a question, they brushed it off with something like, "When you're older…" as if I wasn't important or something. They never used to do that. Their lives didn't revolve around me anymore, but something else, and I couldn't figure out what.

After awhile, all I could think about was how much longer it would be until we arrived in Drell. I wanted to get there soon. Then, maybe Mama and Papa would once again notice me, instead of whatever they had on their minds.

Chapter Two

At the beginning of September, our very slow trip to Drell was almost over. The gates of Drell were finally in view. They were tall, black gates that made my heart fill with excitement. We were there!

As we drew closer to the gate, my father turned to my mother. "Rose, shouldn't Amy lie on the floor or something?" he asked, looking frightened.

"She probably should," she told my father and then turned to me. "Amy, honey, do as Papa said. Lie on the floor."

I obeyed without question, because that was what I had been taught to do, but my brain overflowed with thoughts. *Why do I have to do this? What is going on? How come they wouldn't tell me anything, and then expect me not to wonder why I was on the floor? They'll probably tell me I'll understand when I'm older.*

When we got to the gate, it was easy enough to get in. Papa just pretended to be Mama's guide, who used her maiden name. As little sense as this made, I kept my mouth shut. I now had the feeling that if I said even one word or breathed too deeply, my parents' plan would be ruined. I didn't know why they had to lie to the gatekeeper, but because they felt that way, they probably had a very reasonable explanation. Not that they would tell me, I'm sure.

Once inside Drell, I could sit up again. All I could do was stare at the scenery. I saw a wood not far off, and in the distance I saw a castle. Drell was beautiful, the grass was green, and the skies blue; it seemed peaceful over by the gate, and the roads seemed happy as people waved. I couldn't see why we hadn't moved here before. So far, I liked what I saw. My new home was absolutely breath-taking. The air smelled of honey and as the sun was setting, the sky filled with a pinkish tint that made me wonder why my parents ever left.

My little mouth opened wider than it had ever opened before as I took in all I saw and smelled. I was so amazed that I didn't pay attention to my parents' murmurs in the background. If only I had listened to that conversation, I wouldn't have speculated over many things that went through my mind during the first few months in Drell.

Finally, the carriage stopped in front of the biggest house I had ever seen. It was white and perfect. Not even the pickiest, most detailed person could have found anything wrong with the outside of the house. The garden roses, which grew under the windows, were perfectly groomed, and the lawn was clipped and very green. I was so caught up in the majesty before me that I didn't even realize we'd stopped.

"Ames, it's time to get out," Mama said excitedly and smiled. "Oh, it's so good to be home, John! I can't believe this!"

I looked at her in bewilderment. I had no idea how to respond. One minute she was crying with worry, and the next jumping for joy.

I became anxious as the front door opened; I couldn't wait to see what they looked liked. I had wished to live near them, and now I was finally going to see their faces.

An elderly man smiled as he introduced himself as my grandfather, and said I looked like my father before he picked me up.

When he let go of me, another man walked over and agreed with my grandfather.

"You're right—she does look like my older brother. It's uncanny the resemblance, really."

I had no clue who this man was, except he had just told me he was my uncle. Suddenly another man who looked just like the first walked over to us.

"Hello, I'm your Uncle Greg. I see you've already met your Uncle Ferdie."

Relief came over me. "Are you twins?" I asked, amazed. I'd never seen twins before.

"Yes," replied the first one.

"Amy, pumpkin, come here. I want you to meet some more of your aunts and uncles." Mama called me over and I skipped merrily in her direction.

"Sweetie, this is your Aunt Susan, Uncle Thomas, Aunt Elizabeth, Aunt Samantha, and Aunt Grace. I see you've already met your uncles, Greg and Ferdie." Mama smiled kindly at me as she introduced each person, who also smiled.

"Hi." I shrank back shyly.

This place was amazing! I wanted to explore and ask questions, which I did. I still had many questions that I didn't dare ask; for instance, why did Mama seem so happy but sad about living in Drell? If she really were upset about it, why? Drell seemed more than a nice enough place to live, or was it too good to be true? Was it really such a terrible place?

As I looked around the huge house, I noticed something: it seemed my cousins weren't around. I began searching the house for them, but it seemed to be an impossible task because the house appeared to grow, never staying the same length or size. I could have sworn that every time I reentered a hall, it grew a door and then a room beyond. This new home of mine was surprising, and I didn't understand why all the children were hiding from me. So, I continued to search until I ran into my uncles again.

"Oh, hello, Ames. What are you looking for?" They had found me in a chest. Well, half of me anyway.

"Well, Uncle Gre…Ferd…oh, I mean, how am I supposed to tell you two apart?" I complained as I studied them, looking from one set of green eyes to the next, from the small ears to the big ears.

"I know! You have smaller ears than him!" I yelled as I pointed to the uncle on the left.

"I do? I never knew that. You're very observant!" The one on the right laughed.

"All I need to do is have each of you tell me your name again so I can remember," I told them both, feeling quite proud that I could solve such a problem.

"Well, little missy, I'm Ferdinand," the big-eared one on the right told me.

"And I guess that means that I'm Gregory," the little-eared one added.

"Big ears, Uncle Ferdie; small ears Uncle Greg," I repeated over and over again as I left the room with the chest, which had nothing interesting in it but old, smelly clothes. My uncles stood there laughing, with the question they'd planned to ask me gone from their minds.

I finally found a room, which was full of pink blankets and had a dollhouse in the left corner opposite of the bed. My name was on the door: "Amythist."

This has to be my room, and all my cousins must be in there waiting for me, I thought as excitement mounted inside me. It was very disappointing when I opened the door to find a very comfortable room, with not a child to be seen. Now that I thought about it, even in Hopeville there didn't seem to be any children, and this bothered me. Maybe I was the only child in my family. Maybe Mama didn't want to move to Frindeline because children weren't allowed?

As I tried to process the meaning of this, I quickly climbed on my bed as tears tumbled down my cheeks. Nothing seemed fair; everyone seemed to be in on a secret, which they were deliberately keeping from me. All I wanted to do was scream, which was the only thing I felt I could do to show them all how frustrated I was. The only problem was that Mama disliked it and Papa detested it, but it didn't really matter. With a house this big, no one would hear me, anyway. So I screamed. I found that it didn't make me feel any better, so I cried.

All I wanted was children my age. Even ones that were older or younger, any form of a playmate would do. This didn't matter, though; they all had their secrets and didn't want me to know anything. I knew deep down that my parents must have had a reason—they always seemed to—but I didn't understand and didn't want to understand the reason behind the secrets.

After some time, I stopped crying, but I didn't want to face the world that was probably wondering where I was. I just sat there, staring at the ceiling. Someone knocked on the door.

"What do you want?" I yelled, made a pouty face, and crossed my arms, as the door slowly creaked opened.

"I heard you wanted to meet one of your cousins." Aunt Grace half whispered as she held a tiny bundle in her arms.

I looked at the woman I had only briefly met. Now that I really looked at my aunt, I noticed she, too, had beautiful curls like Mama, except hers were a very rich and comforting red color. Her eyes were different, but the rest of the resemblance was obvious. I smiled at her as she walked in with her nephew.

"Yes, I do, but what can I do with a baby?" I gave a longing look toward the toys. It really did make me happy to know that I actually had cousins, but this baby was too little to do anything but sleep.

"Oh, there are lots that babies like Teddy can do. He crawls, laughs, and likes to play peek-a-boo," my aunt said as she giggled, and the baby began to squirm. She looked around the room and sighed.

"This used to be my room, you know. I hope you like it." Aunt Grace smiled at me as she bounced my baby cousin on her knee.

After talking to my aunt, I was relieved. I knew that I had cousins and would meet them soon. Aunt Elizabeth was very kind and let me hold her son whenever I wanted, occasionally giving me help. I knew now that life couldn't be horrible; it just wasn't always what we hoped it would be.

I almost liked sitting in my room by myself better than when everyone was around smiling at me. In my room I could think, and that's exactly what I did. I thought about how everyone told me I'd meet my cousins soon, never telling me when or why they weren't here now. I was very confused, and none of it made any sense. Could they not leave their houses because Drell was a scary place? I couldn't get these thoughts out of my head; I was scared out of mind and I didn't even know why!

That whole day everyone talked about my cousins and wouldn't stop. They never showed me a portrait, though. I even looked through the house again to make sure that Teddy really was the only cousin present. I had to do something to get my mind off this. I decided to explore again because I knew there was no way I could have possibly seen it all.

I looked around everywhere I hadn't yet discovered. The house was massive. I found a small library, a study, something like servants' quarters, and stairs on the highest story. Confused, I ascended the stairs. They led to a two-room suite. It looked lovely. It was exactly what I had always wanted in a room. It looked as if it had once belonged to a girl my age, but it hadn't been used in years. There was a dust layer on everything. The dollhouse, the pink satin blankets on the bed, and the books on the perfectly organized shelf were all covered in layer upon layer of dust. This room hadn't been touched in years. It was, as Mama would say, "timeless." *If only it were cleaner*, I found myself thinking, *then I could stay up here until Mama and Papa found a place of our own.*

After staring for some time, I left looking for something better. That day I ventured into many rooms. Some were intriguing and others were dull. The most amazing room I found that day was one so high that it took a ladder to reach. This room was full of old toys and dresses. Some fit, but most were too small or too big; I had been trying them on and playing my four-year-old's games.

I didn't have the chance to look at everything, because the boxes in some places were piled too high for me to reach. I could have looked for weeks and never reopened a box.

I found a tall mirror and five boxes of Mama's and my aunt's old clothing. I even found a box from when Grandmere was a girl. I found a doll with brown curls and blues eyes in one of the boxes. This doll was beautiful and nicer than most dolls I had ever seen. I brought it downstairs with me so that I could show my findings to my relatives.

When I came back to where my family was sitting, Mama looked over and smiled.

"There you are. Where have you been? I was just about to come and find you." My mother was beautiful all the time, but when she smiled she had to be the most beautiful person ever to have walked on Delynelle.

"I was in the high room, full of boxes," I told her.

"You were in the attic, and I see you found Lyssi." My mama looked at the doll with longing in her eyes.

"She found Lyssi? That doll you carried everywhere when I first met you?" Papa's voice said as he looked at the doll. "Yeah, that's Lyssi." He laughed.

"This dolly was Mama's?" I asked as my face lit up.

Grandmere nodded.

"Really? Mama, this is a very pretty doll." I smiled the semi-sweet grin that both my parents loved.

So far, my day had been like a dream. I ran around the house without a care in the world...until I found the cellar.

"Aunt Samantha, where does that door go?" I asked curiously.

"Oh, you don't want to go down there. It's the cellar. A dark, damp place," my aunt replied, making it sound scary.

But this was me she was talking to. Did she really expect me to listen to something like that? As soon as I was sure that everyone's backs were turned, I opened the door. You couldn't tell me something was forbidden, not offer a punishment for going there, and then leave me alone with it. I looked inside, but all I could see were stairs upon stairs. It was dark, just as Aunt Samantha had said. There was a leak somewhere—I could hear the dripping noise. It was so quiet that I could hear spiders crawling on the floor. After that, I felt like screaming, but I was determined to go down there and come back alive. I wasn't sure if my ambition was possible; I knew a monster lived down there. This monster was probably a big, fat, black, hairy, smelly, people-eating thing with horns that he liked to pierce you with.

None of this could stop me, Amythist Amelia Grace Jonestone. No, I would kill the beast before it came into the house. I didn't know where the monster was in the cellar or how to kill it, but I had to do it. I started to descend slowly, when I slipped and fell a few steps. I almost screamed.

"I hope the monster didn't hear me." I started talking to myself, telling myself not to be scared and that nothing would happen to me. Then I went to the bottom.

"Now, to find the monster," I whispered, hoping he was lurking somewhere close. I began to search, but without a light, it was, much to my dismay, hopeless. All of a sudden, I tripped and something—*the monster*—was on top of me, and I couldn't get away.

"Help! Help! The monster! It's got me…*Ahhhhhh!*" I screamed, trying to get someone's attention. I wanted out but couldn't get away. When all seemed lost, someone picked me up.

"Let go of me!" I screamed.

Two of them—now I'll never get out of here!

"Amy, it's okay. I'm Uncle Greg. There are no monsters down here. You tripped and a couple of bags of flour and some corn fell on top of you. Look, you're covered in flour. Grandmere is going to need to clean those clothes," Uncle Greg said goofily.

"Oh, Uncle Greg," I said with a smile and a hug, "you saved me."

"Ames, it was nothing."

Chapter Three

I thought that living in Drell would be exciting. It was where all my family lived, but it wasn't what I expected. It had been three months since we moved into Grandfather's and Grandmere's house and I hadn't gone outside once, except on a small, round balcony. I was starting to forget what it was like to be outside for more than a few minutes.

Every day, my parents would leave, saying goodbye early in the morning and not returning till late at night. They were trying to find something or prove something, but I wasn't sure. I only knew what I overheard; they wouldn't tell me anything. If I asked, they would simply say, "You wouldn't understand. When you're older we'll tell you."

I didn't find this reason good enough. It made me feel left out; I'd never felt this way with my parents before. My parents were never home. I was left with

Grandmere or Aunt Grace most of the time. I played in the attic or listened to stories whenever someone was willing to tell them. In the attic I'd pretend I was a princess or a countess, while wearing old clothes I found. My mother was a countess, being the daughter of Count Paul Somner. I had no friends in Drell because I wasn't allowed outside the mansion. They would tell me it was too cold, but I was too smart for that; in Dimple I could play in the snow. It wasn't that cold.

While I felt imprisoned in my home, my aunts and uncles visited often, but they never brought their children. Some of them would tell me stories about my cousins. My favorite one was about my Aunt Elizabeth's daughters. Kyia used to run around in her older sister's clothes, pretending to be her. This made her older sister, Josephine, extremely mad. This story was funny if told correctly, which meant only Aunt Elizabeth could tell it. It was mostly amusing because Kyia didn't care what Josey did. After Josey yelled at Kyia, Kyia would only add more clothes to her ensemble or would imitate her yelling, making Josephine all the angrier. After every telling, I'd have a hard time breathing. In the end, my aunt had to tell Kyia that if she kept it, Uncle Daniel, her father, would spank her.

One time after my aunt told this very story to my mother, she commented on wishing she was there.

"I've got to go Beth, I'm meeting John. We have to keep searching." She sounded concerned, and I wondered what was so important to find.

"Now, you find that evidence, and soon. Poor Amythist can't live indoors all her life." There were most of the answers I needed. They were looking for some sort of evidence and not until they found it would I be allowed to go outside. That made so much more sense—much better than it's cold outside.

After everyone left, all I could think about was why everyone insisted on lying to me. Why wouldn't they just tell me what was going on? I might have been only four and a half, but I was going to figure out what was going on, and I would do it all by myself. Then, with hands on hips, I marched to my room.

The mansion was huge! It might as well have been a castle. I'd seen a glimpse of the Castle of Frindeline when we headed for Grandmere's and Grandfather's. If it wasn't for that, I would have assumed that this mansion was a castle. My bedroom was the smallest of them all, although it really wasn't that small compared to my room in Dimple. I walked into my room, sat on my bed, and contemplated everything that had happened that day.

I had overheard some information that I was sure must have been important. Aunt Elizabeth seemed to know what it was. This is so unfair! Everyone knew except me. It could be about me but they still wouldn't tell me. I might have been living in the biggest house imaginable, but I was a prisoner, trapped inside and allowed to know nothing. Finding all the information I felt entitled to know was going to take a lot of work. I knew it wasn't right to listen in on others' conversations, but if only I knew what was going on, then maybe I could help.

I was awake when Mama and Papa got home. Instead of immediately resorting to spy work, I decided to see if I could get Mama to simply tell me.

"Mama," I began as I walked into the kitchen.

"Yes, sweetheart," she replied as she eyed Grandmere. "Mother, why isn't Amy in bed? It's almost ten o'clock." My mama seemed upset.

"Rose, she wanted to see you. So I told her she could stay up until you got home," my grandmere told my mother.

Mama shook her head. "Mother, that could have been hours from now, you know." She seemed grateful, but frustrated.

"Rosemarie, you know she deserves to see her mama from time to time, just as you are allowed to see me. She misses you; I can see it in her eyes. Look at her, Rose, look," Grandmere told my mother sternly as tears tumbled down my face.

"Amy, I'm sorry. Grandmere is right. You do deserve to see me more often." My mother hugged me as she, too, became teary eyed. "I've missed you too, sweetheart." She picked me up and sat down.

"Anything you need?" she asked.

I nodded as I wiped away the tears. "Mama, I need to know why you and Papa are always gone and why I am not allowed outside," I said as tears welled in my eyes again and spilled all over Mama's dress.

"Amy, your father and I are trying to find something that will make our lives much easier. Until then, or when we feel you're ready to hear what's going on, trust your mama. I love you very much and don't want anything to happen to you. Remember, no matter what happens, I'll always be with you," she told me as she rocked me back and forth.

No matter what, whenever I really needed her, she would always be with me. As I sat there in her lap, she began to sing my favorite song, "Alleluia." With one verse I was fast asleep.

That night I had a dream, a dreadful dream. It started with me, but it wasn't me, all the same time. It was an older version of me and dressed differently than I thought I would. I was dirty—Mama would never allow that—and I was cleaning. I looked miserable. I was cleaning in a huge kitchen. My hair was pulled back into a bun, and I wiped my hands on a brown, shabby apron. Then, out of nowhere a voice repeated, *"Save your family, Amy. It's all up to you."*

As the voice continued, so did the dream. It showed me images of Mama and I visting Papa in prison. Mama yelling at Aunt Grace, "I'm never speaking to you again!" The last thing I saw was Mama getting sick. The voice disappeared and Mama was in bed as I hugged her and yelled, "Come back! Come back!"

I woke up and screamed; I had never dreamt anything worse than that. All I could think about was Mama dead, Papa in prison, and me saving my family. I had to make sure that none of that would ever happen.

Mama and Papa ran into the room. As I hugged my pillow, with my eyes shut tight, I chanted, "Save my family, save my family."

"Amykins, is everything all right?" came my father's concerned voice.

"Amy, what's wrong?" I heard my mother ask worriedly.

As I opened my eyes I yelled, "Mama you're still alive! Papa you're not in prison! I'm still little! Everything's all right!" I hugged them both. I was more excited than I had been in a long time. Everything was the way it was supposed to be. I couldn't have been happier.

"Pumpkin, what are you talking about?" Papa asked. "Why would I be in prison?" He seemed confused.

"Well," I began, "I had a dream—no, more like a nightmare. Everything was wrong. I was working in a kitchen with lots of other people. I was older, but I knew it was me. Mama and I went to visit you in prison, and everyone was dirty and scary. Mama, you got in a fight with Aunt Grace. You told her that you would never speak to her again." I paused before continuing. "Then, Mama was lying down on a bed with really thin blankets. I was sitting there, yelling 'Come back! Come back!' Mama, you died." I watched as my parents' eyes grew twice their normal size.

"Sweetie, that is a scary dream," my mother said as she checked my temperature and pulse.

"I'm not finished," I told them.

They looked at each other in horror. "What else, Amykins?" Papa asked, staring at me. He looked as if didn't know what to do.

"The whole time, there was this voice that kept saying, 'Save your family, Amy, it's all up to you,' over and over again," I explained to my parents, who both looked at me, their jaws touching the floor.

I waited for some explanation for why I would have such a dream. Neither of them seemed to know what to think or what to tell me; they both just glared at each other. Neither of them knew how to handle the situation.

"We might as well tell her. She's going to figure it out anyway, if she keeps having these dreams," Papa said to Mama.

"John, how do we even know this has anything to do with that?"

"Rose, it's obvious—'Save your family'—come on." He told her.

"Do you think all that will happen if we don't succeed?" Mama asked him.

"I don't know, but we should tell her."

"You're right, John. She has a right to know her family history, even if it's nothing to be proud of," she confirmed. "Well, sweetheart, a long time ago a man pretended that one of your ancestors betrayed the country, when he didn't. After that, he went very quickly from lord to servant. Frindeline hated all of the Jonestones. The only way to fix the problem is to prove that our family didn't do it," my mother explained.

"You see, servants aren't allowed to marry above their status. I'm a servant and your mother is a countess," papa said slowly, as if ashamed.

"But your grandfather let us get married, anyway. We went to live in Aldreen. While we tried to prove ourselves innocent, they made us move back, as you know," Mama said.

"And if we don't find the evidence, I will go to prison and you might end up working in a kitchen. I know it's been a hard three months here, but I promise that by Wintereve I'll have an appointment to free our family." He smiled his corny smile, the one that always made me feel better.

I said goodnight to both my parents. As they were leaving, I heard my mother say, "John, don't go making promises like that. Wintereve is in two weeks, and we don't have enough evidence yet." I could tell she was upset.

"Rose, don't worry about it," my papa told her. "I think I figured it out..." Their voices faded as they walked farther down the hall and into some other part of the house.

Now, for the most part, I understood everything: why Mama didn't want me to go outside and why she didn't want to leave Aldreen. I finally had enough questions answered that, for now, I didn't think any more needed to be asked.

As I thought about all this, I began to feel guilty and my stomach began to knot. I had wished to live near my family, and instead of being the great thing I had anticipated, it turned into an awful ordeal for everyone. I was glad that this would all be over in two weeks' time. All I could do was think about what it would be like to have my parents back. They'd have time for me again; I couldn't wait.

That night I slept cautiously and uneasily. It was almost like my subconscious mind was making sure I didn't have the dream again. I couldn't stand to see Mama die again. I woke up earlier than usual but tried to go back to sleep. I couldn't. I was scared that if I fell asleep, my dream would come true.

After lying awake for some time, Grandmere came up to my room, more excited than I'd ever thought possible.

"Your papa just needs to pick up a few things and make an appointment with the king! And then you'll be more than halfway to freedom!" She was crying as she picked me up and hugged me.

"Really, Grandmere?!"

A tear trickled down her cheek. *Everything will be fine; none of that nasty dream will come true.*

"Yes, Amy. Really."

Everyone in the house was excited that day. A new purpose, it seemed, had come about for continuing the day. Usually it was just to make it to tomorrow, but today our purpose was to make tomorrow a better day than today.

That day, everyone told me that very soon I would be able to go outside again; everything would go back to the way I used to know it. Grandmere must have been the happiest grandmother in all Delynelle. And right at that moment, I felt like the happiest daughter to set foot in all the lands. Little did I know that what happens in the past often affects what happens in the future, no matter how long we hide from it.

Chapter Four

A few weeks later, everyone at the Somner Mansion was getting ready for the arrival of Noah and Margaret Jonestone, my other grandparents. They were coming for Wintereve, only a few days away. I was also allowed to meet some of my cousins. It seemed that life was turning back around. I was more excited than I'd been since I'd figured out what was going on, since I knew that freedom wasn't far away. I couldn't wait to meet the gaggle of children that would soon enter the halls.

On the night everyone was to arrive, Grandfather, Grandmere, Papa, and I were all running around trying to make sure everything was ready for the feast. Mama kept trying to help, but every time she tried, Papa told her to relax, and she'd sit on the sofa and sip some tea. Lately, it seemed that this sort of thing happened a lot. I couldn't figure out why Papa was doing this, but I didn't ask any questions. I knew I'd know the truth eventually.

Grandfather was ordering a couple of servants, just as he always did, to clean things. Everything had to be perfect for the announcement of some important news.

"They think we know nothing!" one laundress began. "We're not stupid! We know somethin' queer is goin' about. An appointment of some kind, and I hop' it allows that precious chil' to go outside. She can get in the 'ay, you know."

I liked to tease this particular laundress. She always reacted in the strangest ways, and her accent didn't help her much. She smiled smugly and then pranced off to the laundry room.

My grandfather seemed nervous. It wasn't that he didn't believe in my father, but he had his doubts. No one could be sure that my father would pull it off. How could we? The king might have a completely different opinion on the evidence, or he could refuse to accept it. Either way it might not fix our problem at all; if anything, it might enhance it. Once my parents' secret was out, it would be either freedom or imprisonment. The king would find out about my mama and papa being married, and about me. This could lead to a forced separation for all eternity. In reality, there was a lot to worry about.

That night was wonderful. At dinner, Papa announced that he was going to see the king on my birthday, February 19. It wasn't this that bothered me—it was what came next.

"I'm doing it on this date so that I will always remember that I did this for my daughter, my wife, and the child Rose and I will have in the fall." My father looked so pleased with his announcement, but I felt like screaming.

Everyone clapped and looked at my mother. They were all smiling, as if this was a wonderful thing.

Even the idea of another child…? No! They can't do this to me! I wouldn't be Papa's only anymore, I'd be his eldest. How could they? This new baby would steal my father from me, and he might even forget I existed.

Everyone was so excited, and at first so was I. All my cousins were there. I didn't think a more perfect night could have ever been. For the first time in a long time, everyone I cared about or wished to meet was in my grasp. I could talk to people I'd only heard about in stories, but now I felt like nothing could ever be good again. No matter what, my life could never go back to the way it used to be, and this bothered me. I would have to share my parents. What if they never paid attention to their Amykins again? I didn't understand everything, because I still didn't understand how this could have happened—how a tiny baby could ruin everything.

I didn't know how to express my feelings. The only way I knew was to get up from the table and run. I would hide in the only place where I knew no one would look for me: the cellar. I no longer cared about the monster that lived down there or if it ate me. It might as well eat me; it would save the baby the job of getting rid of me.

"Why can't anything go my way anymore?!" I yelled across the table at my father as I stood up.

"Amy!" He looked at me sternly; he had just finished telling everyone about the baby.

"Papa, *go away!* I don't want to see you ever again!" I screamed as I ran out of the dining room.

I heard my father yell, "Amythist Amelia Grace Jonestone, what do you think you're doing?!" I could tell by the way he yelled that he was more concerned than angry, but at the same time was furious at the way I had acted.

"John, what's wrong? Is Amy all right?" my mother asked my father, as I lingered just close enough to hear the conversation. It sounded as if Mama thought my actions were my father's fault.

"Rose, I promise, I have no idea why she acted that way. I didn't say anything that would hurt her."

Some people laughed as Papa tried to defend himself. Grandmere laughed so hard and shrugged it off, saying it was natural for me to act that way. I decided I couldn't delay going to the cellar any longer, and left.

As I ran to the kitchen, I could hear everyone calling my name from different directions. I heard my father angrily calling my full name to make me come out. That in itself made me want to hide. I hated seeing him when he was mad at me, but he ruined everything. I couldn't go and see him. I hated him now…or I wanted to hate him.

I could hear Uncle Greg and Uncle Ferdie searching for me in the kitchen. I was scared out of mind to be in the cellar. They had saved me last time. They were the only ones who would look for me here, but I hoped they wouldn't. I wanted the monster to attack me, like it had the time before, so everyone could live happily without me. They definitely didn't need me. My parents had proved that. I had barely seen them at all in the three or four months I'd lived in Drell. To top it all off, they go and decide to have another baby to replace me. I didn't need to be here, and I hoped my twin uncles saw that and stayed clear of the cellar. I guess they had no intention of doing what I wished because the next thing I knew, the door at the top of the stairs creaked opened and light flooded the cellar.

"Go away!" I screamed. "I want to be left alone!"

"Amy, please let us come down," one of them called down into the cellar. I pouted and wiped the tears off my face as I thought about letting them come down.

"As long as it's just you two," I called back up.

"We promise it's just us," one of them reassured me as they walked down the steps with a lantern.

"Amy, why did you come down here in the first place?" big-eared Uncle Ferdie asked.

"Well," I started with a sniffle, "I didn't think anyone would look for me down here. Oh, and I wanted the monster to eat me, so that I wouldn't get in the baby's way. No one will like me when the baby comes. Uncle Ferdie, the baby will steal my papa, and I'll never get to be with him anymore. The baby won't share, and Mama and Papa will forget me." I began to cry. Uncle Greg picked me up and gave me a hug. In the dim light I could see Uncle Ferdie trying not to cry at the way I saw the situation.

"Ames, if we know our brother the way we think we do, there is no way he could ever forget you. You're his life. He'll make sure he finds time for you and the baby. Isn't that right, Greg?" He looked over at us with his green eyes full of meaning.

"Amy, Uncle Ferdie is right. Your papa will always have time for his Amykins."

I smiled at both my uncles, wiped away my tears, and hugged Uncle Greg all the harder.

They made me realize that the only person who could make my father ignore me was me. They were right—he would never forget me. Even if I chose to push him away, he would always love me, no matter what I did. I decided to go upstairs with my uncles.

As I was heading to find my cousins, I ran into my mother, who promptly asked worriedly, "Amythist, what on Delynelle happened in there? One minute you're the sweetest little girl, like you usually are, and then the next, you're yelling across the table and running off screaming. What's the matter?"

"Well," I started with a shrug and a crooked smile, "I thought the baby would take my place and you and Papa wouldn't love me anymore." I stood there waiting for her to say something, but she got down on her knees and hugged me and began to cry.

She finally spoke. "Amy, you will always be my little girl, and I could never forget you." I'll never forget that moment when I realized that, no matter what happened or what I did, I knew my parents would love me.

Wintereve was drawing nearer. I wished Wintereve wouldn't come; I didn't want all my relatives to go home. I loved being with all these people I thought I would never meet.

Wintereve finally arrived, and it was the best I ever had as a child. I played with my cousins Kyia and May in the attic, while trying to keep it a secret. We had a beautiful dinner of duck and mashed potatoes, even some things I'd never heard of before. It all was delicious, but I do remember that I found the snails quite appalling. I will never forget that night. It was a dream come true, a holiday with almost my whole family.

The next day, I said goodbye with tears in my eyes, as my grandpa and grandma returned to Hopeville. I didn't know when I would see them again, and with them being all the away across the country, it was hard to determine anything.

A few weeks went by, and now it was the middle of January. I knew that soon I would be allowed to go outside. Soon, Mama, Papa, and I would have our own house, and soon everything would be the way it was supposed to be.

One cold day, Mama, Aunt Grace, and I were in the kitchen where the stove was to keep warm, when we heard a knock on the door. Usually it was a delivery boy, or someone who had no idea what was being hidden in the house. So, it didn't matter if I went to the door with whomever answered it. On this particular day, Aunt Grace and I went to the door, expecting just some delivery boy or one of my aunts surprising us with a visit. Once at the door, Aunt Grace asked, "Who's there?"

"Count McCarthy," was the reply. I watched the smile on her face turn into a frown faster than I'd ever seen before. She turned to me and whispered, "Amy, take your mother and go hide in the attic—now!" Her voice sounded urgent, so I ran off quickly to get my mother.

Once I was in the kitchen and explained it all to her, we didn't go up to the attic but stayed very quiet and listened at the door.

"Hello, Your Lordship. Would you like to speak to my father?" Aunt Grace asked politely.

"No, I need to speak to Jonestone. Well, where is John? I know he's here. He's worked for you Somners all his life. There's no more house in Aldreen, so where else would he be?" The count spoke rudely to my aunt, almost as if he were talking to someone who wasn't there.

"Well, he isn't in right now. I think he's at the library. Why don't you look there?" my aunt told him in the most obviously fake sweet voice I had ever heard.

"Grace," McCarthy began, "you and I both know that he lived in Aldreen with Rose for a reason. I'm sure that—it is only a guess—John and your sister Rose have been married for over five years. They're only back here because your father's deal for the use of that beautiful house in Dimple is over. They had no choice but to come back and prove themselves. I would even be willing to bet that John now has a child that looks exactly like him, and that child is hiding at this very moment," he retorted horribly.

"McCarthy, I really think you have the wrong information, but if you wish to find John, I'd go look at the library in town," Aunt Grace told him firmly as she shut the door.

Mama and I ran up the stairs to the attic, so Aunt Grace would never know we didn't do as she'd told us to do.

Chapter Five

When Papa came home later that day, I told him the whole story—even the part about not being in the attic, as we were supposed to be. I hoped he would explain why we had to hide and who that man was. Mama said she would rather have him tell me. He once again told me that it was against the law for him and my mama to be married, because of something that my ancestors were accused of doing but actually didn't do. This time, though, he pulled out a document that described our predicament in its fullness. It was the law, the decree saying what my family was and wasn't allowed to do.

"Amy, according to all the research I've done, the McCarthys are responsible for this mess, and they blamed everything on us. They betrayed Frindeline, not our ancestors. Amy, we shouldn't be in this predicament, but we are, and the McCarthys will do just about anything to make sure that we stay at fault and they stay innocent—even though they know as well as we do that they did it."

My father took a breath and looked me in the eye as he continued. "Now all you need to do is be a good girl and stay here with Grandfather and Grandmere while your mother and I sort this all out."

"But, Papa, I want to help," I complained. I was tired of feeling useless.

"Amykins, you're doing exactly what I just said will be the most help you can possibly give us. If they find you, or even see you before I prove that the Jonestones are innocent, everything will be ruined. I can't wait to take you to all the places I used to play when I was a little boy, but I'll never be able to if you don't do as I say." He was stressing the importance of the situation much better than he had the night of my dream. It was even scarier now. I nodded so that he knew I understood.

"All right, Amy. It's getting late and you should get to bed and try not to have any more of those scary dreams." He smiled at me, and I did as I was told.

A few days later, I was helping Aunt Grace clean house. I was thinking about something that bothered me. Aunt Grace lived with Grandfather and Grandmere and wasn't married, but why? I had thought about this a lot, considering that all my mother's other sisters were married.

"Aunt Grace, why is it you're not married?" I asked, hoping she would answer. I never knew these days whether people would answer my questions.

"Well," my aunt began, "once I was married and lived in Lanski. While I lived there, they were in the middle of a civil war. I was only married for six months. The baron I married was bringing food to some of the men who were fighting. He was run over by a horse in the middle of a knights' camp. I wish my Charles were still alive today," she whimpered.

Aunt Grace, why didn't you marry again?" I was curious.

"I loved him too much. I could never marry again. I treasure those six months more than anything. The only thing I have to remind me of those months is my wedding dress. It's my most important possession. I don't think I could go on if my dress were taken from me." She sighed as we heard a knock on the door.

We both walked over to the door, as we usually did. I liked to see the different people who came to call on my grandfather.

"Who's there?" Aunt Grace asked.

"It's Count James McCarthy. Open the door," he yelled.

My aunt looked at me and said, maybe a little too loudly, "Hide."

I ran into the living room as quickly as I could and hid behind the sofa.

"Your Excellency, if you're here looking for John Jonestone again, he isn't here, but I'll let him know you stopped by," I heard my aunt say while trying to shut the door.

"Now, Grace, I've known you since we were children. I'll stay if I please. I'm going to say this once and only once. If you don't answer me correctly the first time, you will ache so badly that you'll wish you were never born. Your family will wish you were never born." He threatened my aunt.

"My lord, I don't know..." she moaned with pain, "...much. I won't be able to help you. All I know is that John is trying to give his family the freedom they deserve." I heard something being banged against the wall and then another whimper.

McCarthy then yelled, *"Is that right? Then, who did you tell to hide?"*

Aunt Grace screamed, "That's my wrist you're...*ow!*...twisting."

"That's not what I asked you. Who did you tell to hide?" he said between clenched teeth. I was scared and began to cry. That man was beating my aunt, and I couldn't do anything about it. No one else was home, and even if they were, I couldn't have left the room without being seen. I was just a little girl to that man, and showing myself would have made things worse.

"I said 'hi' to a maid who was on her way to the kitchen." I could tell Aunt Grace was holding back tears as she spoke. I tried to hold my tears in as I listened.

"Grace, you lie. Tell me, before I search the house and hurt you and whoever I find!" The evil, mean man yelled in my aunt's face. He still had her pinned against the door.

I didn't want to listen anymore. This whole situation was bad, and that man was hurting my aunt. I didn't listen any longer, though; I couldn't bear to hear what was going on. I began to cry quietly, making sure it stayed quiet so that he wouldn't hear me. I knew she finally said something to make him go away--what, I didn't know.

"Good day, Your Excellency," I heard the man say mischievously as he turned and left my aunt on the floor. He walked down the path when I heard Papa.

"Your Excellency," he retorted smugly, with no respect and great disdain. Then I heard Mama scream, followed by the sound of a whole group of people running toward the door. I quietly got out from behind the sofa to look at the sight by the door—Grandfather, Grandmere, Mama, and Papa were all standing over my aunt, who lay on the floor crying. My mama looked up and saw me with tears streaming down my face.

"Mama," I wailed, "a bad man was here, and he was being really scary, asking Aunt Grace all of these questions…" I cried into her shoulder. She picked me up and walked me to my room. I continued to cry. That was the scariest thing I had ever heard in my life. I didn't even see what happened, but I knew from the noises what was said until I blocked it out with my tears.

"Amy, it's all right. Aunt Grace is going to be fine. It's okay." My mother rocked me back and forth.

That night at dinner Aunt Grace seemed shaky. She wasn't herself, and she kept telling us that she didn't give him any information and no one needed to worry about her. We just needed to stay focused on February 19. Everyone looked worried.

We also received good news that night. There was a small bit of land in Grandfather's county which had a very small house on it that was vacant. It only had two rooms, but Papa said we would build onto it after we were set free.

The next day we were moving into it. We only put a bed and a cot in the second room and a rug in the first, along with a few other small essentials.

My parents took the bed, giving me the cot. There was a hole dug in the ground, where we were to put our fires, and a hole in the ceiling above to allow the smoke to leave. The door between the two rooms was a just a piece of cloth. The entrance to the house was a wooden door that seemed intact.

"Papa, why can't we just live with Grandfather, Grandmere, and Aunt Grace?" I complained. I was disgusted by the look of the house on the outside, and the inside was even worse. I scrunched up my nose and raised my eyebrows as I looked around.

"Mama, I hate it. I want to move somewhere else," I told my mother disrespectfully.

"Amythist Amelia Grace Jonestone, you need to be grateful for what you have, and you don't speak to your mother like that," my father reprimanded.

"Yes, sir," I told my papa and held my tongue the rest of the night.

After freezing for some time in that new bed, I finally fell asleep. I hated this but I couldn't do anything about it. The next few days were spent making this hovel (if you could even call it that) clean. I absolutely hated my situation and hoped that everything would work out because I couldn't wait till we could make our house better.

A few days later, after Mama finally declared the house clean enough to be homey, Aunt Grace dropped by.

"Rose, don't you think you could get better than this?" she asked as she looked around.

"Grace, this works, and we can always build on later. But this house is just fine," my mama replied as she looked around, unsure.

"I'll help you find something better, or come back and live with Mother and Father. They really don't mind." Grace tried to convince my parents.

"Really, Grace, I think we can make this work. We'll be fine, I promise," Mama reassured her older sister.

"If you say so. And Mother wants you for dinner tomorrow night," Aunt Grace informed us.

As she left, I could have sworn she asked herself what she was doing, and my parents definitely looked at each other strangely, as if they both noticed Aunt Grace wasn't acting like herself.

My birthday was in a week. All our problems might just be solved, but so many things weren't making sense anymore: Aunt Grace, why we moved, my parents. No one seemed to be themselves. I didn't like it very much, and I hoped it would all be over after Papa met the king.

The next day, Aunt Grace came over and told me the story of the maiden. I loved this story. None of it was true yet, but I hoped I'd be alive when the maiden of Delynelle was. That would be amazing to meet the princess of the greatest country. Who would rescue Lanski and all of Delynelle from all its problems? If only I were a princess, I used to think. Now I found myself wishing that my father were a duke.

The fairies were always talking about the prophecies they had about the maiden, making the stories longer. There was a choice that she would have to make, which would give Delynelle peace or havoc. She would have an Authorin (the fairies that look the most like us)-type power. There was just so much about her that was intriguing that I could listen for hours.

Chapter Six

A few days went by and it was February 18, the day before my fifth birthday—the day before my papa would prove our family was innocent. We spent the day at Grandmere's and Grandfather's. Every relative of mine who lived in Drell was there to celebrate my birthday.

It sort of became a good-luck party for Papa as well. Wherever he turned, someone would say, "John, good luck tomorrow," or, "Don't worry, you'll do great." I even heard someone say, "John, no matter what happens tomorrow, we all know the truth." No pressure at all. I could tell that he didn't like the attention and, if anything, it was making him nervous. I remember the whole night he kept biting his lip and scratching his head. His eyes seemed to twitch, which they did only when he felt he would mess things up for someone else.

Besides Papa's acting nervous, Aunt Grace seemed even more nervous and worried. Maybe I should have been distracted by my cousins and by my turning five, but I wasn't. I knew something was bothering Aunt Grace. You don't walk around aimlessly plucking at your necklace for no reason.

"Aunt Grace."

She jumped, and her eyes grew three sizes.

"I didn't mean to scare you," I added quickly.

"It's all right…I know…What did you want?" she stammered.

"You look kind of worried. Are you all right?" I asked sincerely.

"Amy, you're turning five tomorrow and you're worried about me." She smiled and stared at me, as if thinking whether she should answer my question. "Why don't you go play with Kyia? I'll bet that's more fun than asking questions."

She stopped talking, and I stared at her as she looked back at me. I could tell she wanted me to leave, but I really wanted an answer. She continued to give me the "leave" look, so I decided to go. As I walked up the stairs with Kyia, I heard the front door open and close.

I knew something wasn't right. My aunt was walking around as if someone was going to jump out and scream at her. All I did was say her name and she jumped. What was it with that look of hers? She'd never before given me anything like that.

When it was time for cake, Aunt Grace was nowhere to be found. I didn't say anything about being worried about her, because I didn't want everyone else to be worried about her. The cake was great, but I didn't enjoy it as much as I usually would. The adults' murmurs about

Aunt Grace distracted me. As people started to leave the dining hall, Aunt Grace entered looking flushed, and she apologized, saying, "Sorry, I wasn't feeling very well and went to lie down. I sort of fell asleep."

"Are you feeling better?" Grandmere asked avidly.

"Yes, Mother."

Finally, it was time to go home. We said our goodbyes and left for our little house that I was very displeased with. When we stepped in the door, Mama was quick to inform me that it was time for bed. I did as she told and lay down on my cot. I found it impossible to sleep; tomorrow was my birthday and I'd be five. Tomorrow was the day that my little freedoms of playing outside, being allowed to ask questions, and my parents' time would be returned to me. I know that doesn't seem like much, but those things were everything to me at that moment. I stared at the ceiling, waiting for my mind to allow my sleepless eyes to close.

Instead of sleeping, I found myself listening to my parents talking about what they wanted after tomorrow and how they planned to improve our house, but the subject I was most interested in, and hated the most, was the baby-name topic.

"Well, I haven't really thought much about names yet. It won't be here 'til late fall," my father told Mama sheepishly.

"I know, and you've had a lot of other things on your mind, but what names do you like?" my mother asked simply.

That's how it began. They started with boys' names. I figured they did this because they already had a girl—me—and probably were more interested in a boy. They agreed on that name fairly quickly, deciding on the name they would have given me had I been a boy: William John Noah Jonestone. I didn't like it much.

With a girl's name, it took them forever to decide. My mother liked the names Emily, Ellen, Emma, and Everild. Papa and I both disliked that one, even though they thought I was asleep. I heard my father finally get his way, and Everild was out, thank goodness. They had it down to two names for a girl—either Emily Ellen Rose or Ellen Emily Rose. After deciding that either name was fine with me, I fell into a light sleep.

It couldn't have been long before I woke up to a knock on the door. It must have been about midnight.

"Who could that be? It's practically midnight," Mama said worriedly.

A man yelled from the outside. "Let us in, or we'll break down the door! McCarthy sent us—let us in!"

"Shh…Rose, go hide Amy, and act as if no one's home," I heard my papa whisper urgently. I heard about a dozen fists banging on the door. I began to cry silently, just as I did the day Aunt Grace was being questioned. I knew that if I were heard, we would all be in trouble. They were all screaming, but I couldn't understand what they were saying, because there were too many voices at once.

Mama came into the room and grabbed me. She even tried to cover my ears, when we heard the door slam against the ground.

"Mama, what's going on?" I asked as tears rolled down my face much faster. She never answered my question, because before I could even look at her properly, a man ran into the room and pulled me away from my mother. I screamed, I kicked, I cried, I reached my arms out toward Mama. I will never forget the look of anger, fear, and hatred that entered her eyes as she yelled at the man.

"*You put down my baby!*" That simple phrase meant everything to me. Another man, who was just as scary looking, grabbed my mother and pushed her into the other room. I was screaming as the man with a scar above his eyebrow held me, refusing to put me down.

My father was pushed into a corner and guarded by eight men. He sat there crying, knowing there was nothing he could do.

"I was so close. I love you," my father yelled through sobs. Mama tried to push herself free, tried to get closer, but every time she tried, the evil-looking man pushed her.

Finally, I couldn't take it anymore, and I yelled, "Mean man!"

They weren't listening, so I did it again. "Mean man! What do you want with my papa and mama? Just tell us and stop pushing!" I screamed, tears tumbling down my face. I'd never been more scared in my life, and I didn't like this at all. Eight men were guarding my father, who never cried, while he sat in a corner doing just that. A man with a menacing grin on his face was holding me much too hard. Another man held my mother, who was desperately trying to get to me, and at every attempt they'd pull her back and practically throw Mama toward the bedroom.

"So, you're the daughter. A very kind and generous soul told us about you, *Amythist,*" the man who held me said as his black eyes looked intimidatingly into mine. "I promise no one will push your mama again if you tell me where the evidence is," he promised as he showed me a smile. If it weren't for the fact that this man was terrorizing my home and family, I would have believed him to be friendly.

I looked around the room as two men searched, toppling everything over. I saw my papa look at the horror that had arisen around him, and he begged them to let my mama and me go. I watched him plead, and I cried at the sight of it.

When I turned my head to look in the direction of Mama, she yelled, "Amy, sweetie, Mommy will save you. I promise!" She reassured me as she pulled herself free of the man, who then proceeded to push her, her head landing centimeters from the fire.

He laughed. "Woman, what do you think you're doing?"

I couldn't take it anymore. I couldn't stand to see my papa and mama in such a state. My papa was crying, and he never did that. Whenever something happened that wasn't supposed to, he was the strong one, not the one to cry. That was always me. I couldn't stand to see him like this. Mama was being pushed around as if she were some ball that could be thrown about. I couldn't stand all the men searching my pitiful home. I hated these people who thought they had the right to scare a five-year-old out of her mind. I didn't care anymore as the tears rushed down my face. How could I care? I was too scared to care what would happen if I told them where it was. I knew I shouldn't, but I was so scared they'd take Mama and Papa away—so scared they'd take me away—that I did it, anyway.

"It's under the stove, under the stove. Now, please let my mama and papa go!" I screamed at the top of my lungs.

Everyone in the room went quiet, Mama stopped screaming, and Papa stopped crying. He looked in the direction of the stove. The men watched avidly as one of them pulled the wooden box from underneath. The other man who had been searching the house pulled out a piece of parchment and read:

> *"By the order of King Sencraugh, we put you, John Samuel Noah Jonestone, under arrest for marrying above your status and having a child. You are sentenced to a life in prison unless a divorce takes place. As ordered by the king, we take this evidence and burn it."*

He paused as the man with the evidence smiled and dropped it into the fire. It seemed to take that box forever to reach the flames. To make matters worse, all twelve men sat there laughing as we watched all our hopes and dreams burning right in front of our eyes. Once there was nothing left of the wooden box except ashes, two men grabbed my father by the arms and led him outside.

"No! You can't do this! Please don't do this! Please, not today!" my mother pleaded as they let her go, tears welling in her eyes as she watched the man we both needed the most being taken out of our lives.

The man holding me dropped me and, as much as it hurt landing on my butt, I ran to my mother.

As I hugged her, Papa yelled, "I will always love you!"

My mother held me tight and rocked me back and forth as tears ran down both our faces. I looked up at her. I had never seen my mother so upset, so heartbroken. It made the tears fall all the faster.

Finally, all but one of the men had left—the one with the parchment still stood there in front of the stove, as if waiting for our tears to stop, which I didn't think could ever happen.

My mother yelled the worst scream I'd ever heard. *"What do you want?"*

"I just want to read the rest of the sentence," he retorted, as if it were obvious. I stared up at him blankly, wondering what he could do to make my life more miserable.

> *"Not only shall the evidence be burned, but because a child was born out of this illegal marriage, a child who shouldn't exist will start to work as a scullery maid on March 1, 1127. This child will do this all her childhood. If then the child proves that she deserves to be more than nothing, further punishment will not be endowed upon one Amythist Jonestone. If, by her twenty-first birthday, I, King Sencraugh, do not see her fit for life, she will be locked up like her father. I hope you understand how much I stress that the law be followed. King Sencraugh."*

"Why bring her into this? She's innocent. She hasn't done a single thing to deserve this," my mother wailed.

"Your Excellency, I don't make the rules. I just follow them," he told my mother before rolling up the decree and walking through our now nonexistent door.

That night I couldn't sleep. My life had turned into a nightmare in just a few minutes. Nothing could ever be the same again. I spent the whole night crying next to my mother, hoping that somehow this was all just a bad dream, yet knowing it wasn't. I had never been more scared than I was that night. Anyone who watched me lie next to my mother in the bed sobbing would have known.

Those men just stole from me one of the most important people in my life. I couldn't even begin to think how life would be without Papa. I didn't want to think about it at all. I wanted my papa back, but I knew I couldn't. My parents would never get divorced, and I didn't want them to. I was so scared for Papa, for Mama, and for the life I was now forced to live. I would never have guessed that this was how I would lose my father. I had imagined the baby taking him away, his searching taking him away, but not this. This was too much.

Chapter Seven

The next morning we were both still crying. I couldn't stand to look at Mama's face; it was so tear stained and tired looking that I couldn't help but feel her pain along with my own.

Grandfather came by not too long after we should have eaten breakfast. Neither of us could will ourselves to get out of bed and stop crying. Aunt Grace came with him. We heard their voices as they screamed in shock at our knocked down door, but we didn't move. Finally, Grandfather walked into the bedroom, where I'm sure he could hear our tears as they hit our stained cheeks.

"What happened?" Aunt Grace asked as if she was scared to know the answer.

I looked up. I was sure my eyes were red and puffy, and sure they could tell that the twang of pain in my heart would never quite go away.

"They took him. He's gone! He's gone!" My mother screamed somehow through her sobs.

"Who took him? Who's 'him'?" Grandfather asked for more confirmation. I could see in his eyes that he knew exactly who my mother was talking about.

Aunt Grace looked at me and a tear trickled down her own cheek.

"Amy, what happened?" She just stood there, trying to control the tears she knew would come.

Tears rolled down my face in every direction as I tried to grasp what I was about to say, knowing that if I said it again it would be real. "They took Papa. Mean men came and took him away. They burned the evidence. They're making me work in the kitchen at the castle. It was awful. They held me too tight."

I stopped as my tears were now making it impossible for me to talk. "They pushed Papa into a corner and pushed Mama. They were really bad men." As I told them, I covered my face so they wouldn't see the new tears that began to spill.

My grandfather looked startled and sprang over to my mother and hugged her.

From behind, I could see his face as he spoke the next words, "How'd they find out? I'll kill whoever told them." My grandfather looked absolutely frightening as he said this. His face was no longer the kind and gentle one I was used to, but a fierce and awful smile filled his face. If he had looked like that when I met him, I would never have gone near him.

Aunt Grace cowered and began to cry. As my grandfather hugged my mother, I ran to her for a hug, and we cried together.

She simply said, "I'm sorry." She couldn't be sorry—she didn't do anything. She had no control over the situation, yet she was apologizing, and at least it allowed me to know she cared. She rocked me back and forth and hummed to me. I soon fell asleep, getting the rest I desperately needed.

I had that scary dream again. *Amy, save your family. It's all up to you.* It began as images flashed through my mind, showing the same horrible scenes from a life of a grown-up version of me. The one thing that perturbed me was that in this dream, which showed such awful thoughts, my papa was in prison.

I woke up at the same time I had the last time I had this dream, screaming, *"Mama, come back!"* I was relieved to find my mother alive and asleep when I woke up, and I knew she hadn't slept at all the night before.

I decided much before the day ended that no one could have a worse birthday than the one I'd just had. No one except me could know how it felt to have your father taken away forever on your birthday.

Finally, Mama and I stopped crying all the time. We now cried only at night, when there was nothing else to distract us. Everyone still knew that we were upset, but we did our best to hide it. I didn't want anyone to know that I was miserable—most of all, I was angry. I was still mad at those men. How could they have done what they did to the three of us? How could they even look at our faces? I wanted more than ever to beat up whoever told those men about my family.

Not too long after my birthday, I had to start working at the castle. My first day isn't something I would be willing to brag about. As soon as I walked in, a very pudgy woman walked over to me.

"You must be Amythist. Wash the dishes, then make some bread, then set the table for lunch in the dining hall, then wash the new dishes. Oh, and then you can eat, but not until all of that is done. Just so you know, I'm the kitchen supervisor, Dovendella. Now, get to work."

I looked up at her, bewildered, not sure if I should say anything at all. Out of that whole to do list I only knew how to set a table, and not in any proper fashion.

"Uh, excuse me, Duvelyia, call me Amy. And I don't know how to make bread," I told her sheepishly.

"You've never made bread. Well I, *Dov-en-della*, don't have the time to teach you. Prissy over there will help you," my supervisor told me as she pointed in the direction of a whole bunch of teenaged girls. Dovendella left me with only that, not knowing which one I was supposed to ask for help.

I walked over to the group, feeling very uncomfortable as I tugged on one of their skirts.

I asked, "Which one of you is Prissy?"

A girl of about fifteen looked my way. "Honey, how old are you?"

"Five—why?" I answered.

"People these days! Putting a five-year-old to work—that's just wrong," the girl told her friends.

"Which one of you is Prissy?" I asked again, this time more urgently.

"I am," said the one who'd asked me how old I was.

"Doven...um, the lady in charge said you could show me how to do stuff."

"Dove, *hmmph*, I hope this doesn't mean I have to do all the other stuff she told me to do today. So what did she ask you to do first?" She smiled at me, and I knew I liked her.

"The dishes," I replied.

As we walked over to the sink, Prissy pointed out people to me. She introduced me to a ten-year-old named Mary and a boy not much older than me, whose name was Robert Garrison. As she showed me how the dishes were to be done, she pointed out more people and told me their names. I would never be able to remember them all.

I was easily distracted as I looked outside the back entrance of the kitchen. There stood a boy who looked to be about seven, but he didn't look like the people in the kitchen. He wore beautiful clothing, unlike the brown garments we were wearing. I thought he looked like a prince. Not even my cousins would wear clothing that fancy without it being a holiday.

He walked into the kitchen, and no one noticed until Dovendella came in and yelled at everyone. "Where are your manners? Is this how you treat your prince?"

Everyone bowed or curtsied faster than I had ever seen anyone react before. I felt foolish for not realizing who he was. I had never seen a prince before.

"Prissy, I left you in charge here. Why didn't you see to the prince?" Dove glared horribly at Prissy as she whispered through the side of her mouth.

"Your Highness, I'm sorry this wench didn't notice you. If you want, I'll have her whipped," Dove told the prince with a twinkle in her eye.

The prince laughed. "Dove, that doesn't deserve a whipping. She was preoccupied and I don't get offended by not being bowed to. It actually gets quite annoying. You don't ever have to bow to me, but you should in front of my father. He'd be furious if you didn't," he told Prissy.

Prissy nodded to show agreement.

Dove simply said, "Of course, Your Highness."

That was my first encounter with my prince.

Mama and I were having a hard time affording all of our needs. I got very little pay, and Mama refused to move back in with Grandfather and Grandmere. Instead, Mama started dusting Grandfather and Grandmere's house every day and probably received more money than most dusters deserved. Mama couldn't do much else with the baby. We got along all right, but Grandmere made sure we had dinner with her at least twice a week, always insisting that we eat more. I didn't really need the extra nourishment, considering I ate the king and queen's leftover bread every day.

Prissy and Mary were the nicest older people at the kitchen. At about noon every day, they'd take over my and Rob's duties for an hour or so. As long as everything we were supposed to do was finished by the end of the day, Dove wouldn't notice. If she ever did find out, Prissy, Mary, Rob, and I would be in a lot of trouble.

Rob was a nice boy with deep, blue eyes and brown, curly hair. He was funny and kind of a troublemaker. We became friends quickly. I remember many afternoons of tag and fairy hunting, although we never found any. Life definitely wasn't what I had expected it to be after my birthday, but it wasn't awful either. I still had fun with more simple things, and I tried to make the best out of every situation. The only thing I even thought about changing was that I only saw Papa once a month; even then he was always behind bars.

The bad part was that I felt like it was all my fault. Both of my parents reassured me that just because I told the men that the evidence was under the stove didn't mean it was my fault, and that eventually one of my parents would have done the same thing for everyone's safety. That wasn't the only thing I felt guilty about. If it weren't for the fact that I wished to move closer to my family, we never would have been in Drell, and no one would have found out. I didn't want them to know this though; I didn't want anyone to know. My dream didn't help much, either. I tried wishing it all away, but to no avail.

I woke up one April morning with a wet face. There was a leak in the roof and water had been dripping on my face all night. I didn't feel good, but I knew that if I didn't go to the kitchen, Dove would double my work when I came back. So I went, planning to finish my work as quickly as possible so that I could get Grandfather to fix the leak before night.

"Ames, you look sick." Rob was kind enough to tell me as I walked through the kitchen door.

"Rob, you'd be sick, too, if you'd slept with a leak right above your head." I was irritated and didn't feel like talking at the moment. I wanted to get out of there as quickly as I could, but that didn't happen. Dove kept giving me more to do, and at noon, my break, I was tired.

"Rob, can you go to my grandfather's house and ask him to fix the leak in my roof, so I can take a nap?" I asked as I yawned and lay down on the flour bags in the corner.

"Yeah, I guess so. I just need to know where he lives and who the count of the county he lives in is," he told me.

"He lives in the Somner mansion, and he's the count, Paul Somner," I replied without thinking anything of it.

"Amythist, your grandfather is Paul Somner?" He practically yelled, his eyes huge with disbelief.

"Yeah, so?" I yawned back.

"Of course, I will. I'll just go tell Paul Somner," he said as he left the kitchen.

I fell asleep as soon as he left, not quite sure why he found that so shocking.

He was back about an hour and a half later, when he woke me up.

"We fixed it." He looked at me as if I owed him some kind of explanation.

I simply said, "Good," and then, when he continued to look at me like he should be bowing to me or something, I finally asked, "Rob, why are you so shocked that he's my grandfather?"

"Well, because your grandfather, is one of the most well-known counts in all of Frindeline. I never would have thought that one of Paul Somners' grandchildren would work in a kitchen," he explained, still in disbelief.

"Well, my father is in prison for marrying my mother because he's a peasant," I said and then coughed.

"Oh," was all he would say as he averted his eyes.

"I'm going back to sleep. Wake me up at two o'clock, all right?" I asked as I laid my head back down on the flour bags and closed my eyes.

At two o'clock, Rob came and woke me up, saying that Dove was on her way down and I'd better get back to work.

I started back to the loud part of the kitchen, where I began to help Prissy bake a cake.

Rob was baking bread and was looking at me peculiarly again. "Amy, why does your grandfather speak of your papa so kindly?"

I didn't understand why he would ask a question like that. "Why do you ask?"

"Because it's against the law for your father to have married your mother. Wouldn't that make him mad?" Rob asked me critically.

"My father should be a duke. Some family by the name of McCarthy kind of messed that up, though," I told him as I began to cry. "My papa married my mama with my grandfather's permission. Papa was just about to fix everything, when someone found out about Mama and me, and then they burned our last hope." I was trying not to cry, but I wasn't doing a very good job of it, and I wiped my nose. I was standing on a stool, trying to mix the cake batter, and then I began to bawl.

Rob looked at me. "I'm sorry—I shouldn't have asked." He turned around quickly, and I knew he felt bad.

Prissy came back over, "Amy what's the matter?" She looked concerned.

"I miss my papa." I told her as I began to cry more.

"Well honey, you may miss your papa, but that won't change what Dove will do if she finds you crying. I'd stop before she gets over here," she told me sympathetically.

"Prissy is right, you know," Rob said as she left. I stopped.

That night I went home to find my grandfather there, talking to Mama. I said that I didn't feel too well, thanked him, and went to bed.

Chapter Eight

Summer finally found its way to Drell, and it was scorching. I found it very difficult to work on the days when it seemed that not even dunking myself in the water would help. Prissy made things easier, though, by continually covering for Rob and me.

"I'll go find Rob," I remember telling her once, in a way of accepting her offer. It being a very hot August afternoon, we of course went straight to the lake.

"I bet I'll beat you there," I told my best friend as we began to run.

"No you won't—you're a girl."

"So? I bet I'm faster than you, Robert Garrison!" I yelled as I began to leave him in the dust.

"Well, I bet you're not!" He, too, began to run.

I can almost remember that afternoon as if it was yesterday. Rob was not far behind me, yet I felt like I had done something extraordinary. To this day, Rob will never admit that this happened, and if he ever does, it'll take another twenty years or so to convince him that I won. I don't really care what he thinks, because I know it happened. I know the exact words I said once I reached the lake: "See, girls aren't wimps. I told you I could beat you."

"Fine, but I'll beat you next time, Amy!" he yelled as he jumped into the water.

"Is it cold?"

"Yes, and it feels so good." He told me as I put my foot into the water.

My nose squished as I shook off the cold, feeling refreshed. As soon as my body was completely in the water, a splash fight began. I don't remember how long we splashed each other, but it was a long time to spend splashing someone. When we'd had enough of that, we lay out in the sun to dry.

"Amy," Rob began, as if remembering something, "what time are we supposed to be back in the kitchen?"

"Rob, we need to leave now!" I told him, as I remembered Mary said to be gone for only an hour.

We both shot up and ran much faster than either of us had run on the way there.

"Ames, Dove is going to kill us," Rob informed me as we slowed down, the kitchen in view.

"I know, but let's just keep moving."

When we walked through the door, Dove was waiting.

"Where have you two been!?" Dove yelled in our faces without warning. "You were supposed to be here helping us get ready for the banquet tonight!" she continued to scream.

"We know, but Prissy—" Rob started to explain.

"Prissy didn't look like she needed our help, so we decided to go swimming," I interrupted, trying to giggle, as if I thought it was funny.

"Amythist, you think you're so funny," Dove told me sweetly, *"But you're not! Get back to work now!"* she screamed, her face redder than a tomato.

She turned around to leave, and we just stood there until she looked back, giving us the most maniacal grin ever.

"We're going," Rob managed as we turned to do our work.

Dove made me stay later than usual, so I was up very late, which made me tired the next day. Usually, that wouldn't be such a bad thing, except that the next day was the day I was allowed to visit Papa.

The next morning when Mama woke me up, I didn't want to move.

"Amy, get up. We're going to see Papa," she told me quietly as she shook me awake. When my eyes opened, she smiled.

"I know, and I really want to go, but I'm so tired." I yawned.

My eyes were full of sleep, and I kept blinking to keep them open as I walked through the middle of the cells. This wasn't my first time at the prison: I'd been here once a month since my father was arrested. I hated walking through the cells; most of the people in this nauseating place were robbers and murderers.

Most of the time I cringed as I walked down the long hall until I reached my father, but today I was so tired that I hardly realized what was going on.

"Amykins, are you all right?" My father looked at me with concern in his eyes.

"John, she worked late last night. She was caught after sneaking away from the kitchen," Mama explained as she put her hand on her very round stomach.

"Well, I hope that doesn't happen again. The getting caught part, of course," my father joked.

"John!" Mama shrieked.

"Only kidding," he explained quickly as I began to laugh.

"Rose, do you think it'll be a boy or a girl?" He smiled as he looked at Mama's bulging stomach. The baby was due in about a month.

"I think it'll be a girl." she smiled. "But a boy would be wonderful as well." She, too, smiled as she thought about the baby.

I stood there, hoping that everything would still be all right once my brother or sister arrived. I could tell that my papa wasn't happy about not being there when he or she was born. He kept looking away from us, as if he thought he was letting us down. There was nothing he could do about it.

My life was something I was still getting used to. I worked in a kitchen, my father was in prison, and my mother was expecting a baby very soon. It couldn't get much worse. I was now used to the kitchen work and the fact that my papa was in prison. But I still wasn't used to him not being home eating with us, or the fact that he lived with scary people. I never could get used to that. I missed him.

Soon it was September, and the temperature was beginning to cool down. I still wished Papa could be at home and he didn't have to live with all of those dirty people.

My mother had received special permission to visit Papa the day after the baby was born and the last Friday of the month. It was the only good I could see that would come from a baby.

On the seventeenth, McCarthy decided to drop by and see how we were doing.

"What are you doing here?" My mother screamed as she tried to slam the door in his face.

He caught the door and said, "Mrs. Jonestone, please let me come in. All I wanted to do was apologize for getting your husband arrested at such an inconvenient time." He smiled at my mother's stomach and chuckled to himself. I wanted to hit him.

"Well, the only convenient time to arrest my husband would have been before we wed, so there would have been fewer people to hurt!" she yelled again.

"Well, if that's how you feel, maybe you should contact one of the people you hold most dear, because if it wasn't for her, your dim-witted husband would be here next to you. I assume you have no idea what I'm talking about—that is only to be expected. You'll figure it out, but if you don't, I'm more than willing to inform you."

My mother sneered at him, as I began to yell at him. We did not hear who he wanted us to thank, but he definitely told us to thank someone. That someone I wanted to hurt, that someone was the reason I worked and Papa was in prison.

As he left, my mother began to cry and I yelled at all McCarthy's evil being.

My mother got down on the floor and began to scream. I thought it was because she was angry, but I soon realized it was because of pain.

She yelled, "Amy, get your grandmere quickly." She was gripping her stomach.

I ran to my grandparents' house faster than I normally would run. I wasn't sure what was going on, but I had a hunch.

Grandfather answered the door.

"Mama—I think she's having the baby!" I yelled, out of breath, but Grandfather couldn't understand me.

"Amy slow down," he said, but before I could catch my breath and repeat myself, he yelled, "Oh my

Delynelle, she's having the baby!" He put his hand over his mouth and ran to find Grandmere.

I stood there waiting. It seemed as if they still thought they had months to wait when, for all I knew, I was a big sister already.

Finally, Aunt Grace walked by.

"Aunt Grace," I yelled to get her attention, "Mama is having the baby." I waved my arms urgently in the direction of my house.

"Do Mother and Father know?" she asked. I knew who she was talking about.

In an annoyed tone that usually would get me into trouble, I answered, "Yes, now let's go. You can help her." I grabbed her by the arm and began to run back to Mama.

When Aunt Grace and I ran into the first room, Mama was still on the floor, and Aunt Grace helped her into the bedroom. When Grandfather and Grandmere arrived, we all went into the bedroom. I only stayed for about an hour. That's when I was tired of watching my mother go into pain every five minutes or so. I decided to go outside to wait, hoping it would be an Emily and not a William—not that I wanted either.

After being outside and playing with Rob for a few hours, I decided to go back and check on Mama. That whole day while I played, I tried to convince myself that having a brother or sister would be a good thing, but I just didn't want to share my parents. I wanted to be the only one, not one of two, no matter what.

I found myself wishing for over the millionth time that I could start over in Aldreen, before I ever made that stupid wish to live near family, before Mama became pregnant. I wanted life to be the way it was then, but I wanted Grandfather, Grandmere, Aunt Grace, and Rob, too. I wanted the impossible.

There was a small—a very small—part of me that was excited, too. I liked the idea of being a big sister, and not an only, but hated the idea of sharing. I was more confused than I'd ever been in my life. I had so many thoughts and emotions that I didn't understand. I was excited, yet not. Curious, yet I wished I wasn't.

When I entered the small bedroom, my mother was screaming, and I thought my ears would burst. Finally, five hours after I went to get my grandparents that morning, a head was seen. In less than ten minutes after that, I had a brother, William John Noah Jonestone. He was cute, after Grandmere gave him a bath.

It was now around bedtime. Mother insisted that I go to bed, because we were going to see Papa the next day. That was impossible. Will wouldn't stop crying. By the time I finally went to sleep, Mama was waking me up. I now wished even more than before that William didn't exist. I didn't want him to begin with, and now, because of him, I couldn't sleep. I felt like everything was out of control.

When we arrived at the prison the next day, Mama told the guard that the baby was born and showed my brother to him.

"All right, you have my permission to enter." The guard smiled as Will cooed.

We started to walk toward Papa's cell, when another guard came up behind us.

"We almost forgot that today you have special permission to go inside the cell." He then led us to Papa's cage, that awful thing that kept me from hugging him every time we visited. But because of William, today I was allowed to hug Papa again.

I secretly said to myself, "Thanks Will." I'd never admit it, though.

The guard unlocked the cell and I skipped into my father's arms.

"Hey, pumpkin, they let you in this time," he said as he hugged me.

Then my mother chimed in, "Well John, that's because this is a very special occasion." I hated it when she did that sometimes.

Mama was smiling, though, and I knew she loved little Will. My mother looked very tired. In her arms was a bundle of blankets, and inside that slept my little brother.

Papa immediately let go of me and ran over to Mama. "Is it a boy or a girl? When was the baby born?" My father said all this without a pause. I stood there, watching my father look at his son in awe, as a tear of joy trickled down his face. My parents were talking, but I didn't hear them.

A few minutes later, I opened my ears again, and my father told my mother, "Rose, he's beautiful."

I couldn't help myself as I interrupted, "I'm beautiful, too, aren't I?" I crossed my arms, turned around, and began to cry.

"Sweetie, of course you are. You will always be my prettiest little girl." He hugged me again: I'd missed his hugs.

"Forever?" I asked, wiping the tears from my eyes.
"Yes, Amykins. Forever."

I smiled as I realized that Will changed everything and nothing. My papa still loved me and it didn't matter if I had to share my parents. They both would still be right where I needed them, when I needed them. I looked up at the bundle in my mother's arms. I couldn't help it—as much as I tried not to, I loved that little boy.

I couldn't understand—well, I could, but I didn't see why I'd ever wanted him to be gone. I wanted him to stay. I wanted him to grow up and be my little brother.

We stayed with Papa the rest of the day. We talked about everything. That day, I figured out something very important, which might have been the reason for Will's life; I learned that no matter what happened or who came into our lives, no one could take my place in my father's heart.

A week passed and finally I started getting used to my brother being around and the fact that he got all the attention. I disliked that everyone crowded around him and didn't notice me. I liked that everyone liked Will, but I couldn't help feeling jealous of him. I tried to act as if that were no big deal, but when no one was looking, I once again had too much. Under my breath, not meaning it, I wished away the little boy that took away all my old attention-givers; not expecting it to work.

"Amy, go get your grandfather. Will won't eat." Mama shook me awake roughly sometime after midnight. "He has a fever."

I was scared, not knowing what to do. My two-week-old brother was sick. How could someone who had only been alive for two weeks get sick? I was much older than that the first time I got sick.

I ran to my grandparents' house, much like I had two weeks earlier.

"Wake up! Wake up!" I pounded on the door. I kept yelling until someone answered.

Grandfather opened the door with a sword in his hand.

"Amy, what are you doing here in the middle of the night? Is everything all right?" he asked too calmly, letting me know that he was worried.

"No, Grandfather. Will has a fever and won't eat. Mama woke me up and told me to run for you." It had started to rain while I was pounding on the door, and now my clothes were just about soaked through.

"We'd better get moving, then," he said as he picked me up and ran all the way to my hovel.

William was crying, his face red with fever, and he looked hungry. Mama was crying and yelling for Papa all at the same time.

It was scary. I couldn't do anything. I wanted my brother to get better. I wanted Mama to stop wailing. I wanted Grandfather to figure out the problem. I wanted Papa to be home; maybe he would know something. I was tired, and even though I knew I had to go to the kitchen the next day, I couldn't sleep because I had too much on my mind. I was worried about the little boy I now loved just as much as Mama or Papa. What if something serious was wrong with him? I tried to figure out why this would have happened, when I remembered the wish. But I didn't really want him gone. I didn't want him to die, but if he did, it would be my entire fault.

Chapter Nine

It was a long three hours later when Grandfather left. William had finally eaten something, and with it being close to five o'clock in the morning, Grandfather took Will's eating as a good sign that my brother would be better after some rest. He told us all to get some sleep as he closed our door.

How was I supposed to go to sleep? This was all my fault. My baby brother would have been fine if it wasn't for the fact I had been so selfish. I hated feeling that everything was my fault. I hated thinking that if I'd done something different, everything would be better. I was only five and already I was blaming myself for more things than most adults did.

I finally fell asleep, but I didn't like my dream very much. It was the same dream I seemed to have from time to time, the one where Mama dies in the end. Although, the dream had stopped scaring me, it did tonight. Will wasn't even in my dream. Papa was in it, Mama was in it, and I was in it, but where was Will? Why wasn't he in my dream? This dream took place when I was older; shouldn't a little boy be running around inside my head as I dreamed this awful dream? I was now really scared, but as I began to think about it, I came to the conclusion that Will wasn't in my dream because Mama wasn't pregnant when I first had it. How could he be in a dream I started to have before he was even thought about?

I went to the kitchen, tired and upset. Rob could tell something was bothering me.

"Amy, what's up?" he asked simply, as if it were that easy to answer. I guess it usually is, but today I was still trying to grasp exactly what that was. I didn't respond and just went to work, silently.

He didn't give up. "Ames, there really is no use hiding it. I'll figure it out eventually." He seemed sure of himself, and he was probably right. Most likely, he would find out eventually, even if I wasn't the one to tell him.

"I'm sure you will find out that Will is sick. I'm sure someone who knows will tell you. I also feel like it's my fault! Rob, you don't know how much it hurts to see someone you'd wished were gone get sick, when you didn't really mean it." I began to cry as I crumpled up into a ball on the floor.

"Will's sick?" Rob asked in a whisper.

"Yes, and let's just hope he gets better. Don't tell anyone, okay?" I told him as I quickly stood and wiped my eyes before starting back on the dishes.

"I won't tell anyone."

My brother's fever didn't go away, and he was beginning to lose weight. Mama tried not to cry for my sake, but when she thought I wasn't looking, I saw the silent tears flow from her eyes. I cried as well; it was hard not to.

A doctor came every day to check on Will. Mama and I would watch him as he looked at my helpless baby brother. The first four days he had a chance of living if we could get him to eat, which he wouldn't. On the fifth day, the doctor sadly and almost silently informed us, "I'm afraid, Mrs. Jonestone, that your son won't live any longer than a week."

My mother began to wail; as did I. Will wasn't even a month old yet.

Mama told me to go to the prison to tell Papa. I ran all the way there. I had never run that far; the prison was very close to the castle.

As I ran, I found my cheeks stained. I was mumbling promises under my breath. "I will never forget the name William John Noah Jonestone, never." I might have only been five, but I promised myself that when I grew up and if I had a son, his name would be William. I wanted Will to be well, I wanted him to live. I wanted my little brother to grow up so I could take him tree climbing and swimming, and teach him how to do everything I knew how to do. I promised myself that if by some miracle the doctor was wrong, I'd make it up to Will. I'd make up to him that there had ever been a point where I wished he would disappear. I would do anything to make sure he stayed happy—anything, as long as he would live.

I started to cry harder as I tried to come up with a way to tell Papa his son was dying. I didn't even want to say it, because saying it would make it true, and I didn't want this to be true. I didn't want to believe it.

When I arrived at the prison with tears in my eyes, I walked up to the guard. "I'm John Jonestone's daughter, Amythist, and I've come to tell him that my brother, his son…is…is…the doctor…"

"Come on, girl, spit it out!" the guard yelled at me.

"The doctor says he's dying." I finally threw the dreaded words at him.

"Little girl, go home. We'll make sure your father is notified," the guard told me as he pointed his finger away from the prison, to indicate I was to leave.

"Wait! I must tell him. If I don't, he won't believe you. If I don't tell him, how am I supposed to go home?" I tried to make the mean guard understand.

"I told you, go home!" he yelled as he put his hand on the tilt of his sword.

"I won't leave until I can talk to Papa." I crossed my arms stubbornly.

He began to laugh, and kept on laughing until finally he gave in and let me enter the prison.

I ran to my father's cell.

"Amykins, what are you doing here?" my father asked when he saw me.

"Papa," I began, and then the tears began to flow, "Will's sick." I continued to cry, just barely able to sob out the words.

"What? But Will isn't even a month old. How could he be sick?" he asked, confused as he looked at me with tears flowing from my eyes.

He needed to understand. He needed to know why I was here. I had to finish what I'd started.

"Papa, the doctor says he won't live longer than a week."

All of a sudden, I wasn't the only one crying. Papa had joined in with the tears. I wanted to hug him, but the cell bars were in the way. We just stood there, me looking up at my father's usually kind, gentle face, which was now in tears as he looked down at my small, tear-filled eyes.

Nothing was right. Nothing was fair. No one seemed to care how I felt in any of these situations. All they did was say that it must be hard, but they didn't offer sympathy or compassion, only pity came from everyone's lips the next few days. They didn't care, but if they did, they figured I was just a small little girl who didn't understand anything that was going on. How wrong all those pity givers were. I understood my brother was dying and I knew what that meant: he'd leave us forever. All those who thought my five-year-old life was a pity case, I simply didn't want to see. I wanted everyone to ask me how I felt, how I was doing, instead of saying they were sorry and giving me things, as if that could compensate for the loss of a brother.

Mama and Rob were the only ones who understood. Most people think that a few gold Frindelins could make up for the world. Well, they're wrong; nothing could have make me feel better.

The rest of that week, I didn't show up at the kitchen. I didn't care if I was severely punished. I wanted to be with my brother as much as I possibly could, if all he had were those few short but sweet days promised to us.

Will lasted longer than expected. He wasn't supposed to last as long as he did. He made it to a month old and a little longer. My precious brother died on October 21, 1127. I cried like I had never cried before, but he was smiling. At least he was happy with his very short life.

For a little boy who'd lived barely long enough to even recognize his family, he had more people show up at his funeral than anyone anticipated. Papa, Rob, Mary, Prissy, Mama, my grandparents, and all my aunts and uncles were at the funeral.

William was a cute baby boy, who was my brother, Mama and Papa's son, and the only brother I would ever have, the only son my parents would ever know.

My parents didn't deserve being apart, and they didn't deserve losing their son. Will didn't deserve to die, but he did. There was nothing anyone could do about my brother's death, nothing I could do to control any of it, yet I felt all of it was my fault. Everything had gone wrong because of two wishes I had made—two wishes that had put my father behind bars and killed my little brother. I was the reason my family was in positions that they didn't deserve to be in.

I knew that wishing to be close to family wasn't awful and that it wasn't really my fault, just like it wasn't really my fault that Will had become sick. I knew this, but I just couldn't help thinking that if only I'd kept my mouth shut, maybe—just maybe—Mama, Papa, Will, and I would all be together.

Mama grieved more when she saw my father at the funeral than she had with anyone else present. She gripped his shirt and wailed. She cried so loudly that everyone looked at her. Papa hugged her and cried. He cried silently, but the tears were many. I hugged them both as tears streamed down my own cheeks. After awhile, I couldn't stay there anymore. I couldn't watch everyone be so sad.

I was wearing a very nice black lace dress that Grandmere had picked out for me. I found myself running. I tripped, and dirt spilled all over my gorgeous gown. My home was finally in view, but I couldn't go there, because that's were Will died. I turned and ran into the Wood of Drell, once again not caring if I were killed by something. I didn't deserve to live, anyway. I didn't care if a dragon ate me or an evil fairy captured me; I just wanted out. I just wanted away.

As I walked into the wood, I looked around, trying not to be caught by surprise if anything jumped out at me. When all of a sudden, a little boy I'd seen somewhere before jumped out at me saying, "Hello."

I screamed in response.

"Sorry, I didn't mean to scare you," he said rather sweetly.

"It's all right. I just thought you were a monster or something," I told him shyly.

He looked to be about seven or eight years old.

"Have I seen you somewhere before?" he asked me.

"I don't know, but I was thinking the same thing. I just don't know where I would have seen you," I told him as I studied his face.

"I think I saw you in my kitchen."

I was taken aback. That didn't make any sense. The only kitchens I could think of where I would see anyone but Mama were the king's and Grandfather's. I definitely had never seen him in Grandfather's kitchen, but he wasn't dressed like a prince.

"What do you mean?" I looked at him, confused.

"Don't you work in my kitchen?" the little boy asked.

This was insane; a scruffy little boy in rags didn't own the kitchen I worked in.

"King Sencraugh owns the kitchen I work in, not some peasant boy," I told him crossly.

"Oh!" he exclaimed, "I'm Prince Henry, just not in my usual clothes."

As I realized what I'd been doing, I bent down into a curtsey. "Your Highness, I didn't recognize you. I'm sorry." I became very nervous as I thought about what he might do to me.

"My costume worked, then. I dressed like this so I could go outside and play and no one would recognize me," he explained. He was smiling, as if everything was perfect.

I didn't think I'd ever smile again.

"Why so glum?" he asked as we walked toward the center of the wood.

"Everything, and anything, and almost nothing," I told him as we came upon a willow tree in the middle of the woods. I would never forget this particular tree for many different reasons, one of which was that most of its branches looked like chairs and was great for climbing.

The prince grabbed my hand to help me.

As we climbed, he asked, "What do you mean by that?"

So I told him how my brother died only two days before, and how I had wished he would disappear. We talked for a long time. I felt like I could tell him anything, and all he would do was listen. I really needed someone to do that. When it was his turn to talk, he gave me advice and told me it wasn't my fault.

He was like no one I'd seen or heard. He wasn't like most little boys, who made fun to try and make you laugh, expecting to make everything better. He gave real, useful advice, as if he were all grown up. I liked talking to him.

Finally, after I figured it was about time for me to head back to the funeral, I told the prince, "I'd better get back to the funeral. Maybe I'll see you around."

"Maybe," was all he said.

When I was back in the graveyard, Mama was sitting next to Will's gravestone, still crying. The funeral had been over for some time, but my parents didn't want to leave the grave. Papa stood there, sniffling, his eyes red. I knew this was hard on all of us, but I couldn't help but wonder if my mother's mourning would ever end. I didn't think mine would.

The sun began to set when the guards returned for my father. I didn't want them to take him. I actually begged the guard to let Papa come home with us for the night. It was to no avail, of course, because they took him back to his dreaded cell. I wished for once I could have what was left of my family together.

Mama and I walked home in silence, and as soon as we got in the door, we sat on the bed and cried ourselves to sleep. I fell asleep in my very dirty and torn black lace dress, and Mama in her wrinkled black silk. I didn't think life could ever go back to normal. In the short time my brother had been alive, I learned what it was like to care for something little and small.

My brother taught me two other very important lessons, which I'm not sure I could have learned from anyone else. He taught me that time is a precious gift and we shouldn't waste it, he also was the only person who could ever teach me that no one or nothing could take my place in my parents' lives. I thank my little brother almost daily for those two things, but mostly for giving me my confidence and taking away my biggest fear, the fear that I could be forgotten. The fear that anything could make my parents forget about me. That was my only fear until Will came along. He rid me of that fear by showing me it wasn't something I had to be scared of. Thank you, Will.

Chapter Ten

~~~

"Rob, you're messing it up. You don't make a cake like that. That's the salt, not the sugar." I was feeling a little stressed, because there was a dance at Grandfather's that night and I didn't know what I was going to wear. I was now nine years old, and I was still the same wavy brown haired, blue-eyed girl I had been when I was five.

I was now an excellent cook. In fact, it was a known fact that my cake was the only cake the prince would eat. I hadn't seen him since Will's funeral, and I doubted he even knew who baked his favorite chocolate cake with raspberry filling and white, vanilla frosting. I do remember the day his personal maid came in and told Dove that I was the only one allowed to bake cake for the prince. It was the only cake he would eat. Dove didn't seem to like the news that much. I was only six.

There were a few times when Dove had other people bake it, just because she didn't think he'd be able to tell the difference. I remember one of Prince Henry's maids marching into the kitchen and telling Dove that the prince knew it wasn't baked by the right person, and ordered his real cake baker to bake it. That was the comment that made me realize he didn't actually know who baked his cake; he just knew it was done by some extraordinary cook. It made me feel special.

In most eyes, I was only a kitchen girl, but even that didn't stop me from being Amythist. I was very independent and hated being bossed around. Dove absolutely hated me, yet she couldn't do anything about me because His Highness would complain.

"Ames, I'm trying my best. I can't cook cake as well as you, remember," Rob teased as he quickly stopped himself from ruining a cake with too much salt and not enough sugar. It seemed that today he couldn't cook anything correctly.

"Come on, Rob. Yesterday you baked a perfectly good cake for the queen. You should remember how," Agithus Dartain remarked in her usual, mean drawl.

"Bug off, Agithus. We don't need your help. Aren't you supposed to be cleaning the oven?" I told her, knowing confidently that she would switch jobs with us in a heartbeat.

It was the middle of July and extremely hot. I was having a hard time concentrating on anything. "Rob, I can't breathe, it's so hot. I wouldn't be surprised if I became a raisin." I smiled as I said this, knowing Prissy, whom Dove called "Softy," would overhear.

"Amy, are you hot? Rob, how do you feel?" Prissy asked. "When you two are done with that cake, why don't you go swimming for an hour—but only an hour. I can't cover you for forever." She smiled as she went back to work.

An hour later, everything but the frosting was done.

Mary walked over. "If you want to get wet, I suggest you go now, before Dove comes back."

Rob looked at the cake he had almost ruined earlier with salt and sighed.

"I'll frost the cake. Now run along, you two," Mary told us as she rushed us out the door.

I stuck out my tongue at Agithus. I couldn't help myself.

"No fair," I heard her yell as we left the kitchen.

Rob and I were the favorites when it came to children. Mary and Prissy always covered for the little ones' first year, but we'd been working in the kitchen for four years and they still covered for us. Aggie thought this unfair, but she had at least two things that made me want to shove her to the ground at least twice a day. Aggie was so offensive and foul, not to mention that her mother was the one and only Dove. That in itself made me want to hit her. Not to mention she was always complaining and was never without a snide comment in her mouth. The only person who seemed to care how she felt was her mother, and even she seemed to get annoyed with her own daughter's behavior—not that it was any better than her own.

When we arrived at the lake, I came up with a brilliant idea. I yelled, "Rob!" and as he turned, I pushed him right into the water. I laughed as his head became visible.

"Ames, you should get in," he said as a sly grin spread across his face.

I knew something was up, but I wasn't sure what, as I looked at his brown, soaked hair and tried to figure out what he had up his sleeve. I jumped in and tried to swim back up, but I couldn't move. I couldn't reach the top. In my head I screamed, but Rob couldn't read my mind. I needed air; I couldn't breathe. Finally, he pulled me up.

He laughed. "So there, I got you back!"

I felt like screaming; I couldn't believe he thought this was funny. Once I caught my breath, he was going to get it. "Robert Garrison I'm going to kill you!" I yelled as I turned around and swam for shore.

"Amy, what do you mean?" He looked hurt and confused. He seemed to think he deserved to feel that way—for a second, that is.

"Robert, I almost drowned!" I yelled and then looked the other way.

"You're serious. I didn't mean to hurt you, only to get you back for pushing me in." He actually sounded like he meant it. I couldn't believe that he was never serious about anything.

"It's okay, Rob. Just promise me you won't do it again." I looked at him sternly to show him I meant it.

I loved when Prissy and Mary let us get out of kitchen work. It made life more interesting. Made it seem as if I never really had a routine; it was the way I thought every child's life should be, routine-less and enjoyable.

I now know that no life is without routine or without some sort of work, no matter what a person's rank in society is. I guess most children think that life should be workless and that everything should be done for them. I no longer agree with my own thought process as a nine year-old, but then it was a perfectly fine thing to think. I would hope that every child has a way to relieve him or herself of the monotonous way life can sometimes be.

Rob and I did get back in the water and by the time we had to head back, everything was normal between us. That's one of the great things about being so young—we hadn't yet come to terms with what a grudge is. When we stepped back into the kitchen, we had to do the dishes before heading home.

Rob and I didn't quite live in opposite directions, but it was faster for Rob if he went home another way. So, I walked home with Johannah, who also worked in the kitchen and lived only two hovels away from me. Johannah and I tended to skip and warble our favorite song.

"Maiden, Maiden, Maiden fair, grace us with thy presence, to see thy shining face, a world unknown be shown to thee. Oh, Maiden, Maiden, Maiden fair, grace us with thy presence. With your skin so fair and your hair so luscious, oh, Maiden, Maiden, Maiden fair, grace us with thy presence."

That was our favorite song, "Maiden Fair." It was an old, well-known song based on the maiden story, as I called it. Really it was based on the prophecies about a maiden who was yet to come. A lot of people we knew thought of me and Johannah whenever that song was sung.

"'Bye, Johannah!" I yelled, as I walked in to find my mother cooking. "Mama, I'm home," I told her as I walked over to the stove where Mama was working. I was confused, though; I thought there was a ball at Grandfather's that night, but I could have been wrong.

"Why are you making dinner?" I noticed that my mother didn't look too happy.

"Sweetheart, James McCarthy was here today."

I looked at her, even more confused. What did that have to do with dinner?

"Mama, aren't we going over to Grandfather's and Grandmere's tonight for that ball?"

Mama looked at me, smiled, and then sighed. She looked as if she were about to answer, but then stopped after what seemed to be much thought.

"Amy, honey, before your brother was born, His Lordship McCarthy came by and said that a loved one told him of our situation. Today he came by and told me directly who to blame. Amy, I don't want to believe it, but it explains a lot. He said your Aunt Grace told him everything. I completely forgot with all the thoughts that have been flying through my head. Grandmere picked you out the prettiest dress for tonight, and it's on the bed. I'll show it to you."

She obviously didn't want me to ask questions and hoped the excitement about my dress would make me forget what she just told me. I hated when she did that; besides, she knew I would ask later. I could always tell by the way she changed the subject so quickly.

But all I wanted was to know more. I just told myself that this time I'd figure it out for myself, and I planned to ask Aunt Grace about the whole thing.

We both changed quickly into the elegant ball gowns that Grandmere had picked for us. She had a way of knowing the fashion for every age and just what would look good on everyone. I put on the white satin dress with a pink sash around the middle, which became a bow in the back. I loved the puffed short sleeves, and the gloves just made the outfit complete.

Mama's dress was pink and yellow. It flowed all the way down to the floor in the back, and though shorter in the front, it was only short enough that she wouldn't trip over it. Pink and yellow flowers were attached to her wrist, continuing up her arm slightly, and more of the same flowers rested on her shoulders. There was even a matching headpiece. I thought she was the most beautiful person in all Delynelle, and I doubted she could ever be considered ugly to anyone.

All night, Mama ignored Aunt Grace. I couldn't stand it. Finally, I went over to my aunt.

She spoke first. "Amy, why is your mother avoiding me?"

I noticed she wasn't looking at me but in the direction of my mother, who was turning down a dance partner.

"Funny you mention that. You see, today McCarthy sort of paid Mama a visit. He told her that you told him our secret." I was nervous to say something like that, but I knew it had to come out.

"Oh, no!" Aunt Grace shrieked. "Amy, I didn't mean to. He said that if I didn,'t he'd hurt me and whoever else was in the house. I had to, or he would have hurt you. He guessed...he knew...your parents were married...I told him—"

"So you told him to protect me," I interrupted. "That's understandable. I forgive you, and I'm sure Mama will, too." I left to get my mother; I was going to solve this problem before it ever became one.

I walked up to Mama in that dress. I'll never forget how she looked in that dress. It was and always will be imprinted in my mind. She was yet again rejecting a dance. Once she was done, I told her everything about what I found out, but she reacted differently than I'd expected. Instead of understanding, she stormed off toward my aunt.

"So, Grace, you did it to save Amy. Then why didn't you tell me? We could have prevented John from going to prison. But no, you kept it to yourself all along!" My mother yelled at my aunt, as heads turned from every corner of the room.

"Rose, please listen to me," Aunt Grace pleaded.

"I'll listen if I want to, and don't call me Rose! Call me 'Your Excellency,' like almost everyone else here, or 'Mrs. Jonestone.' I forbid the word 'Rose' to ever leave your mouth again," Mama whispered in a deadly tone that turned my aunt's face white.

"But I'm your sister, Rose. I didn't tell you because I didn't want you to worry about it." My aunt began to cry.

"No sister of mine would ever betray me."

I saw McCarthy smiling from the other side of the room as my mother sternly yelled, *"Grace, I never want to see or speak to you again."* Then she stomped her foot, grabbed my hand, and angrily walked at a very fast pace toward the door.

All heads looked to my mother. I gulped and wished I were anywhere else as we walked toward the exit.

"Goodnight, Father, Mother," Mama said as we walked past my grandparents. She gave me a look that let me know I was to do the same. So I did, just to make sure she didn't channel her anger in my direction. The look in Grandfather's eyes was sad. I couldn't tell exactly how he felt, but if he felt anything like I did, he must have thought the whole situation was ridiculous.

Once at home, my mother looked at me. "Amy we need to change your name."

I was shocked. Why did my name need to be changed? She gets into one fight with her sister and she goes crazy.

"Why?"

"I don't want any of my children to have the name Grace!"

Chapter Eleven

My mother looked determined. I knew she was going to do everything in her power to have my name changed.

"I'm going to talk to your father, but I'm sure he'll agree with me. I think I'll go with my second choice for your name: Amythist Amelia Annette Jonestone. How do you like it?" She smiled at me, as if this were the best idea she'd ever come up with. But all I could do was shake was my head.

"Mama, she did it so McCarthy wouldn't hurt anyone. I know it didn't exactly work, but she had good intentions. You can't be mad forever." I smiled and nodded trying to make her see my point of view.

"But, sweetie, she should have told us. We could have done something different, something that could have kept your father from being put behind bars," Mama told me sweetly as she tucked me in and kissed me on the forehead. "Goodnight baby. No more talk of this tonight." Then she left.

I couldn't sleep that night. Aunt Grace didn't deserve this. Sure, some things should have been dealt with differently, but what was done was done. Mama should have forgiven her. She was her closest sister, and now she didn't even want to speak to her.

To make matters worse, she was changing my name. I liked my name, but it already had too many *A*s in it. Why did she have to take away the *G* and add another *A*? I guess I might not have understood where my mother was coming from, but was this really a good enough reason to act this way?

"Wake up, Amy," I heard my mother whisper as she gently shook me awake.

"Hmmm." I yawned as I opened my eyes to see my mother smiling.

"We need to get ready. We're going to see Papa today."

I looked at her, confused, because we weren't supposed to visit him until next Friday.

My mother recognized my confusion. "I moved our monthly meeting, because I have some urgent matters to discuss with your father. We talked about it last night, remember? Do you still like Annette?"

I sighed. "Mama, I like Grace."

She looked at me disapprovingly as we changed our clothes and left.

At the prison Papa looked at us with a smile but added, "I wasn't expecting you until next week." He grabbed my hand and I smiled, wishing we had a better motive for coming a week early. Papa looked ecstatic to see us, but Mama had to go and ruin it by telling him the events of the day before. I didn't want my name changed, but Mama wouldn't let me say anything.

"John, I think we should change Amy's name. I don't want her, or anyone for that matter, to be named after that wretched betrayer." The way my mother described it, it sounded so much worse than it really was. She had my father convinced. That was the end of it. My two determined parents were against me, and I no longer had a chance.

After realizing this, I didn't feel like doing much of anything. I walked away from my parents who were talking about what they thought 'Grace' should be turned into, as well as other things that had to do with name changing.

Once I was far enough away to still see them but not hear them, I sat down, grabbed my knees, closed my eyes, and began to repeat my name over and over again. "Amythist Amelia Grace Jonestone, Amythist Amelia Grace Jonestone." I would not forget that name. My parents might have the authority to change it now, but one day, I promised myself, I would change it back.

I sat there for a long time, just repeating. I wanted and hoped one of my parents would come to their senses and change their minds, or maybe start to think about how I felt. As I sat there, the prison was silent, but then in the midst of that silence a scream that shrieked through the whole building was heard. The worst part about that shriek was that it sounded much to like my mother.

I ran back to Papa's cell like the end of the world was upon us. When I was close enough, I saw my mother on the floor, breathing deeply, holding her wrist. She held the exact spot where the flowers were placed so perfectly the night before. I wrapped my arms around her, hoping everything would be fine.

"Mama," I yelled, as I realized Papa was holding her the best he could with the bars in the way.

"Mama, are you all right?" I bit my lip. It looked as if something had bitten her. It was a deep bite. I held in the tears that wanted to flow, but I didn't want to cry in front of Papa. I hadn't done that since Will's funeral. I was glad Will wasn't here now, because he didn't need to see his mother in so much pain.

"Amy, I'm fine…really I am." I wondered if she meant it or if she was trying to convince herself. She was looking at her wrist, studying the wound. Some of her blonde curls fell from her neat bun onto the blood that was flowing from her wrist. Something wasn't right, I could see that in her eyes. They weren't the same pretty blue eyes that always gazed at me, showing me passion, care, feeling, but now they just looked…dead.

"Papa, what happened?" I asked as a tear began its way down my cheek.

He looked scared and frightened, and I was sure he, too, saw the deadness in her eyes.

"A…a…a…rat, it…just bi—bi—bit her and she screamed." He was in shock. I don't even think he noticed the tears that were landing on his cheeks.

That rat was evil, I decided, and to this day I think that very same thing. At the moment, I didn't realize just how much I would come to hate that rat and all rats.

After Mama assured Papa that she was fine at least twenty times, we left. I was still worried, but hid it. I could tell that Papa was worried, but he wasn't very good at hiding it. Mama seemed to get light-headed and almost fell down at least five times on the way home. She was scaring me. I thought about asking her if we should call a doctor, but with the way she reacted after we asked if she were all right, she told me that there was no way she would abide that.

"Mama, are you sure you're all right?" I finally asked as I helped her stay on her feet.

"I'm fine. It was only a rat bite. People probably get bitten by rats every day," she said as she breathed harder. "I'll be better in the morning."

I wished I could believe her. Maybe she was right, maybe people were bitten by rats every day. But I could only think of one person I knew; and she stood in front of me, trembling as she held on to the walls of our house for support.

Sure enough, in the morning she seemed to back to normal. I was glad.

"Amy, we're going to see the king's council today, to change your name. I received permission from Dove."

I couldn't think of when she had the time to go and talk to Dove, but a day off was a day off. I still wished that somehow I could keep my name. I really liked being Amythist Amelia Grace, but I guess Amythist Amelia Annette would suffice…unless.

"Mama, do we have to do this?" I know it was not the greatest plan, but it was all I could do.

"Amy, do you not like the name Annette? We could find something else."

"No, I want to keep my name the way it is. I've had Grace in my name for nine years. Do I really have to change it? I'm kind of used to it," I told her.

Looking at her, I could tell she was upset. I couldn't tell by her eyes but by the way she bit her lip, crossed her arms, and tapped her foot. Mama's eyes still looked dead.

"Amythist, your father and I have already decided to change your name, and that's that! Now let's go!"

So we left and went to the council. We waited in a line. Mama told the lords why we were there. They gave Mama a paper to sign, and I was no longer Amythist Amelia Grace but Amythist Amelia Annette. I hated it and didn't understand it.

I now fully understood the meaning of grudge, but that is a lesson I would much rather have learned from a book or an explanation, but not from watching it with my own eyes.

Besides that, not much else happened that day. Rob came over and was curious about where I had been lately, because I hadn't been at the kitchen for two days straight. So I told him of the dance and my dress, but mostly of how my mother looked. How she was gorgeous in her dress and so much prettier than me. And of how I wished I looked more like her, with her long, curly, flowing, blonde hair. Rob always found this annoying, and I don't really blame him. I probably complained too much.

"Ames, give it up. Now tell me the good stuff!"

I thought that was the good stuff. Everything else had just led to something much worse than the thing before. I didn't really want to remind myself of the past few days. I told of how I came home and found my mother all upset, and then of her yelling at my aunt. I told him how Mama decided my aunt's name couldn't be a part of me, so we had to change my name ever so slightly to make sure she was never spoken of again. I told him how I was scared and that Mama should see someone, because I knew that no emotion in her eyes couldn't mean anything good—that the rat bite would do something to her. I told him everything.

"Amy, your life is the most interesting thing I've ever heard. It'd make a great book someday, if there was a happy ending. And even if it didn't, I'd read it. It keeps me entertained," Rob chimed sarcastically.

I pushed him for his comment, before I laughed. I told him I'd better go check on Mama, and I left. He smiled, and we decided to go fishing the next day.

When I went inside, Mama was in the bedroom. I walked in smiling, but abruptly stopped. Mama was kneeling on the floor, rocking back and forth, holding her right wrist with her left hand, with tears streaming down her cheeks. As soon as she noticed I was there, she stopped and looked up, her face was pale. She was shivering and sweating all at the same time. I just stared, not knowing what to do, because I'd never seen anyone like that before.

"Get your grandfather or a doctor!" Mama stopped, breathed in deeply, and then added, "Hurry!"

I ran out of the house, with tears in my eyes.

Rob was still close enough to see me. "What's wrong?" he asked.

"Rob, get a doctor. It's Mama!" I yelled.

He nodded and ran in the opposite direction.

When I reached Grandfather's house, the first person I ran into was Aunt Elizabeth and—not that I cared—Aunt Grace. I didn't know if I should keep looking for Grandfather or tell Aunt Grace and risk Mama being angry with me. I risked it.

"Aunt Elizabeth, Aunt Grace, Mama is sick. She's sweating and shivering with fever, and she's pale. I'm sure it's because of the rat bite."

They both looked at me. Each took one of my hands, and I practically flew all the way back home. As we ran, they asked me questions about how the rat had bitten her. I told them how Mama and I had gone to see Papa. Aunt Grace didn't care that my mother would be furious. She didn't care that Mama hated her, because she loved her little sister.

When we all ran into the house and Mama saw Aunt Grace, she mustered enough courage to yell. "How dare you come within ten feet of my home?! You know what you did, and you know you're not wanted!"

"Rose, please, I told you I'm sorry. I will always be sorry. I'll never stop wishing there was something better I could have done. If I knew this would happen, I never would have…"

"Grace, leave! I don't want you near me or my daughter ever again!" My mother's voice was shrill and raspy as she spoke. If I weren't so scared that she would get sicker, I would have stood up for my aunt. Aunt Elizabeth didn't say anything. She was busy trying to calm my mother down, and Aunt Grace just watched, her lip trembling and eyes welling up in tears. I was torn and didn't know what to do.

A few minutes later, Rob showed up with the doctor. Everyone stood around watching, as I told him about the bite. I didn't tell him anything more about the last couple of days, because he wouldn't care. He looked at the bite and gave me something to rub on it and told me sympathetically that it was all he could do. The doctor left and didn't seem to be bothered.

Let's just say that after that, nothing would ever be the same again. I guess that's how things work in life. As soon as something small changes, it affects everything else and can never go back to the way it used to be.

I was known for skipping kitchen work and getting into trouble for it. It was the Amy thing to do. I never cared what people thought, so when all of a sudden people started complimenting me on my attendance, it was a very foreign thing. I couldn't afford to skip anymore. It didn't once matter if a frindlin were taken here and there, but now I needed every gold piece I could get.

Mama's fever kept getting worse, and I wanted to help pay for her treatments. Most of the money I was saving was swept away too quickly by every treatment for fevers known to man. Grandfather helped a lot, but I would not let him pay for it all. I didn't want to be a charity case. Mama always hated when people tried to help, and she didn't want Grandfather to help at all.

I hardly slept at night; I couldn't help but wonder if I'd have a mother in the morning. After Will, I wouldn't have been surprised. I was hungry, too; I only ate scraps from the castle because all my money was going toward everything my mother needed. I slept in the first room on the floor, with lots of blankets supplied by Grandmere, so I wouldn't catch the fever.

I worked harder than I had ever worked in my life, partly to keep myself busy and partly because I had to. Dove gave me a little extra money—I think not because she cared for me specifically, but because she thought no one should be motherless.

"Amy," Rob said as if he were scared.

"Yeah, Rob? Make it quick. I have to get home to Mama." I was in a rush, as always those days.

"Do you think your mother will be all right?" That got my attention.

"Rob, I don't know. She doesn't seem to get better. All she does is tell me she will always be with me, that she loves Papa and me, but sometimes it's like she can't remember anything that's happened, like she's delirious." I turned away as tears trickled down my cheek. I wiped my eyes and turned back to hug him. I continued to cry as I talked. "Mama keeps telling me to take care of Will, when everyone knows he's dead. Rob, I don't know what to do." I lifted my head and looked at him. He looked back.

"Amy, if you ever need any help with anything at all, with your mother, or if you just need to talk, I'm here." He looked at me intensely to show he meant every last word. I smiled at him before he continued. "Ames, that promise is for eternity, not just now while your mama is sick."

I smiled at him before replying. "All right, as long as you live up to it, I'll call on you. And know I'm here for you, too.

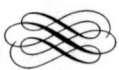

"Amy, honey, come here I want to talk to you."

"All right, I'll be there in a minute," I told Mama as I walked to her bed.

When she talked to me, it was as if everything were normal. She talked to me in the same manner she used to. "Honey, I'm sorry I've been so sick lately, but I think and feel a little bit better. I want you to know that I will always be with you and I will always love you, your father, and your brother. Now, Amythist, I want to tell you something very important."

She stopped and waited for me to nod my head, and then continued. "Sweetie, I want you to know what I think about that dream you had when you were little." She paused for breath. "The one about saving your family, where I die at the end."

I started crying. I was scared about what might happen once our conversation ended.

"Amythist, I didn't mean it that way. What I meant was when I get all the way better, or no matter what happens to me, you have to promise me something." She stopped.

I took the pause to cut in, "Mama, anything. What is it?"

"Amy, you have to do what that dream told you to do. You must save your family."

I felt important. Papa even failed at that. She smiled at me; I loved it when she smiled, and I just wished the life would come back to her eyes. She sang me a song and I fell asleep knowing she loved, with the hope that her speech was a sign that she was getting better.

When I finally woke up, I realized I'd had my dream again. And it finally hit me that if my dream was correct, just like it had been in the past, Mama would die. I already knew my mother knew I had promised, but just to make sure, I looked her straight in the eye and said, "I promise," before leaving to get her some water.

Chapter Twelve

The next day I went to visit Papa. The king had recently granted me permission to visit Papa once a week because of Mama.

"Papa!" I yelled as I ran toward his cell.

"Amy, how's your mother doing?"

"Well, better. She talked like a normal person." A tear trickled down my face. They seemed to do that more often lately.

"Hey, Ames, stop your crying. You said yourself that she's doing better." He smiled at me and grabbed my small hands in his big ones.

"But, Papa, she told me to listen to my dream."

Papa gave me a puzzled look. "What?"

"Remember, Papa, the dream about saving our family?" I tried to make him understand which dream I was talking about.

"Oh, that dream! Yeah, pumpkin, what about it?" He stood there waiting for my answer.

"Somehow, Mama remembered she died in that dream and kept telling me that no matter what happened, I had to listen to that dream and save the Jonestones." Tears were not just trickling down my cheeks but tumbling off my nose and chin.

"Amy, why are you crying? Isn't that a good thing? Then all the Jonestones will be free." My father obviously didn't understand.

"Papa, stop it!" I yelled. "Mama died in that dream! I had it last night. I know if that dream is correct, as it has been before, Mama is going to die. Papa, I'm scared." I could barely hear myself, because I sobbed those words as I looked into my father's concerned, scared eyes.

He looked like he wanted to cry, but probably for my sake he held them in.

"Now, Amy, dreams can be misleading. Mama won't die. You said she was getting better."

"Just a little bit," I interrupted.

"Now, a little bit can turn into a lot. You know I want you to do as your mother told you. Listen to that dream but don't pay attention to the pictures. Your mother is not going to die!" He looked so sure, but at the same time it looked as if he was trying to convince himself.

"All right, Papa," I said, "but I really need to leave now. Dove is expecting me in the kitchen." I smiled at him. "Papa, I love you." I ran to his cage, and he put his cheek against the bar and I kissed it.

I ran to the kitchen, the whole time trying to make it look as if I hadn't been crying.

I walked in, smiled, and asked Aggie, "Where's your mother? I need my list of chores."

She just stared at me in disgust. "She gave them to Prissy to give to you."

"Thanks," I yelled back. I didn't like her very much, but that didn't mean I didn't have any manners.

I walked to the other side of the kitchen, where Prissy was telling Rob how to bake a pie. "Rob, you have to shape the dough in the pie pan to make the pie crust."

I interrupted, "Prissy—"

She turned her head and smiled.

Rob blurted, "Hey, Ames, where have you been?"

I looked at him as if he should know before saying, "To see Papa."

Then Prissy decided she should figure out why I had said her name, so she asked, "Amy, what was it you needed?"

"Oh, Aggie told me I was supposed to ask you what my chores are today."

She looked at me funny. "Sweetie, you didn't believe Aggie, did you?"

I felt so stupid. Why would Aggie, Dove's daughter, tell me what I was supposed to do? All she ever did was try and make things more difficult. Why make them easier today?

"Look!" Rob pointed to the corner, where Aggie was sitting with her only friend, laughing.

"I know," I said under my breath. I hated Aggie more than ever.

Johannah walked over to tell me that Dove was looking for us and had been for awhile.

When we went over to where she was, she was quick to inform me that even if I visited my father, I still should have been here sooner. Then she told Jo and me that we were to make crumpets and tea for the princess and some of her friends, clean up the mess, do the dishes, and then report back to her.

"So, how's your mother?" Jo asked as we walked to the pantry for ingredients.

"All right, I guess. It's kind of hard to tell." I didn't know what else to say. I wanted to tell her of my dream and Mama's speech. I wanted to tell her everything, but I didn't know where to start. I just decided to make things simple by not say anything.

"How about you?" she asked next.

"As good as I'll get until she's better," I answered, even though I knew if my dream was true, that might not happen. A tear found its way down my cheek, and I wiped it away quickly, hoping she didn't see.

"It's okay, Amy. You have a reason to cry. If my mother were as sick as yours, I'd cry, too." She smiled encouragingly. "Amy, if you need anything…"

I smiled up into her eyes. I needed that.

Rob and Johannah walked home with me that night. Most of the time we walked in silence, but even silence meant something to me. I could tell by the looks on their faces they didn't want to make me cry or say the wrong thing. They wanted to help but weren't sure how. I felt sorry for them as we walked. They wanted to help so bad, but I knew that no human being could help. A healing stick or a fairy were the only two things in Delynelle that could do anything.

When we reached my house, Rob finally said something. "Amy, I'm really sorry about your mama. I wish I could do something but I don't think I can do anything that would help."

I smiled. "Thanks for being honest, but you've already helped by being here for me."

He smiled, and I smiled back before turning to Johannah. "Jo, I couldn't get through a day without your asking how Mama's doing. It tells me you care and I need that. Thanks."

Her eyes were watering as she nodded. That's when it hit me—my family were not the only people affected by this. Everyone I knew and everyone she knew was affected. I wasn't the only one suffering.

Tears started to well as I opened the door. I ran to my mother's side. She was sleeping, so I kissed her on the cheek and started a fire in the other room.

More than anything else, I wished that my dream would be wrong. I kept telling myself everything else was coincidental. Mama was not going to die, I told myself. I told Mama every day that she was going to get better. Every day I told the world that she was going to get better. She had to get better. I didn't care what she said. How could she be with me always if she were dead? She told me that all the time, and I believed her because she wasn't going to die.

Mama seemed to get weaker, and the doctors were starting to get nervous. It was almost November and very close to the Feast of Eternal Thanks, a holiday that all Delynelle celebrated. I was going to eat at Grandfather's and Grandmere's, but only because they insisted. I wanted to stay home with Mama. I knew they wanted me to come so that I actually ate a full meal. Ever since Mama had become ill, I hadn't been eating properly because I was too miserable.

I remembered Mama at all times in that gorgeous pink and yellow dress. I swear that's the prettiest she ever was. She was wearing that dress the night before she was bitten, which might have been why I remember it so well. I wished at dinner that I could make a new memory of Mama in an even prettier dress than that, but she could barely stand, let alone take the noise of a party.

I walked into my grandparents' mansion in a very pretty dress that Grandmere picked out for me. It should have fit exactly right, but instead it was baggy. It told the whole world I wasn't eating properly. Everyone stared at me, even my aunts and uncles, not realizing who I was. Finally, Grandfather said to the woman next to me, "Annette, how dare you look at your niece, Amythist, so?"

Immediately she curtsied. Her beautiful blue dress with lace on the ends looked marvelous on her.

As I walked away, I heard her ask, "Father, has Rose been feeding that child at all?"

I started to bawl right there in the hall. My aunt looked at me and then at Grandfather for an explanation.

"Annette, sweet, haven't you heard that your sister has fallen dreadfully ill and her daughter Amy hasn't being eating well ever since?"

Aunt Annette gulped, with silent tears streaming down her cheeks as she walked to my side. "Amythist, or is it Amy? I'm not sure which to call you."

I kept sobbing, and she kept rambling, I think to keep from crying. Finally, she began to make some sense. "Sweetie, I had no idea your mother was ill."

I smiled. "It's all right, Aunt Annette."

She looked at me again, put a wave of hair that had fallen from my bun behind my ear, and hugged me. She sang me a song; her voice was practically identical to my mother's. I would have fallen asleep expect that I forced myself stay awake to listen to that voice, imagining it was Mama.

"Mother, what are you doing?" came a voice. The girl looked alarmed.

"Nastya, this is your cousin, Amy. Your aunt, her mother, is very ill, I'm comforting her."

Her daughter was wearing rich garbs that made me want to puke. I really didn't understand my cousin's taste. She still thought her mother was doing something wrong, because the smirk on her face did not leave or go anywhere toward understanding we were related. I thought she was a spoiled brat.

"Mother, this *girl* is a starved little vixen. I don't have time for those."

"Young lady, take that smug look off your face and apologize to your cousin. Now!" Aunt Annette ordered.

"I apologize for my horrid choice of vocabulary. I doubt you even know what that word means, with the schooling *you've* received."

I pulled my hand into a fist as I tried not to let her rude remark affect me.

Aunt Annette looked at her daughter and sighed. Nastya curtsied with a evil grin and left, followed by her mother, who first apologized for her daughter's behavior.

After that encounter I went to find food. I did feel a little hungry.

As I grabbed a plate, Nastya came over. "So you're my no-good cousin Amythist Amelia Grace Jonestone. Your mother was definitely the odd one out, just like my elder sister Meila. Your mother is ill and probably deserves it." She smirked.

I don't think I hated anyone as much as I hated her then. I didn't understand why she acted this way, so I went to the only aunt I knew would tell me.

"Amy, your Aunt Annette did not raise that child to act that way. She just fell in love with a man who has a problem disciplining his children. He thinks they can do no wrong. He's too soft."

"Aunt Grace, can't she punish them?" I asked.

"Well she does, but the two middle children, Sigurd and Nastya, pay no heed to her warnings. They don't care what she does. She's only their mother, and to them, if their father wouldn't do anything about it, they have no problem doing it. Meila and Edwin are her eldest and youngest. They are the sweetest things you could ever meet."

I nodded, showing that I understood.

"I find it funny, though. Your Aunt Annette may be one of the sweetest people to ever exist, but when she was your and Nastya's age, she viewed the poor exactly the way her daughter does. Nastya will grow out of it, I promise."

I smiled, knowing that she would never lie to me.

When I walked through the door to our hovel, I checked on Mama. She was sleeping. I put a new cold cloth on her head and went to bed in the other room.

That night I had my dream again. The pictures flashed by as I saw myself working in a kitchen and visiting my papa in the very cell I went to once a week. I saw Mama yelling at Aunt Grace. The whole time the words *Amy, save your family. Save your family; it's all up to you* repeated over and over again. Finally, I saw myself sitting next to Mama's bed. The words stopped and were replaced with *Come back, come back!* I was holding my mother's dead, limp body in my arms.

I woke up and cried that fear was so seemed imminent. It could happen at any time and I knew it. I wanted her to heal; I wanted her to live.

"She is going to live. Mama is not going to die," I whispered to myself.

I didn't understand why my dream showed me things that were going to happen to me, especially if saving my family wasn't going to stop them. It didn't make any sense. Why me, anyway? I was only nine years old. No other nine-year-old had the weight of huge a family problem on her shoulders. Why me?

Chapter Thirteen

I wasn't expected at the kitchen until ten o'clock, but I woke up at nine-thirty, and it took at least twenty minutes to walk to the castle from my house. That meant I'd be lucky if I arrived on time.

"Well, Amy, is it just me or are you slipping back into old habits?" Dove looked at me, "Well, girl, I didn't hear an answer, and guess what I want?"

I gulped and looked at my feet. "You want an answer."

She smiled at me and then gave me my chores. I tried to tell her why I was late, but as usual, she didn't listen but continued to tell me my duties for the day.

"Now, Amy, when you're done with that, I need you to mop the floors. Then you need to do the dishes. The…Amy, are you listening to me?"

I hopped back into reality. "Of course, Dove, I always listen. I like to listen…" I told her weakly.

"Well, Amy, if you like to listen so much, then you won't mind repeating what I just said."

I looked up at her in disbelief. I had no idea what she'd just said.

"Aggie never listens to you, but you don't do this to her," I complained, knowing that was the wrong move the second after I said it.

"Amy, that's a daughter's privilege. You, on the other hand, might as well be parentless, so you'd better listen this time. I will not repeat it again, and I'm the only one who knows what your chores are today."

After she said that so *nicely*, I felt like crying, but I held it in. I listened to every last word she said, and I knew she added more to the list because there was no way I could finish that anytime before dinner.

I immediately went to work. It took me two hours to mop the floor. Aggie told her mother that I was rushing, and therefore missing spots, but I wasn't. I don't think a kitchen floor has ever been cleaner. It should have been done an hour and a half before I was allowed to be done.

The whole day, I didn't see even one of my friends, not Prissy, Rob, Mary, or Jo. It was as if Dove wanted to make my day miserable.

Finally around four o'clock, Rob and Jo found me. "Hey, do you want us to walk home with you?"

I looked up at them and smiled.

"I can't go. Dove gave me a really big workload today, and I'm just over half-finished now. I'll probably be here for a few more hours."

They looked at me, shocked, but I just sighed.

"Amy, what are you going to do? Should one of us go watch your mum?" Johannah looked as if she thought Dove was mad, which she was.

"How could Dove do this? You need to take care of your mother, not work here!"

I smiled. "Jo, if you want, you could go look after Mama for me."

"You would let me do that?" She seemed happy that she could help.

"Yeah, go," I told her as she ran for the door.

"So, Ames, could I help you with anything, like that oven you're scrubbing?"

"Yeah, if you want to." I smiled; my best friends never let me down. "So, obviously, you have nothing to do today," I said thinking that was the only reason he would stay to help.

"Actually, I was supposed to help Ma with the twins, and when Father got home, I was supposed to help him mend a leak in our roof, but they'll understand."

After he said that, I realized he was more considerate than I'd ever thought. I smiled.

We scrubbed and scraped the oven and the sink, and set everything up for tomorrow. We were finished by five. If it had been just me, I would have been there for at least another hour.

When I arrived home at about five-thirty, Jo was still there with my mother.

"Thanks," I whispered to them as they began to leave.

"I offered, remember?" Jo told me, smiling as she tried to let me know that no thanks was necessary.

After they were gone, I walked over to Mama's sleeping body and kissed her on the cheek. I looked at her wrist, with the scar from where the rat had bitten her. Mama's arm was red all the way to her shoulder. I remembered when first her hand turned red, I ran to the doctor to ask him what it was. He proceeded to tell me that her infection was spreading and they would try to drain it. Those draining processes were ones I could not watch and seemed to hurt dreadfully. Now the infection was all the way up her arm.

The infection never improved. I was starting to wonder if the doctors knew what they were doing. Mama kept getting worse and worse, and it scared me. Was Mama going to die, as the dream said? I started to cry as I looked at my mother's sleeping face and her sunken cheeks, something she never had before she became ill. I cried because this sickness was taking everything from her—her beauty, her energy, and maybe even her life. As the tears started to fall, Mama woke up.

"Amy, honey, are you crying?"

I gulped the rest of my tears down and struggled to keep them there. "Now Mama, why would I do that? Everything is going to be fine." My lip was quivering and I hoped she didn't notice.

"Now, Amy, listen, you're a whole lot stronger than I ever was at nine. I would have been crying constantly. I know you don't want to cry in front of me, but it's okay. You can. It's not going to scare me or make me worse, I promise. I want to know how you feel, so no more of this business of hiding your tears."

I was now crying in front of her, more because I was happy than because I was scared. She was talking like she used to, something she rarely did.

"Ames," she continued, "you're the strongest nine-year-old I've ever seen. When you were five, Grandmere told me she was amazed with how you coped with everything that happened that year, and she didn't think most grown women could handle something like that. Amy, you dealt with it better than I did. I wasn't much of a mother that year. I screamed and wailed and acted like a child. You tried to make the best of it, tried to go back to normal, while I did everything I could to make sure the world knew I was hurting. I'm very proud of you."

I smiled. I had to tell her how I was feeling now or she might never know.

"Mama, but now I'm more scared than I ever have been before. If you leave me, Mama, I don't think I could live."

My mother looked at my tear-stained cheeks and ran her finger down it until her hand was placed over my heart, and she smiled. "Amythist, I'm not going anywhere right now, but if I do, then here," she said and looked at her hand covering my heart, "I'll always be with you."

I looked up at her, confused.

She looked me in the eye and said, "Sweetheart, no matter what happens, I'll always be with you in your heart."

I nodded.

Mama continued, "Amy, I'll always be with you because I love you and you love me. Our hearts are combined, so we are connected and we will never leave each other."

I didn't know what to say after that, so I didn't say anything at all. I hugged Mama and she hugged back. She sang to me just like she did so many nights ago.

The next morning, I woke up next to Mama. She was still breathing. I went to get up and get ready. Today I needed to visit Papa. I left a note for Mama so she wouldn't worry, and I left her to sleep.

A few minutes later when I arrived at the prison, a guard asked, "Haven't you been here once this week already?"

I looked at him with remorse. Most of the guards thought I was a nuisance. "No, but I was here sometime last week."

They all mumbled as they let me pass.

"Papa!" I yelled as I ran down the prison hall. Everyone looked out through their bars at me; I hated when they did that.

"Amy, is that you?" There was my father looking out at me as I ran to him. I wished he were out of that cage they made him live in. I wished he could come home.

"Papa, Mama isn't getting any better. The infection keeps spreading, and now it's snowing. Papa, the cold won't help her. I wish it would stop snowing." I told him as I looked out his window. It had been snowing for three days nonstop. I wished it was the middle of summer, because heat would have been good for Mama.

"Pumpkin, stop worrying. Nothing is going to happen to your mother," he said sternly, as if he was so sure, but a tear trickled down his face.

"Papa, you're in denial. You don't hear her when she talks. She keeps talking about important things that everyone should hear, but I don't know, it's hard to explain. She sounds like she will die, but then she tells me she won't. I don't know what I'll do if she dies. How am I supposed to go on living if she does?" I was crying. This had been on my mind a lot lately and I'd tried to push the feelings away. I really didn't want to think about the possibility, but I found that I couldn't help myself.

"Amythist." I was shocked he used my full name, "No matter what happens to us as a family, we will always be family. Amy, she will never, ever, really leave."

Tears were wildly tumbling down my face. "I know."

"You do?" he asked, surprised.

"Yes, I do. That's what Mama talked about last night when she told me that she will always be with me. She told me it's because I love her and she loves me." The tears were running down both of our faces now.

"She's right, Amy. She'll always be with us."

"Papa, I know she's right, but what if she's wrong? How can we go on?"

"Well, if that were the case, which it's not, we would do just that—go on."

I could tell he hated his answer to my question, but I knew there was no better one. "But how, Papa?" I was now crying so uncontrollably that I didn't think I'd ever be able to stop.

"Amy, if it comes to that, we just will. I can't tell you how, but we will over time." Then he started crying harder than I had ever seen him cry before, yet he did so silently.

"There, there, Jones," said a prisoner from across the room. "Calm down. At least you'll get outta here."

My father gave him the ugliest look.

"Sorry, sorry. Just tryin' ta sho'ya the brighter side." As he looked away, I could have sworn I heard him say, "I wish I'd a wife ta cry about."

If I hadn't been so sad, I probably would have laughed at that remark, but instead I ignored it. "I have to go. Dove will be furious if I'm late," I told Papa regretfully.

I couldn't go to the kitchen though. I wanted my mama. I wanted her to get better. All I wanted to do was take care of my mother.

When I walked into the bedroom about half an hour later, Grandmere was sitting next to the bed, running her fingers through Mama's golden-blonde hair.

"What are you doing here?" I asked, shocked.

"Amythist, I could ask you the same thing. Why aren't you at the kitchen?" She looked stern and strict at the moment, something I wasn't used to seeing in my grandmother.

"Well, I decide not to go today. I wanted to stay here with Mama." Tears were gathering in my throat as I struggled to keep them intact.

"Amy, I guess you could say I'm here for the exact same reason. I just wanted to make sure my baby was all right." A single tear left her eye as she looked at her daughter and stroked her very pale cheek.

I ran over and hugged her. I knew this had to be just as hard on her as it was for me.

Finally, when we stopped crying, she looked at me. "Amy, have you eaten anything today?"

"No," I answered honestly.

"Well, then, I must insist that you do. How about lunch?"

I smiled at her as she smiled at me.

"And that you spend Wintereve with us."

"Well, lunch sounds good, but the king has given Papa permission to spend Wintereve with Mama and me, so I'll stay here with them."

Grandmere smiled at me.

"Well, then, we'll just have to come here, won't we? And a few of your aunts and uncles. We'll supply the food. It'll be wonderful to see your father again. It's been a long time." She continued to smiled as I ran over and gave her hug to show how happy she made me.

"Grandmere, I would love that, and I'm sure Mama and Papa would, too." I almost left it at that, when I remembered something, "Aunt Grace can come, but don't let her get too close to Mama or Papa, but *I want her to come.*"

She smiled, "I'll let her know."

Chapter Fourteen

A few days passed, and I went to get Papa from prison. This was the first time since the bite that he would get to see Mama. I didn't tell him about everyone being there, because Grandmere and I thought that it would be a good surprise.

As we walked to the shack I lived in, Papa held my hand. I couldn't remember the last time we walked hand-in-hand, but it was probably at Will's funeral. I quickly disposed the idea of my brother being buried, as I put my mind back on how surprised my papa would be.

Finally we were home, where Papa should be. The door creaked open. As soon as I lit the candle next to the door, seven or eight people yelled "Surprise!" What surprised me was that my mother was sitting there, right in the middle, yelling along with them. She still looked sick and pale, but she was smiling.

Papa smiled at the sight of her, as a tear trickled down his cheek. I knew it was both a happy and sad tear. He hadn't seen her since the bite, and she had lost at least twenty pounds since then and was very weak. As I realized this I began to cry. I knew this could very well be the last time they saw each other alive. That thought was not comforting, and I quickly got rid of it.

"Stop it, you two," Mama finally said as a tear made its way down her cheek. "It's Wintereve and John is home to celebrate. Let it be a happy one, with only smiles and no tears." She smiled as she stifled her tears, and Papa and I quickly did the same.

In my opinion, it was the best Wintereve I ever had as a child. Papa and Mama together, and seeing that after all this time they still loved each other. Mama might have gone to bed only an hour after Papa arrived, and Papa sat by her side for almost another hour, just watching her sleep. It made me feel as if everything was all right, that nothing could stop us from being a family. I knew that if Papa were here with us all the time, where he was supposed to be, he would take care of Mama, as he should. I liked knowing that everything they said about their loving each other always was true. I had no reason to doubt their words, even though they hardly saw each other. It was comforting.

After awhile, Papa ascended from the bedroom, and he spent the rest of the night catching up with everyone else, especially me. It was true that he saw me once a week, but that was for very short amounts of time. We talked for a long time about lots of different things, mostly about my friends. That was one thing he knew almost nothing about. I told him almost everything there was to know about Rob and Jo. We both laughed at a lot of the things those two did. I had a good time with Papa, and everyone seemed to think it best not to bother us; I was glad of that. I needed to be with him alone, when he wasn't behind bars, to hug him and feel like we weren't in the situation we were in.

When Papa finally had to go back to the prison, everyone was upset. They all told him they wished he didn't have to back and they thought it was atrocious the way he was kept locked up. I didn't want him to leave, either. I remember that I even tried to persuade him to run away so he wouldn't have to go.

"Amy, you know I can't do that. If I did and I were caught, King Sencraugh would never let me out."

I frowned, but I let him go.

I hated the day after Wintereve. I always had to be at the kitchen extra early, to clean up the mess from the parties and the feast the royals had the day before.

"So, Ames, how was your Wintereve? Did your father faint when he saw your mama?"

"No, Rob, but he cried."

He looked at me quizzically.

"I mean it. So did Mama and I—we all cried, but it was a good thing, if that makes any sense."

He looked surprised but didn't argue with me.

That day was quiet and so were most days after that. There wasn't much to talk about. Mama now seemed to think there wasn't much left to hold on for. It seemed that I was the only reason she was still alive. She would tell me every day that she loved me, but she'd also tell me to tell Papa that she loved him.

As January approached, it looked as if she wouldn't even make it to my birthday. Her infection now covered her whole arm, and the doctor told me that once it reached her heart they couldn't do anything about it. My birthday came, and Mama was still alive and holding onto life dearly. She gave me hope that she really was fighting for life, but I could tell it was costing her.

The rest of February went by slowly, and I thought it would never end. Now I sometimes find myself wishing it never did. Mama seldom talked anymore, and I knew it was because she no longer had the energy to do so, but I could tell she spent most hours, when she wasn't sleeping, thinking. I didn't know what she thought about, but it didn't matter, because she was still alive. When she did talk, it never made much sense to me.

Finally, it was March 1. Mama had made it to March, and I was so happy. I didn't think she could last much longer, and knew it would probably be easier on her if she just died. But I knew I could never voice that, because I needed her alive, not dead. I wanted her to live. I knew she knew it, too. I knew that was why she kept fighting for me—not for anyone else, but for me.

It was hard to look at her sometimes. I remembered her once being the most beautiful person I had ever seen, but now she was pale and sickly, her cheeks were sunken, and her hair was thinning. She was nothing more than skin and bones. I wished she would get better, but at this point I could tell that every breath was a struggle. I wished that she could feel better and wasn't in pain, but she was.

On March 7, something happened. Mama had not spoken for the past few weeks, but that day she called me over.

"Amy," she said and took a breath, "come here." She breathed wildly for a few minutes as I walked over to her bed.

"Sweetie, I can't hold on much longer...I've bare... barely been...able to...breathe the...last couple...of days. Now listen to me...my time is...running very short. Tell...Grace...that I was...stupid...I wou...would have done the...same thing...but...was too...stupid to rea...realize it. Do what your...dream...told...you to do...save your fam...family. Amy, I lo...lo...love yo...I love you."

And then she was gone, just like that. I didn't know what to do. Tears came in torrents from my eyes. Everything was a blur through my tears as I lifted her dead body into a hug. And then I screamed at the top of my lungs.

"Mama, no! Mama! Come back! Come back! Please come back...come back." I sat there on her bed,

holding her and crying, not able to move. I probably cried for hours.

The door creaked open, and I didn't care who it was. I didn't care about anything anymore.

"Hey Am…" My grandfather stopped mid-sentence when he saw me crying inconsolably over my mother's body.

He leaned over and picked me up, but I resisted as I kicked at him to let me go.

I screamed into his chest until finally I hugged him and cried into his shoulder, hoping he would never let go of me. After a few minutes, I looked up to see a blurred version of my grandfather. I heard him trying to suppress his own tears.

"Grandfather, Mama is…Mama is…Mama is dead." I started to say loudly, but ended in a whisper as I realized I had a difficult time saying those words. I didn't want to say those words. How could she be dead? Was it because I didn't take good care of her? Was there any way I could have prevented this? Was there anything anyone could have done? I hated those words, but now that I had said them, I knew it was real.

"I know," he choked back. A steady flow of tears burst from his eyes.

"Do you know what this means?" he asked as he set me down, before he walked to my mother's lifeless body.

"I no longer have a mother." Tears once again made their way down my cheeks. I no longer knew where they were coming from, but they still came. I watched Grandfather look up at me as tears splattered his face.

"Amy, you will always have a mother. Rosemarie Rachel Reality Jonestone will *always* be your mother, no matter the conditions you face, no matter how far apart. She will always be your mother. She will always be my youngest daughter." He told me all this with a steady flow of tears and his this-is-important look on his face.

I nodded, not sure I could trust my voice anymore. But what he said sounded familiar; it was him confirming what Mama had told me over and over again. "I'll always be with you" is what she had told me, and Grandfather made me think that maybe she was right, that Mama would always be with me somehow.

"I still have a mother, but I don't understand what you're asking," I told him as soon as I found my voice.

"Your father, Amy, he's free. You have to go and tell him the news. He's free."

I looked up and a quick smile came to my face, but it quickly disappeared. My father was free at the expense of my mother. It wasn't fair. I'd wanted him out more than anything ever since I was five years old, but I'd wanted him out so that Mama, Papa, and I could all be a family again. Why was I allowed only one of my parents, while all the other children were allowed both? I wanted Papa, but I wanted Mama back. I wanted life to reenter her body.

"I'll go get him," I told my grandfather as I wiped my eyes.

"Do you want me to come with you?" he asked as he wiped his own eyes.

"No, Grandfather, I want to do it myself. But I would like it if you could stay with Mama's body," I told him as I tried to stem my tears.

"Amy, for you I can do that."

Through my tears I saw a smile appear on his face for a fleeting moment.

I left after one more look at Mama's dead body, and a tear trickled as I opened the door and ran. I didn't want to see a single face or hear a single voice; I just wanted to get what I had to do over with.

I hated the world, I hated everything, I hated that rat, I hated Papa for letting it bite her, and I hated the doctors for not fixing the problem. I hated myself for not stopping her from seeing Papa a week early, I hated that I couldn't make her better. I hated myself; it was all my fault.

Then I found myself hating her for not holding on longer, for leaving me, but I stopped that quickly. I stopped because I knew she held on longer than she should have. I saw how much pain she went through those last few weeks. She even told me the only reason she lasted that long was for me. I knew she didn't want to leave me. I cried harder as I realized this whole thing was my entire fault, just like everything else.

When I reached the prison, the guard saw my tear-worn face and looked at me as if he were sorry. He didn't ask why I was there; I think he already knew, and I didn't feel up to telling a complete stranger. I just walked in. I don't think I could have told him if I'd tried.

I ran down the corridor. It was so familiar that I didn't even watch where I was going. I couldn't see anything in less than a blur, anyway.

When I knew I was close to Papa's cell, I yelled, "Papa!" I looked up and tried to stop my tears as I looked at his blurry appearance.

"Amy, what's wrong?" he asked.

I couldn't tell if he was concerned or if he already knew. His face was too disoriented from my consistent tears to tell.

"Papa." More tears came as I tried to will myself to tell him what he needed and deserved to know. "Papa... Mama is...is..." I didn't have to finish my sentence and I was grateful for that.

He grabbed my hand and joined me in tears. I was glad he didn't ask questions, because I couldn't answer questions yet.

"All because of a rat!" My father wailed. We continued to cry until a guard I hadn't seen earlier came over.

"Be quiet! Why do you have to make so much noise?" the guard complained.

"Please, sir, my daughter just informed me that my wife...my wife died this morning. Let us be." I was still crying while he told the man. I was thankful he did it and I didn't have to.

"Come with me. I must take you to the king."

"Why?" I asked through my tears, as I thought of how awful the king could make this day.

"Don't you want your father back?" he asked me, as if I should know how a prison release was supposed to work.

"Yes, of course I do." I sniffled.

The next thing I knew, he unlocked Papa's cage door. Papa then picked me up, and I cried into his shoulder as we walked to the castle.

When we reached the throne room, Papa put me down but held my hand. I heard him gulp, as if scared about what might happen next. The guard pushed open the door and we entered, grief stricken.

"Sir Charles, what have you brought me? A pauper's child and a prisoner? What is this about?"

Prince Henry sat there looking at us. I thought he found the sight of us disgusting, and maybe he did. I'd have to ask him.

"Your Majesty, I present to you John Samuel Noah Jonestone and his daughter, Amythist Amelia Annette Jonestone. This man has been in your prison for a little over five years, after the discovery that he married above his status." The guard paused and looked up to the king, who nodded. "In his case, the only way for him to be set free was for him to receive a divorce or for his wife to die."

The king nodded again. "Well, this morning I was told that his wife, Rosemarie Somner, died." The prince whispered something in his father's ear and left.

The guard continued. "I thought they should be brought here so you could make sure these claims are true and to make sure this was definitely what was required for his release." The guard bowed and motioned for us to do the same as we waited for the king's response.

"Fetch me the Jonestone records!" he told Sir Charles as he told us to rise. After what seemed forever, Sir Charles returned with my family's file.

"I remember Rose when she was a child. It was quite sad what she did with her life, actually, and it ended so quickly," the king said as he thumbed through our records.

Some time later, he sent a messenger to see if my claim was true. I didn't think it was necessary; anyone who looked at me for more than a minute would have to know that something wasn't right in my life. Why did they have to see her dead body for themselves before they'd believe me? When the messenger returned, confirming everything I had said, they let us go.

The walk back to our small house was quiet, and my tears had subsided for the time being. I figured that as soon as I looked at Mama again, they would come rushing out. All they needed was to restock.

Once we walked through the door, I saw so many people: Mama's sisters—all of them except Annette—Grandmere, Grandfather, and Papa's side of the family, too. Our little house had too many people in it, especially since I just wanted to be left alone.

When we reached the bedroom, everyone left. My father knelt over her limp, no longer fun-loving, perfectly beautiful body, grabbed it up in his arms, and allowed his tears to flow. I began to cry all over again. I hugged him as he hugged Mama, and we both wailed.

Papa would never know how I felt, how seeing your mother die right in front of you felt. Papa wasn't even there to watch her grow sicker and sicker! I knew he wanted to be, but he wasn't. He could never understand how it felt to be nine and have the weight of the world on your shoulders, because to a nine-year-old, your mother is your world.

"We're in this together." He hugged me and whispered in my ear.

"No, Papa, we're not! You weren't here when she died, and you didn't see her in pain every day! Papa, you will never understand how it feels to know that your mother might die and you have no control over it, yet you have to watch what you can't control every day! How can you understand? Papa, you never heard her mumble things that didn't make sense. How can you say that?" I took a deep breath as tears poured down my face.

"Amykins, you know I would have done anything to be there. You have to believe that I wanted to. You may think that I can't understand, and for the majority you're right, but I had less control over the situation than you did. Like you said, I couldn't even watch the infection make its way through her. I couldn't even try. At least, you could try," he told me as a tear trickled down his cheek.

I was furious. I already knew all of that, but that didn't mean I would admit it, and I still couldn't see how it related at all.

Still, I found a way to calm my voice and tell him, "I know you wanted to be, but you weren't. I know you're just as much upset as I am, but you're not ever going to know what I went through." Tears were pouring out my eyes; it was as if I had never cried before, and now ten years worth of tears were coming down my cheeks.

"You were not there when the doctors were estimating how if she'd live or if she didn't recover how long she had. You weren't there when people figured that I might as well be considered parentless. You weren't there when I was at Grandfather and Grandmere's and no one recognized me; when all my relatives who hadn't seen me since I was four thought I was some beggar girl they'd let into the house and were feeding for the simple fact that they felt sorry for me. Papa, you will never know how that feels," I yelled at him. I was breathing wildly, and my heart was beating faster than I ever imagined it could.

"Amy, I know it's not the same, but I would have… oh, Amy I wish I'd been the one who was bitten, and not your mother." He said this so sincerely, before his tears cam back again.

How could I really be upset with him? He wished he'd been bitten instead, but I wished it wasn't anyone.

"Papa, I'm sorry. I know you wanted to be here. I'm just angry that she's gone and angry that everything I did didn't work and…I'm sorry," I told him as he hugged me, and we both cried all over again.

Two days later was the funeral, and all my family, and mine and Mama's friends were there. Not many of my mother's childhood friends were there. I learned at the funeral that many people had rejected her once they found out who she'd decided to marry.

The man who spoke at the funeral talked about how my mother was determined and strong-willed, but most of all that she was kind. I didn't hear most of it, because I was to busy trying not to cry, yet wanting to all at the same time. My efforts failed, though, because about every few minutes a single tear would draw a line down my cheek.

When it was time for them to put the casket in the ground, I started to bawl, I couldn't stop myself. Papa hugged me and told me everything would be all right. I knew nothing could ever be the same, because she was gone.

At one point that day, I realized that for one little boy this was a good thing, and maybe in a sense it was fair. I'd had my mother all to myself for practically my whole life, and now maybe it was Will's turn. For him, this was wonderful; he'd get to see his Mama again. At least someone was happy.

That night I had my dream again, but this time something was added. I was standing in a room and heard myself yell, "I did it!"

When would that day come, and what did I do? I hated this dream. This dream told me I'd lose my father and I did. It told me I'd see him in prison, it told me I'd work in the kitchen, and it told me my mother would die. It showed me how messed up my life would become before it ever was even messed up. My dream never even bothered to include Will, probably because it knew he wouldn't be around long. I wished—no, I hoped—that I wasn't as old as I looked when I said, "I did it," because I needed that part sooner. It looked like I'd be an adult.

I stayed away from everyone for the next couple of days and cried my soul out. Then, one day a breeze came through my window, and everything seemed better. After I sat up, I felt a hand on my shoulder. It felt like Mama's, and that's when I realized she was right—she would always be with me.

Chapter Fifteen

Over the next few months I began to remember why I loved my papa so much. I never really forgot, but five years is a long time to be without a father. I remembered what life was like when he was around, but I had forgotten how it felt. I remembered loving it, but until now I would have had to dig so deep into my mind to find it. I was as happy as I could get, considering that my mother had just died, but if it weren't for Papa I don't think I ever would have moved on with my life.

Papa put life back into the house. Even before Mama died, our home had started to feel like no one should live there. Nothing ever happened there; all anyone ever did was sleep and take care of the sick. With Papa there was music, awful music, but still music. There was laughter again and fun.

My father started practicing his instruments about a month after Mama's death. I remembered his playing the harp, violin, and piano as being not very good, but if anyone could imagine, it was worse. His violin went from scratchy to—I don't know how to describe it except to say scratchier. His harp playing had been loud before, but now it was even louder. I didn't think a harp could get that loud. His piano was worse. His flute wasn't perfect, where it had been before. Aunt Grace told me one night that his flute playing used to sound like an angel.

Aunt Grace had been forgiven by both my parents, and I was glad. This made life easier.

Kitchen life went back to the way it used to be before Mama became sick; if anything, I went far beyond my old habits of skipping kitchen work. I probably was only at the kitchen for, at most, an hour every day. Rob and Jo skipped every once in awhile, but not anywhere near the amount I did. I loved coming in the morning, working for about an hour, and then leaving, only to return the next day to see Aggie eyeing me in a way that made me grin with pride. She never told on me, but I could tell she was jealous. To be honest, I really didn't care how much work I finished; instead, I was perfectly content with not doing any of it.

Papa got a job as the lamp lighter. He walked on stilts and lit the candles on all the lampposts in Drell. So, every night we would eat dinner, and then he'd light the lamps, come home, sleep, and then wake up too early for me and put them out. I thought it must be the best job in all of Delynelle; it had to be so illuminating walking on those stilts and saying hello to everyone. I remember telling people what my father did when I was ten, and all the children would *ooh* and *ahh*. I was considered as the daughter of the man on stilts. It was grand the way they all acted, compared to when I said he was a prisoner.

Unlike me, who loved what her father did, he hated to see me work. This was one of the main reasons I didn't. I really didn't need to work. Papa was making enough for the two of us. I hated to listen to Dove, and Aggie was a pain in the neck, so I just didn't go.

One day, Rob came over and asked, "Amy, when are you going to stop being a no-show? Come back to work, please." He looked upset.

"I don't know. Why?"

"Ames, it just isn't any fun without you. Prissy and Mary think that Dove might go to the extreme of whipping you or something if you don't come back soon."

I knew why he wanted me back, but I really didn't know how to answer. "Rob, she can do whatever she likes to me. I've been doing everything she's ordered me to do since Mama was sick, and I just needed a break." I paused to think. "I'll be back to normal Monday, I promise." I smiled and he looked at me contently.

"Which 'normal'? Before your mother became sick or after?"

"Before," I told him as I thought about how much grief I had been giving Dove lately.

"Good!" Rob replied with a smile. I was glad that he seemed happy about it. "So we'll sneak away every once in awhile?"

"Yeah," I retorted, "this is me you're talking to, remember. I have to get away from that kitchen every now and then."

We both laughed as he told me how true that remark was, and I playfully punched him in the shoulder.

I was still rebel Amy Jonestone to Dove. I would never be some suck-up, like most of the people in the kitchen. I knew they were scared of her, but still it was pitiful. That reason was as good as any to skip kitchen work.

Most of the time when I skipped kitchen work by myself, it was to visit the people I felt weren't visited enough. That's when I went to see Mama's and Will's graves. I went here only when I really needed to think or when I needed one of them for some reason. I still wasn't over my mother's death, and Will's—well, I still felt it was my fault even if it happened almost five years before. I missed them both equally. I couldn't express to anyone how much that was, and I felt that they should still be right here beside me, but they weren't. Most of the time I would talk to them, even though they weren't really there. Or I would just read their graves over and over again. Will's read:

William John Noah Jonestone
September 17, 1127–October 21, 1127
Sweet Son
Darling Brother
Precious Child

I always found myself thinking it was sad that he'd never had the chance to accomplish anything. What his tombstone said was true. I had helped decide what it should say, now almost five years ago. I hated thinking that today he'd be four-and-a-half and running around like any little boy who doesn't have any cares or worries. I imagined he'd have blond curls and gray eyes, as he did when he was alive, and he'd still have a sweet, round face. I knew he would look like Mama. She deserved to have a handsome son, since she didn't have a very pretty daughter.

I knew he never really left, and deep down I could still see his precious smile whenever I needed a smiling face. I knew he would never leave, because he hadn't left yet. I only hoped that Papa and I would be able to keep each other, because I knew that neither of us could go on for long if we lost the other—no matter how much we told ourselves the others hadn't really left us.

After looking at Will's grave, I'd go over to my mother's, which read:

Rosemarie Rachel Reality Somner Jonestone
August 10, 1103–March 7, 1132
Kind, Gentle, Sweet Women
Loving Mother and Wife
I'll Always Be with You

It took me awhile to truly understand my mother's tombstone, because that last line was confusing. I wondered why anyone would want that said on their tombstone, but it was in my mother's will. She distinctly said that saying had to be on it, so how could we not if it had been one of her wishes. She told me that all the time when her health was failing. When I was a very little girl, she told it to me so often that I remember asking her stop, because I was so annoyed with her little saying. I find myself wishing I didn't ask her that, because by now I knew what she meant by it. I felt what that saying meant every day. No matter what happened, she would always be with me. I could feel her. Whenever I needed strength for anything, I could feel an invisible hug. I received one, every night before I went to bed, whether I needed it or not. I knew it was her, my mama, hugging me goodnight.

I missed that loving, kind, sweet woman I called Mama more than ever in the three months since she'd been gone.

June had begun, and with it the first summer without Mama. I couldn't imagine what that would be like, but then again, it was my first summer in a long time with my papa. We had lots of picnics together, we talked, and we played tag by the lake. Mama was never there, though, to scold us about getting our clothes dirty, or sing, or do any thing we used to do together. I missed all of it so much. I wanted a real, physical hug from her. I loved the invisible ones I felt every night, but they weren't the same.

This might sound odd, but I even missed her yelling at me for doing the stupid little things that all children do. I missed it all, from her smile to her singing to her scolding and everything in between.

By Mama's birthday, everything was getting easier, but it still seemed harder for that day to pass.

It was long and sad. There was no cake and no smiling face to say, "I can't really be this old," as she would say every year. Thirty, that's how old she would be today on August 10, not an age before which most people die, but she died, just as my brother did. Life didn't seem fair at all today.

"Papa."

"Yes, pumpkin," Papa answered, with his corny smile all across his face.

"Why can't everything be the way we want it to be?" I knew this question was impossible to answer. I didn't really expect him to have the answers to our world.

"Well, Amykins, that question does not have an easy answer. I know that lots of things have happened to us which we never would have wanted to happen." He paused.

I was curious as to how he would answer me, but I had to say something. "Papa, I'm glad you're back, but I want Mama and Will here, too. And I don't want someone to have to give our family its freedom, but I want to already be free." A teardrop fell from my eye onto my nose, and Papa took his index finger and wiped it away.

"Amy I know you would prefer life to be perfect, but imagine if it were: it'd be kind of boring. No one would get into trouble or drop anything, and everyone would be serious and lack a sense of humor." He smiled, so I smiled.

Papa was probably right. If no one was funny, then no one would laugh, and that was one of the things I loved about people and fairies–they all laughed. If a perfect world would take away laughter, it wasn't worth it. But maybe…

"But what if things could be changed—would that be different?"

"Sweetie, it would be the same because everyone would make their life perfect and so, eventually, it would be just as boring."

"Oh." I really didn't want life to be boring, so I guessed I would just have take whatever life threw at me and deal with it as it came.

"Wintereve, Grandmere." I sighed, with a tear in my eye, one cold December morning.

"Sweet, what's the matter?" She looked at me and I saw the same sadness in her gaze that I felt.

She already knew what I was feeling, but I figured I should be polite and answer her question. "First Wintereve without Mama." I started to cry all the more. She had been dead almost a full year, but I still missed her as if it happened yesterday.

"Her favorite holiday," Grandmere told me. "Rose would hate to see us crying like this. You should know, Amy, that she will never leave you. Remember that. Do you know who that last line on her tombstone is for?"

I shook my head. I had no idea it was for someone specific.

"Amy, she put that there for you and your father. When did she really start to say that phrase?" She looked at me in a way that told me a simple "I don't know" wouldn't do.

"Well, she had always said it, but it was shortly after Papa was taken away that she started to say it all the time. I told her to stop when I was seven because it bothered me for some reason."

"Well, sweet, do you remember your dream? You said your mother died in it, right? At first we all thought that was what it was, simply a dream, but then your father really did go to prison and you did go to work in a kitchen."

I was starting to catch on to what Grandmere was trying to say. "So, Mama realized that she probably would die before I was grown." I had never thought of it that way, and I don't think I could live while thinking that, or knowing you were going to die before a certain time. But knowing when would scare me away from life.

"Amy, she wanted you and your papa to know that she will always be with you."

I had kind of already figured this out, but she had figured out my dream before I had.

That Wintereve was the worst one ever. Everyone kept asking how I was doing and telling me how much they loved my mother. I hated that all anyone seemed able to do was remind me that she was dead. Only Aunt Grace and my cousin Kyia seemed to realize how I felt, so the three of us went up to the attic to talk.

"Aunt Grace, can't people just stop it? It's already hard enough without all my relatives reminding me why it's hard. Couldn't they just talk about food or something?"

"Well, Amy, they're worried about you," she told me gingerly.

"And, Ames," Kyia began, "you look worse and worse after you talk to a new person, giving someone else the idea that you're not okay."

"I know, but that's because they're asking me questions about how Papa and I are dealing with it, and if I miss her. I don't want to talk about Mama on Wintereve." Tears started to run down my cheeks.

"Amy," my aunt and cousin said in unison.

"Sweetheart," Aunt Grace continued, "if you don't want to talk about your mother, then that's fine. We'll be quiet."

"So how's the kitchen?" Kyia interrupted. "Seen the prince lately?"

I giggled at where the conversation had turned. "No, I haven't seen him in months. I don't really care, though. The kitchen wouldn't be any fun without Rob and Jo, my friends there. It would be one of all Delynelle's top ten boring places." I yawned. "See, even talking about it makes me want to yawn."

"So, these friends of yours are both boys?" Kyia asked, her eyes growing with excitement.

"No, Rob is, but Jo is short for Johannah."

"Amy, how long have you been friends with Rob and Jo?" Kyia asked.

"They've been friends since she started working there, almost six years," Aunt Grace answered for me.

Now it was my turn to change the subject. "Kyia, what's it like to have both parents, two brothers, and a sister?" I really wanted to know this, because it was something I wished I had.

"Well, for me it's normal, but it's not perfect. I get on Josephine's nerves all the time, and the rest get on mine." She smiled. "I wish your mama was still around. She always had a way of making everything seem worthwhile."

This made me smile.

"Me, too!" Aunt Grace added. So Wintereve wasn't a complete waste of time, and I lived through it.

My birthday came and went, just like everything else that year. Without Mama, I realized, nothing could make things go back to the way they used to be.

Chapter Sixteen

On my twelfth birthday, I was working at the kitchen. I couldn't wait until that night, because Grandfather was throwing me a dance in my honor, just as did for all his grandchildren on their twelfth birthdays. That was why I decided to stay at the kitchen today. I couldn't take the chance of Dove making me stay late, and I couldn't be late for my own party.

"Amy, concentrate; you're going to get in trouble. You've missed about ten spots," Rob informed me.

"Oh, yeah, right," I said as I looked at the floor I'd been scrubbing.

"Amy," Jo called, "your Grandmere picked out the most beautiful dress for me to wear tonight. I'm going to look like royalty in blue satin. Thanks." She winked.

"She's good at that," I responded.

"Thanks for inviting me." I received one of those from everyone I had invited from the kitchen. They were never invited to this sort of thing—they were paupers and peasants, not lords and ladies.

Rob was the only one to complain. "Amy, do I have to open the ball with you?" He had already expressed nearly a thousand times his disdain about dancing in front of the others.

"Yes, Rob, you do. And don't worry, you can't be that bad a dancer."

"Ames, can't you just replace me?" he whined.

"No. And even if I did, who could replace you?" I asked sternly.

"Don't you have a boy cousin or someone who's about our age?"

"No, Rob, I don't! I'm not going to change my mind, so just make sure you're there tonight."

He mumbled that he would be and smiled as I watched him go back to work.

That night I was going to wear a green satin dress that opened in the front to lace. Two white roses were on either side, and long strings of pearls went down the middle on the edge of the green white lace. Around my neck I wore a gold chain with an emerald-green pendant. My sleeves were straight and didn't quite go all the way to my wrists, and green beads went around the bottom. I curled my hair for the occasion. Although my hair wasn't blonde like my mother's, I thought I looked prettier with curls than without.

I wished Mama could have been there to see the prettiest I had ever been. When I felt an invisible pat on the back, I knew she was there. Papa was there, and he gaped at the sight of me. He was quick to inform me that I was no longer his little Amykins but a young lady. He hugged be before we left for my grandparent's mansion.

When I walked through the door I was amazed—there was a tower of tiny boxes for me. There was lots of expensive food, too, the kind I was used to cooking. The music hadn't started yet, but lots of people had already arrived.

Grandmere found me and told me to follow her. She took me through the back way to the library, at the top of the grand staircase where you could enter the ballroom through. After waiting a few minutes, as Grandmere said, I ascended the stairs. I saw Rob at the bottom waiting for me, as he was supposed to.

The herald saw that I was there and announced, "Amythist Amelia Annette…Jonestone." He went over my last name so quickly it was almost as if it wasn't even there; I knew no one understood what he had said as he continued to announce who I was. "Granddaughter of Count Paul James Connor Somner and his Wife, Countess Penelope Rose Grace Elizabeth Somner."

I walked down the stairs as everyone stared at me. I thought they were all probably trying to figure out which of the Somner daughters was my mother. Usually they would announce the parents' names, too, but they didn't. It was probably for the same reason the herald went over my last name so quickly.

When I reached the bottom, I took Rob's arm and the music started. I saw Prissy wink at me as I walked by, and I gulped. Rob and I danced while others began to join us slowly on the ballroom floor. Finally, when there were enough people dancing that no one would notice, we went to get some food.

"See, Rob, you weren't that bad; you only stepped on my foot twice."

He smiled. "Amy, I'm glad you didn't let me out of this."

We both laughed.

"Me too. It wouldn't have been the same if you didn't dance with me."

We were talking about how my birthday would have been ruined if Rob hadn't shown up and how I would have been deathly embarrassed to dance with anyone else. We were laughing our heads off, when another boy who looked to be about a year or two older than us came over.

"Hello. You're Amythist, right?" he asked

I laughed because no one ever called me Amythist.

"Sorry, it's just that most people call me Amy." I curtsied as I explained my laughter.

"Would you like to dance, Amy?"

He emphasized my name, making me want to laugh more, but, I held it in. I was trying to cover my shock and figured that I wouldn't get asked to dance. I wasn't all that pretty, and most of the people here didn't even really know who I was.

"Sure," I answered, "I'll be back." I told Rob.

"So who's that?" The boy I was dancing with asked.

"Who, Rob? He's my friend. I've known him since I was five," I told the mystery boy. I thought I recognized him but couldn't put my finger on it.

"Which daughter of Count Somner is your mother?" I didn't think anything of the question, so I answered it, just as any normal person would have. "Rosemarie."

"Hmm, my father has never mentioned a Rosemarie," he said and suddenly made a very strange face. "That doesn't make sense," He told me, looking confused.

"Why not?" I asked. To me it made perfect sense.

"Well, Paul Somner has five daughters, Annette—"

I tried to interrupt, but then I thought better of it; I remembered where I had seen him before.

"—Susan, Elizabeth, Samantha, and Grace, but I don't remember there being six."

"Oh," I replied, "she died young. Not many knew of her," I told him, I didn't feel like explaining my family history at the moment.

"Amy, what was your last name again? I couldn't really understand the herald."

I thought quickly and remembered Mr. Lyode from Aldreen, so I said, "Lyode."

"Oh, no one of importance with that name," he murmured, and then he seemed to remember I was there. "Sorry, excuse my manners. It's just that the Somners are thought of highly by my father, so I find it strange that I don't remember his ever mentioning your mother."

This was exciting. It made me excited, but then it didn't.

"Really, the king and queen find my mother's side of the family favorable?"

"Yes," he answered.

I never knew this before, although it had never affected me that they didn't find my mother favorable. That meant they didn't find me favorable, either.

"Well, if you'll excuse me, Your Highness," I said as I curtsied before departing.

As I left he yelled, "Call me Henry."

I kept walking. I was furious; the king respected my family but pretended my mother never existed.

I imagined the king and queen before my fifth birthday: *"Oh, that Rose. Darling, isn't she beautiful. Have you seen her since she returned from Aldreen? It did her wonders."* Then the conversation a few days later: *"Oh, sweet, can you believe how that Rosemarie Somner ruined her life by marrying a pauper? What was she thinking?"* The queen would be interrupted, *"Who, darling? I've never heard of her."* Then they would both laugh.

How could they pretend she didn't exist? My mama was an amazing person who always saw the good in almost every situation, Aunt Grace being the exception. She was kind and loving, yet they chose to say she was an outcast simply because she married beneath her.

Grandfather found me as I was waving to Johannah, who really did look like royalty. I was happy she was there, too, because wearing that dress was fulfilling one of her dreams.

"Amy, having fun?" Grandfather asked.

"Yes, I was until I found out my mother was forgotten long before she was even dead." I wanted to cry, but held in the tears by fixing my hair and hoping it would distract grandfather from seeing my quivering lip.

"Amy, maybe now would be a good time to show you your birthday present from your grandmere and me."

I didn't quite understand why I would open it now and not in front of everyone else when I opened the rest. He took me into another room where all my relatives were. Grandmere came over and gave me a tiny box, and I opened it. Inside was a heart-shaped locket. Engraved on the front were the words: *I'll Always Be with You.*

I was stunned. I couldn't believe it. It was so beautiful. I opened it and inside was a picture of Mama, Papa, and me as a baby in my christening gown. Mama was a wearing a simple purple satin dress, and Papa was all dressed up in his best clothes. My mother was well and had no idea how her life would end about ten years later.

I took off the emerald pendant and replaced it with the locket, with the help of my father. Tears were rolling down my cheeks, and I wiped them away.

Papa pushed me toward the party. "Go on, have some fun."

I danced with many boys I didn't know, with Rob too many times, and one more time with the prince.

"So, I see you've switched necklaces," the prince decided to inform me.

I smiled. "Yes, and I prefer this one."

"Well, I think the one you're wearing is much prettier than the one you were wearing earlier, but you're easily the prettiest one here."

I blushed because the prince had complimented me. Even if he didn't know who Mama was, I had just been complimented by royalty.

"Thank you."

Prince Henry wasn't as bad as I thought. As we danced that second time, I realized it wasn't his fault that he didn't know who Mama was. His parents were the ones who'd decided she shouldn't be a part of the family, not the prince.

When midnight came and my grandparents announced that everyone had to go home, I found myself wondering why time had to fly when you didn't want it to, and move like a slug when you wished it had wings.

I thought my twelfth birthday went rather well. I did everything I had wanted and a little more. I never expected to dance with the prince—serve him dinner maybe, but not dance with him. He was much more fun to dance with than Rob, that's all I can say.

I don't know if it was because of his compliments, but he was different than I expected. At Will's funeral he'd helped me understand that my brother's death wasn't my fault, but I doubt he even remembered that. It was almost seven years ago. But I decided he never could see kitchen girl Amy, not after he had seen me all dressed up at a noble ball.

The next day at the kitchen I went about my usual business. I was beyond tired from the night before, and I wasn't the only one. Dove was meandering around the kitchen, as always, when Jo was found asleep while mixing something.

"Johannah, what do you think you're doing?" Dove yelled as she pounded the table, making everything jump.

It successfully woke up Jo, who looked horrified. She was never in trouble, but if she was with us when we snuck out, we'd tell Dove she wasn't, because Jo absolutely hated being in any kind of trouble.

"I think I fell asleep," Johannah replied nervously.

"Oh, well, isn't that obvious!" Dove retorted sarcastically before returning to her rounds.

Today was also strange because a laundress had come down into the kitchen, automatically taking everyone's mind off what they were doing. Laundresses never came down into the kitchen; they stayed mostly in the laundry room and bedrooms, but not the kitchen. The laundresses thought themselves higher than those who worked in the kitchen. They thought that just because they bumped into a royal now and then, they were better than all the rest.

"Hi, Dovendella?" The laundress asked sweetly. Anyone could tell by the look on her face that she really didn't want to be there, no matter how sweet that voice of hers was.

"Yes," answered Dove in a very fake sweet voice.

"Well, Lavender, the head laundress, was told by the king that a certain Amythist could assist her for free."

Dove looked thrilled as she rubbed her hands together. "She could as long as..." she said and stopped. Rob and Mary were both asleep, Rob in an uncooked piecrust and Mary over dishes.

Then, from the other side of the room I heard snoring. I didn't want to look to see who it was, and hoped Dove didn't hear.

I didn't need to look; Dove looked at the laundress. "Excuse me."

"Prissy!" Great, that's who I thought it might be. "Mary! Rob! Johannah! Amy! Report in line now!"

They all woke up at once when they heard Dove call them in her maniacal voice. We formed a line faster than anyone could say a word.

"I know all of you are good friends," Dove started as she walked back and forth in a line in front of us, "and all of you seem to be tired on the same day. You all have either fallen asleep or almost have."

We all looked guilty, but we couldn't help it.

"So," she continued, "what did all of you do last night after leaving this kitchen?"

I gulped as she asked the question, and so did Jo. Prissy looked confused, and Mary stepped on my toe. All of these things were okay, but Rob looked at me.

"Robert, why are you looking at Amy?" Dove asked sternly.

"Was I looking at her? I didn't mean to look at her." he said nonchalantly.

"Yes, you did," Dove told him assertively.

"Amythist, what did you and all your friends do last night?" She stared at me with those horribly evil eyes.

"Well, my twelfth birthday was yesterday and…"

"And what?" she practically yelled, even though her pudgy face was already an inch in front of mine.

"And…well, my grandparents, Paul and Penelope Somner…sort of…had a ball…in my honor." I knew this meant trouble, but I didn't know what else to do. I couldn't come up with a clever enough lie to get us out of any trouble, but I knew the truth would make her furious.

"Hmm," was all Dove said as she stood properly and far enough away from my face that I could no longer smell her halitosis.

"Amy, was everyone in this room invited?" she asked, as a grin that I knew meant nothing good made its way up her cheeks.

"No, Ma'am, but if I had known this would happen, I would have invited more, so no one would feel left out," I said as I looked over to Jo, who looked about ready to cry.

"Well, I don't care. If anyone in this room falls asleep, no matter where they were last night, I'm taking you to see the king!" She smiled at me. I saw the victorious look in her eyes, as she saw the look of contempt upon my face.

"Oh, and Amythist, along with kitchen duties today, you also have to go with this laundress. When you're done doing whatever it is they ask, report back to me."

How can they do this to me? The sentence said I was a kitchen maid, a scullery maid—whatever you feel like calling it. You can call it a dirty kitchen tramp for all I care, but it never said I had to do anything other than that. Both? Whoever heard of anyone doing both at the same time? I doubt it had ever been done before.

The laundresses hated the kitchen maids, so life was about to get terrible for me. All the laundresses were going to make fun of me—it was the only thing I'd ever known them to do, the snobs!

"Well, you must be Amythist. You *reek* like the kitchens. How do they expect you to do laundry? You're absolutely filthy," Lavender, the head laundress, told me with her nose held high and a smug look on her face, as if she thought herself better than everyone in Drell.

"Yes," I replied back.

"Well, I see why you can work for free. You are only going to make the clothes dirtier before they are washed."

I hated the way she said "you," like I was some disgusting bug she could squash.

"Free?" I asked curiously.

"Yes, free. We needed another person. We were running behind schedule and Princess Daffodil had complained to her father, so he said you would work for free, or something like that. He also told me to mention that it's an order." She seemed all the more smug about this, as if it proved that laundresses were superior.

"Well, then, I guess I'll do it, but I might try and have a word with him about this," I told her sweetly. I was not going to stoop to her level.

"Like his royal self would talk to the likes of you. Anyway, Kim will show you to the king's, queen's, princess's, and prince's sleeping chambers where you will collect the clothes every other Tuesday. Understood?"

I nodded. My brain wasn't allowing me to speak as Kim said "hello." I couldn't collect clothes from the prince's room. What if he were in there? What if he saw me like this? How would I explain it?

"Hi. I'm going to show you this only once, so you'd better pay attention."

"Yes, Kim," I answered as we walked through the laundry room. I almost felt sorry for her, because all the other laundresses laughed as we walked by and whispered to the girls next to them.

"Kim, I'm so sorry. I hope this doesn't ruin your reputation for good," said one girl sarcastically as we reached the door.

I paid very close attention as she showed me where to go. I didn't want to get into trouble with the very rude and smug head laundress, but I also didn't want to ever ask for help from these girls. They wouldn't help me, because helping me would ruin their reputations. I didn't want any grief from them, either. When I did have to collect the laundry, I wanted to be able to do it first thing and get it over with as early as I could, without the prince seeing me and without many of the laundresses being there yet.

Later, back in the kitchen Rob asked, "So Ames, what did you have to do?"

"Oh, I only have to collect the king's, queen's, princess's, and prince's laundry every other Tuesday. Without pay." I sighed.

He stared at me in amazement, and then he yawned.

"Don't fall asleep. I really do not need a visit to the king added to this perfect day," I told him sarcastically as I heard a plate drop.

I turned to see that Jo had fallen asleep again. I ran, but Dove was already there.

After waking up Jo, she turned to me. "Amy, with me, please."

I walked behind Dove, praying that no one would be present and that the royals, especially the prince, would be in town or something. Thankfully, it was just the king and queen sitting in the dining hall, enjoying afternoon tea. I sighed in relief as I realized I wouldn't have to explain myself to the prince.

"Your Majesty, this girl keeps falling asleep in the kitchen." She put her hands on her waist and tapped her foot on the floor.

"Oh, I see," said the king. "Name?" he asked, turning to look at me.

"Amy," I told him, but he laughed.

"Well, Amy, please don't fall asleep again. I'd hate to be bothered over nonsense twice in one day."

I curtsied and smiled. "Thank you, Your Majesty."

I skipped back to the kitchen, but first I stuck out my tongue at Dove. King Sencraugh laughed when he saw it. I will never forget the look of horror—no, embarrassment or even anger—on Dove's face as she realized I had beaten her.

Chapter Seventeen

That night Papa and I ate dinner together, as we usually did, before he had to light the lamps in the square and on the important streets. We talked as usual, but tonight's conversation wasn't pleasant.

"Papa, today I was assigned to do laundress chores as well as my kitchen ones," I started, and I was surprised at his reaction.

"They what?! Amy, you're a scullery maid, not a laundry maid!"

"I know that, but the king ordered that I collect the laundry every other Tuesday. Without pay," I complained.

"They're not paying you?!"

"No," I told him, in almost a whisper after he screamed.

"Amy, I'm going to fix this…well, try to. They don't really listen to us all that much, but I'll do my best. Now

I have lamps to light," he said, his voice full of contempt as he grabbed his stilts and marched out the door.

I know Papa tried; I saw him enter the king's councilor's room, but they declined him an audience. He told me he'd try again, but I convinced him not to because it wasn't really worth the effort. I still had to collect the laundry and I still wasn't getting paid for it, but I would live, I assured him.

Dove was making everything difficult for me; she never took her eyes off of me. I knew it was because she was humiliated that I didn't get into trouble with the king. I knew now that she would do everything in her power to get me in trouble with His Majesty. I couldn't sneak away because Dove was watching me so closely. I went for almost two months without skipping once. I didn't have a choice.

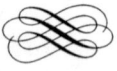

When April arrived, Dove was not watching me as closely, and I took advantage of that—probably a bit too soon. I left two days, after it seemed she had stopped tracking my every move. Not smart, I know, but I hadn't gone that long without skipping since Mama had been sick.

I went to Mama's and Will's graves, and I did a lot of thinking that day. I played with my pure gold locket.

I took it off my neck and read the engraving: *I'll Always Be with You.*

I loved this saying; it meant almost everything to me. I now understood it to its fullest. I felt my mother all the time; she was definitely with me always. I would go to Mama's and Will's graves, mostly when I needed to think about difficult things, such as how I was never going to run into the prince, or when I needed to be alone or just needed to cry.

Today I just needed to be alone—everyone needs that sometimes—and today, after it seemed that I hadn't had a day to myself in ages, being alone is just what I needed. I didn't care if I got into trouble. Today I was going to do what I felt was overdue. I didn't get to leave the kitchen on March 7th, the day Mama died, and I felt awful.

I knew Mama understood because she gave me one of her huge, invisible hugs that morning and again that night before I went to bed. I wished she were still alive.

Well, I should have waited a little longer before skipping kitchen work. Dove had finally gotten me; I finally did something worth being punished for. I'd skipped kitchen work for the millionth time.

"Amy," Dove said, smiling as she began to punish me, "the prince is having a ball for his fourteenth birthday tomorrow night, and the next night King Sencraugh is having a huge feast. You will be the main server, first to the prince and then to the king."

That wasn't so bad, being the main server at two banquets in a row. Serving maids always received the day of the banquet off, too, so that they wouldn't fall asleep while serving an important person. Wait until the laundresses heard I served the king; they wouldn't be able to make fun of me now.

"Okay," I replied, as she watched the smile spread across my face.

"You didn't think that was all did you? Amythist, *this—is—a—punishment*. You'll also have to do all the dishes afterward, and you won't get the days off." She smiled, as if pleased with herself.

"But, Dove, that isn't fair. I'll fall asleep while I'm serving the king!" I complained.

"Yes, Amy, and then you'll be in trouble for falling asleep, won't you?"

I looked at her menacing smile and gave her the meanest look I could muster, before stomping off to the table, where Jo and I were preparing a chicken for the king and queen's dinner.

"Ames, what's going on?" Jo asked, as she looked at my face, which was all squished up and tight from trying not to explode.

"I have a whole lot of extra work to do and I'm not going to get any sleep." The half chicken that I was preparing looked more like a lump of nothing, and then a chicken because I kept pounding it.

"Amy, stop it, or you'll make things worse for yourself," Prissy told me as looked at the chicken. She had Charles with her.

Prissy's son, Charles Daniel, was now three and still hadn't started talking. He was always quiet except when he laughed. This made his mother very upset. She was scared that he couldn't talk at all. Charlie usually went with his father, Phillip, to deliver the mail, but now and then he went to the kitchen with his mother.

"Hi, Charlie, how are you?" I bent down to talk to him.

"Amy, don't waste your time. You know he doesn't talk." Prissy looked as if she could cry.

"Prissy, he'll talk sooner or later. If you want, I could try and teach him, starting next week after kitchen work," I offered with a smile.

"Oh, Amy, you'd really do that? Phillip and I would love it if you could." She almost jumped because she was so happy.

Mary had recently become engaged to a blacksmith. He was a commoner, but he made plenty of money. The king often used him to make cups and things. So after Mary wed Cornelius Smith, she would no longer be working in the kitchen. The money wouldn't be needed. I knew that Prissy especially was going to miss her. I'd miss her, too, but I knew I would still see her, because she had promised to come and visit.

The rest of the day was a complete waste; I was too frustrated to get anything done. When I trudged home I was still the angriest I had ever been with Dove.

Papa happened to see me as he walked home from town square. "Ames, what's the matter?"

"Papa, Dove's the matter. I'm a serving maid in the royal feasts at the castle this week. I don't get those days off and I have to stay and do the dishes afterward. Papa, why does she have to be so mean? Can't she try to be nice for once?"

I ran into the bedroom as soon as we arrived home and lay on the bed.

"Amy, I can't control Dove, but if I could I would do everything possible to make her be nice to you."

I appreciated his sincerity, so I gave him a hug and whispered, "Thanks, Papa."

The next day was a busy one, and everyone was running all over the place. In the middle of all the hustle and bustle, I realized that I would be serving the prince tonight. What was I going to do? I couldn't serve him—he'd wonder what I was doing and run after me. Then again, maybe he wouldn't even recognize me. He probably thought me the daughter of a duke, a count, or a bishop, but not the daughter of the lamp lighter.

Thinking that he wouldn't recognize me was a relief. I was mad at myself for a multitude of reasons. I was also embarrassed. Everyone in the kitchen knew why I was given the simple dress, and I didn't like the looks they gave me.

The dress was nicer than those I normally wore; it was a royal blue color made of simple cotton, like all the other serving maids' gowns. I was allowed to pin my hair back and was told it was preferred so that no hair would find its way into a royal's food. I didn't make myself as pretty as I had been on my birthday because I didn't want to be recognized. I left my locket on; I would never take it off, except to look at the picture inside.

All the serving maids lined up in order, with plates of food in their hands. I was in front because I was serving the birthday boy. I didn't want to be in front. I didn't want to be there at all. I wanted to be at home in my bed. It didn't matter, though. I was there, at the castle, in the front of the line, about to serve the prince—the one person I never wanted to see me working, or in rags, or being anything less than what he believed I was.

A bell rang, which meant it was time to serve the food. I didn't start walking until someone pushed me, and I almost dropped Henry's food. I walked all the way to the top of the table.

"Your Highness, your dinner is served."

He looked up, looked at me as if puzzled. "That's a pretty necklace. I think I've seen it somewhere before."

I gulped. "Thank you, Your Grace."

The bell rang to signal us to turn around and go back to the kitchen for the second course, which was soup. Once I had that on my tray, I stepped in line to wait for another bell.

It rang, and I walked up to Henry. "Your soup, Your Majesty."

"I know where I've seen that necklace--it belongs to Amy."

Then a bell rang. I was glad, but not sure what would happen once the bell rang to tell me to bring the main course, chicken, to his royal self.

The bell rang. I gulped as I walked slowly to the head of the table, trying to form some sort of plan in my mind. What if he accuses me of stealing?

"Your Highness, your…"

"I thought I told you to call me Henry."

"Your chicken." The bell rang, so I turned, glad that the main course always took the longest. I didn't have to serve dessert and face the prince. I was scared of what he might say next and wondered: had he recognized me or just my locket? I think it was both, but I was too nervous to be sure.

Finally, it was time to serve the dessert. I brought a piece of chocolate cake with vanilla frosting and raspberry filling, Henry's favorite. I'd known this since I was five, which didn't really matter. I didn't even care if he enjoyed the cake that I'd never tasted but had baked over a million times for him.

We were all in line again. A bell rang, and I walked after taking a deep breath.

"Your dessert," I began.

"What are you doing here, Amy?"

I was afraid of that. "Working like I always am." I didn't look at him to see his reaction, but just picked up his plate from the main course. Then the bell rang again. I only had to go back one more time, to pick up his dirty cake plate, which was relief in itself. He couldn't interrogate me much longer.

I was already tired, and it was only ten o'clock. The worst part was that after I was done trying to avoid Henry's questions, I still had to do the dishes. After a few minutes, we all lined up again. A bell rang, and we walked in.

I grabbed the prince's plate.

"Why do you work?"

"Long story."

A bell was heard, and I turned around and left right behind all the other serving maids. I went to sit down in the kitchen; I was the only one there. I just sat, not wanting to start the dishes, procrastinating, I guess. I listened to the music coming from upstairs. I heard footsteps, but I didn't think anything of them; it was probably someone coming to make sure the dishes were being done.

"Hey."

I turned around at the sound of that voice and curtsied. "Why are you here? I mean, why aren't you at your party?" I didn't know what else to say.

"I have time, so I was wondering what's the long story about?"

"Oh, you want to hear that? It's kind of boring."

He looked at me. "I think it'll be interesting to know how the granddaughter of Paul Somner became a serving maid."

I smiled. He wanted to know, and I doubted he'd leave until I told him, so I did. He'd probably figure it out eventually if I didn't. I told him about my papa being sent to prison, about Will dying, about my real name, about Mama dying, and about all of it.

"So it was you I talked to in the wood all those years ago. Didn't you come to the throne room crying a couple years ago with a prisoner—your father, I'm guessing."

I was surprised he remembered both of those events. "Yes, that was me." I was crying, as I usually did when I relayed my story to others. I looked down and saw that my locket was opened.

"So, is that you?" he asked, pointing to my baby picture.

"Yes, that's me." He made me smile; a tear was on the tip of my nose.

"Well, I'd better get going. May I see you soon?" he asked eagerly.

"I don't…maybe," I answered, smiling back. I couldn't believe this was happening--Prince Henry knew who I was, yet he still wanted to see me. He was much different than I'd imagined.

I was at the kitchen really late that night; I didn't get home until close to four in the morning. Papa was up waiting for me.

"You're home finally. I was just about to go out and look for you," he told me as he gave me a hug.

"Sorry, Papa, too many dishes. Now I know why we usually do them in shifts the day after a feast. I didn't finish until about half an hour ago and I have to be at the kitchen an hour early tomorrow morning." I yawned. "I'm going to bed now. Wake me up at eight-thirty."

I went straight into the other room and lay on the bed, and was asleep within seconds. I had a dream—not my usual dream, but a dream all the same. I was sitting and eating ice cream when my locket fell off. Henry picked it up and put it back around my neck, and smiled.

"Amy, eight-thirty. Get up."

I sat up, rubbed one eye, and yawned.

"Papa, I was having a good dream. Let me go back to sleep." I lay back down.

"Ames, you know I can't do that. Come on, you're running late as it is."

"Fine, I'm getting up."

I stood up clumsily, put on my clothes, and ran for the kitchen without breakfast. There were still many dishes to do from the night before.

Mary arrived at the kitchen early. She was shocked to see me and asked if I had been there all night. I told her no, and she helped me with the rest of the dishes.

Dove came in two minutes after we finished. She looked pleased with how tired I looked.

"Now, Amythist, don't forget you have to stay late again tonight after the king's banquet."

I tried to ignore the sparkle of joy in her eyes as she spoke the words of my doom.

I yawned. Aggie stuck out her tongue at me, and then skipped over to the ice cream maker, where she was going to make the queen her favorite chocolate ice cream. Usually I made that, but at the moment there was no way Dove would let me.

I almost fell asleep while mopping the floors, while baking a cake with Rob, and as I cleaned the oven. Dove was thrilled.

Chapter Eighteen

~~~
  ❧
~~~

The king had invited the king and queen of Lavenlee to the banquet. They had four daughters: Sofia, Levina, Hellena, and Malia. King Gelgar and Queen Almea came from a country that had never produced a prince.

It was said that a pixie gave their land the gift of beauty, and along with that gift came only princesses. Because a prince had not been born in Lavenlee for five hundred years, their next ruler was the youngest princess, or the fourth oldest depending on how many there were. No one is quite sure why it was the fourth oldest who got priority over all the rest. Some say it had something to do with the fairy gift, and others just think it is Lavenleian nonsense. I've never been sure what to think; maybe someday I'll meet a pixie and ask her.

No one was sure if the rumors were true, but they were saying that all four princesses would be present. Everyone thought they would stay for a month or so.

I felt bad for the normal serving maids waiting on six extra people for a month.

I put on the royal blue serving dress I'd worn the night before. I pinned back my hair in an elegant bun, except for one strand that I let fall gracefully on my face. I was wearing my locket again; I knew that tonight it wouldn't make things difficult for me.

I didn't serve the king that night. The head serving maid complained, saying the king wouldn't approve of me, a twelve-year-old, serving him. So I didn't know whom I would be serving. Dove swore she'd get me to serve one of the princesses. I only hoped I didn't have to serve a relative or someone sitting next to one. That would be embarrassing not only to me, but also to them. I wanted to serve the prince again, but I didn't have a choice.

I found out moments before we were to serve the salad course that I would be serving Her Highness, Princess Hellena. The schedule was different tonight, I noticed as the head serving maid talked to all of us. Tonight we were allowed to join in the festivities. Supposedly, Prince Henry wanted as many people as possible to hear an announcement. I really didn't plan on joining in; I'd find out what it was the next day, and I was sure everyone would know by then.

Finally, it was time to line up and wait for the first bell. The bell rang, and I stopped one seat before Henry's at Princess Hellena's spot. He looked at me and mouthed, "I'll talk to you later."

I nodded before turning to the princess. "Your Highness, your dinner is served." If I had to serve at all the feast, I was sure I'd die of boredom from saying the same things over and over again. The bell rang, so I turned.

The next time the bell rang, I walked to Princess Hellena, set down her soup, and picked up her salad plate. The prince mouthed, "Dance with me later."

Without thinking, I mouthed, "I will," and Hellena saw me.

"Who are you?" she asked as a bell tinkled in the distance.

When I was back in the kitchen grabbing the next dish, I realized I'd be here all night.

I served the next few courses while avoiding questions from Hellena. *Why is it that every time I serve, I have to avoid questions?*

Finally, it was time for the announcement. All of the serving maids went to the ballroom. I went, too. The kings of Frindeline and Lavenlee stood to make it.

"I, King Gelgar, give my third eldest daughter, Hellena Hannah Honour Lavenlee, to…" He stopped, and King Sencraugh continued, "…my son, Prince Henry Edward John Frindeline."

King Gelgar continued, saying, "As his betrothed."

Everyone in the room clapped, except me. As they walked down the stairs together, I realized I probably should be clapping, too, but found it hard to.

After they started to dance, others came onto the dance floor. A royal door opener came over and asked me to dance, and I consented. I watched the prince the whole time. I wanted to dance with him—he told me we would. I danced with many others until finally, around midnight, he found me.

"Would you like to dance?" he asked, his dark hair as neat as it was at dinner.

"Yes, Your Highness, I would love to dance."

He took my hand.

"Henry, I'm surprised you'll still dance with me while you're betrothed to another." I was frowning.

"Amy, if I had my way, I wouldn't be betrothed to such a brat. If it were up to me, I'd be allowed to choose whom I marry." He was obviously not pleased with his situation, either.

"Well, I hope it works out the best for you." I really did. I felt he should be allowed to marry an ugly girl with wavy brown hair or a very pretty blonde with straight hair, like Hellena.

We kept dancing until Hellena came over and took one look at me and was disgusted. "What are you doing dancing with him?" she asked, as if dancing with my betters were against the law. She stopped and gaped at me as she realized who I was. "You're my serving maid! How dare you dance with a prince!" she shrieked.

"Wel—" I started, but Henry interrupted me.

"Hellena, I asked her to dance with me. I knew perfectly well what her station was."

The princess looked amazed and surprised at the man she would someday be married to.

"I'll go then," I told them both and curtsied.

"No, you don't have to," he said and paused, "but if you must, good day."

"Goodnight, Your Majesty." I turned toward the princess. "Your Highness," I said and left.

The ball went on for hours after I started the dishes. I listened and sang along to the music I knew.

"*La dee, la la love. So love is what they call it, love.*"

I yawned. The music had just ended. It was three-thirty in the morning, and I still had lots of dishes to do, but I decided to lie on the flour bags and rest my eyes for a bit. The last time I had lain there I was only a little girl with a cough. I didn't mean to fall asleep…

I was awakened by Henry about three hours later. "Henry!" I yelled as I stood and wiped the flour off my dress and out of my hair, but it didn't help.

"What are you still doing here?" he asked, alarmed.

"Oh, I had dish duty and was tired. Oh, Papa is going to be so worried." I bit my lip and walked over to the sink and started the dishes again.

"Want some help?"

I was shocked at his question, because the prince never did dishes.

"If you want to, but you don't have to." I smiled.

"Amy, it's okay. You'll never get this done before Dove shows up if I don't."

I looked puzzled. "Why, what time is it?" I was curious.

"Around six-thirty." He smiled as he grabbed a plate.

"Dove will be here in half an hour to make your breakfast. Why are you down here?" I asked. I'd been wondering this ever since he woke me up.

"I often come down here about now to get a drink of water." He smiled.

I couldn't help but smile back.

"Today's meals I will eat and be proud," he told me as we were finishing up.

"Why's that?" I asked playfully.

"In my heart I will know that I might have cleaned the plate I'm eating off of."

I laughed as I dried my hands. "I'm sure for you that will be delightful. If you want, I can guarantee one of the dishes you cleaned will have your breakfast on it." I smiled.

"Really, you'd do that for me?" he asked playfully.

I nodded.

"Then, today I will be proud of my breakfast plate. I'd better go. Dove should be here any minute," he told me before bowing and leaving

I mimicked him by curtsying and followed suit, just out the other door. I had to go home and change because I couldn't stay in my flour-covered dress all day. When

I arrived home, I changed and took down my hair, and then went back after leaving Papa a note.

I met Rob and Johannah on the way to the kitchen. "So what was that ball for?" Rob asked.

"Oh, it was to announce the betrothal between our prince and Princess Hellena of Lavenlee." I giggled.

"Really, and you got to be there. Lucky." Jo thought it wonderful.

"All that fuss over a betrothal!" Rob shook his head.

"Especially when Henry doesn't want to marry the brat." I didn't realize what I had said until Johannah's smile dropped and Rob's eyes became huge.

"You called him Henry!" Jo yelled.

"I didn't tell you? He gave me permission to call him that at my party." I wasn't sure how they'd react to that, either.

"Really? Do you think he gives everyone permission to call him that?" Rob asked as he tried to close his mouth.

"I don't know, but Princess Hellena calls him 'Prince Henry' and I don't." They both just stared at me in amazement.

My summer was normal. I skipped kitchen work, and Dove was furious that I never managed to fall asleep while serving a royal. She was also upset that she couldn't punish me further because I'd finished all of the dishes. I loved making her angry, especially when it was because I outsmarted her.

Nothing of great significance happened until sometime in October. I was walking up to my grandparents' house when I saw Aunt Grace running to meet me.

"Amy!" she yelled.

"What?" I yelled back.

"The prince came by earlier looking for you!" I didn't know what to say or if I'd heard her right.

"He was looking for me?" I asked as she hugged me.

"Yes, love, and I told him you'd be here later tonight. He's waiting for you in the sitting room." She jumped up and down as I stood there unable to move.

I walked into the room right off from the front door. I was wearing my usual rags, but that couldn't be much worse than his seeing me covered in flour. I curtsied. "How do you do?"

"Do you always run around like that? Beg pardon."

I blushed at his question. I was a little embarrassed. "Yes, I do." There was nothing else I could say.

"So, about all this—I'm sorry for intruding, but I haven't seen you since April."

I blushed again.

"Well, Henry, that's because I'm not usually a serving maid, and I've never felt the need to sign up for the empty spots." I couldn't believe this: he wanted me to serve at the banquets just so he could see me.

"I'm surprised you even talk to me when your father obviously despises my family and, as his son, couldn't that get you into trouble?" I couldn't believe I was having this conversation with the Prince of Frindeline.

"What if I told you my father doesn't know I ever talked to you, and if he did, then yes, I would be in trouble."

I blushed, but he continued. "Do you think that in two weeks from today you could meet me in the Wood of Drell at the willow tree in the middle?"

I smiled. "Is that the tree where we talked all those years ago?"

"Yes, but I don't remember your being very happy on that occasion."

We began to laugh.

"Yes, I think I could." He wanted to meet me in two weeks, but why me?

That night at dinner, all anyone talked about was the prince's visit. All I could think about was our meeting in two weeks.

No one knew about the meeting except me, and I didn't want them to know. When they asked why he had come, I told them that he was just making sure I was a kitchen maid and not a serving maid, and he left as soon as he found out. Even though it wasn't very encouraging, they were impressed he'd come there to figure out something like that. I was quiet most of the night.

A week went by, and Rob and I were teaching Charlie how to talk. Rob, who only helped because I'd begged, thought I was trying for the impossible. I disagreed.

"Charlie, say Mama…Dada…Papa…anything…" I tried. Nothing. I'd been giving him lessons for over six months now and he still didn't say anything.

Crash!

"Rob, what did you break this time?" I scolded.

"Amy, I didn't mean to break the cup!" he retaliated.

"Yeah, Rob, like you didn't mean to break the plate, or the lamp, and you didn't mean to spill wine on the rug. Oh, and you didn't mean to break—"

"Ames," he interrupted, "I never mean to break stuff on purpose!" He yawned, "Are we done for today?" He looked done.

"Yes, Rob, we're done." I could never continue teaching after yelling. Every three days Rob would break something and we'd have to end early.

"Good job, Charlie. We'll try again tomorrow." I smiled at him, and he smirked back.

I personally thought Charlie could talk if he really wanted to; he would just rather not. He felt no need for conversation, so why should he talk? I felt sorry for Prissy and everyone else who worried about him, though, and I wish Charlie could have realized how much he made people worry. Maybe then he'd talk.

The next day and the day after, nothing changed. He still didn't ever say a word, but whenever Rob broke something, he'd laugh—that was all.

Chapter Nineteen

Finally, the day I was going to meet the prince in the Wood of Drell came. I was excited. I wanted to look good, so I put on the nicest—well, newest kitchen clothes, rags—I had. I put my hair in a very neat ponytail. When arriving at the kitchen at ten, I signed up to be a serving maid on New Year's Eve, collected the laundry, and then left. If I were going to get into trouble for having Jo cover for me, I didn't care.

I walked into the wood, and I wasn't scared this time. No monsters or dragons lived in this wood, as I'd thought when I was a little girl. I now looked back to when I was five and realized just how silly I'd been. This time I was twelve and knew that the Wood of Drell hadn't had a dragon or monster in it for over a hundred years.

I walked into the middle of the forest without a doubt. I saw the willow and Henry. He was sitting on the ground next to the tree, with a picnic basket and a wide smile. I sat next to him on the blanket.

"Henry, this is perfect. I never would have thought of this," I told him as his smile widened.

"Really, I just thought a picnic would be fun. And afterward you can show me a place that's important to you, since I showed you mine."

I smiled. So, this was his special place. That meant I'd have to take him to Mama's and Will's graves.

"I'll show you my special place, the place where I think, but just so you know, yours is much more cheerful." I frowned as I remembered my brother and mother and thought of Mama's last words. She had died almost three years ago and I still wished she hadn't.

We ate lunch, and then climbed the tree and sat in its chair-like branches as we talked. Then I took him to the cemetery.

He looked at me, confused. "This is a graveyard."

"Yes, it is. Follow me."

We walked to the place where Will and Mama were buried. Henry looked at the graves and then looked at me.

"I'm sorry, we didn't have—" I interrupted him.

"No, it's okay. I come here a lot."

I looked at my mama's grave and then at my locket. He read Will's tombstone to himself:

William John Noah Jonestone
September 17 1127-October 21 1127
Sweet Son
Darling Brother
Precious Child

"He only lived a month." He looked at me as a tear came down my cheek, and continued. "That must have been hard." He looked at me again.

"You have no idea," I told him as I walked away.

When we reached Mama's grave, Henry read aloud, "Rosemarie Rachel Reality Somner Jonestone." He looked at me. "She had a pretty name."

I nodded as he read on: "August 10, 1103 to March 7, 1132; Kind, Gentle, Sweet Woman; Loving Mother and Wife; I'll Always Be with You."

After reading the last line, he looked at me in confusion and then glanced at my locket. "What does it mean?"

"Oh," I said and twiddled my locket, "it's something my mama used to always say. It means that no matter what happens she'll always be there for me, and Papa, and all those people she cared about." I paused. "It's my favorite saying. I don't know what I'd be doing if she never told me she'd be with me. I'd probably still be in bed, crying for her to come back." Tears were finding their way down my cheeks.

"Amy, I don't know what to do. You sit there like this is normal, and that it's all right, but I feel like I have to do something to help. But don't know how." He scratched his head.

"Henry, just that is enough. I had to tell Rob that a long time ago." I smiled, but the prince didn't look too happy.

"You and Rob are just friends, right?" He looked concerned as he spoke the words.

"Yes," I reassured him, "nothing more."

He smiled, so I smiled. Then I told him I had a wonderful time, but really had to get back to the kitchen. Otherwise, Dove would wonder where I'd been all day. So we said goodbye and went our different ways, deciding to meet every two weeks at the willow tree.

Life went on normally and nothing really happened until the day before New Year's Eve.

"Amy, I'm supposed to tell you that you have serving maid duties tomorrow and the prince is allowing the serving maids to dance, so you have tomorrow off. You still have your dress, right?"

She looked like she was upset, as I smiled with glee. I could tell I had defeated Dove again.

I skipped home with Rob and Jo, talking happily.

"So, Amy, I'll see you at Prissy's in thirty minutes?" Rob asked.

"Yeah, I think today will be the day."

It wasn't. Charlie didn't say a single word, and then Rob backed into a table, knocking a picture to the ground and breaking the frame. Rob and Charlie laughed. I scolded, and we all went home.

When I walked through the door and told Papa that I had the day off tomorrow, he was thrilled. He quickly suggested that I sign up to be a serving maid more often.

The next day Papa and I ate breakfast together—something we rarely did, because I was always in too much of a hurry in the morning and he was always tired from putting out the lamps. We ate a picnic lunch by the lake, even though it was snowing. Papa threw a snowball at me, and the only thing I wanted to do after that was get him back.

Rob and Jo decided to skip some of their kitchen duties and they joined in the snowball fight. We all played tag; I even scared Papa by jumping on his back. It was the most fun I'd had with Papa in awhile.

Our fun came to end when a light snowfall started and we all stopped to gaze at its beauty, reminding us what time it really was.

"Rob, we're supposed to be at Prissy's in an hour. You and Jo had better get back before you're caught. You've been here nearly three hours," I urgently explained.

Rob and Jo ran back to the kitchen, laughing and talking about the day.

Charlie didn't talk that night, either. Rob was lucky enough not to break anything. We left early because I had to get ready for the New Year's Ball. It was always the longest one of the year. I had even heard that they didn't make anyone leave until five in the morning. I wasn't serving any of the Lavenlee princesses, but our own Princess Daffodil.

I'll Always Be With You

Rumors were flying around that tomorrow after the Lavenlee royals awoke they would be heading home. I would be ecstatic if the rumors were proved true. Everyone working anywhere near the castle courtyard felt they had overstayed their welcome.

They were all pretty but spoiled girls, except maybe Malia, but she was under strenuous training to become queen. Princess Hellena was a nightmare, but King Sencraugh and Queen Neeuqa spoiled her beyond belief; I wanted to smack her.

I prayed that Hellena would change as she grew older, because I really did hope that one day Henry could be happily married to the witch. Somehow, I doubted he'd ever feel any fondness for her. He was always talking about how annoying she was and about how his father wouldn't listen to him whenever he tried to talk to him about the situation.

"Hellena just needs to back off. I wish my father would stop babying her and realize what she really is..." is just an example of some of the things he would say.

A bell rang off in the distance, and it was time to serve the last course, dessert. After taking away those dishes, the dancing would start and even I would be allowed to dance. I had to be home around two, but that still gave me plenty of time.

When the dancing started, the son of a duke asked me to dance. After him, I danced with the son of a count, after that the son of a bishop, and so on, until finally I sat down around eleven-thirty. I was sitting for only a few minutes and still very out of breath when the prince came over.

"Will you dance with me, fair maiden?" he asked very formally.

I curtsied. "Yes, of course, Your Grace. How could I refuse a prince?" I answered just as formally to continue his game.

He grabbed my hand and we began to dance as we talked.

"How did you get away from Princess Hellena?" I asked curiously.

"The way I always do—I just leave when her back is turned." He smiled as he answered my question, and I giggled.

I loved dancing with the prince. He had a way of making me feel special. I also never felt that I had to hide anything from him, as I did with Rob. It was strange, really. I felt that Henry would never let anything happen to me, that he wanted to know everything about me. Rob cared and also didn't want harm to come to me, but he didn't want to know everything, like Henry did.

Midnight was fast approaching and, as was the tradition in Frindeline, all the members of the royal family would pick someone to dance the midnight waltz with. Usually the king and queen would dance, as was expected. Henry, I assumed, would dance with Hellena, because that's what would be right in most people's eyes. Princess Daffodil, I assumed, would pick among the dukes, counts, bishops, and any other boys of noble blood from whom to pick.

Midnight struck, and Henry was still dancing with me. There were only three couples on the dance floor, as there should be, but I felt out of place being part of one of them.

As everyone watched, I was surprised. "Henry, shouldn't you be dancing with Hellena right now?"

"Yes," he answered, "but she went to bed early with a stomachache, and I'd much rather dance with you."

I smiled as we danced. I saw Grandfather as he spotted me and told Grandmere. They looked shocked as they pointed. Soon my whole family, except Papa, was watching with their mouths wide open.

After the dance Henry's sister came over, and she didn't look very pleased.

"Henry, where's Hellena?" she snapped.

"Daff, she went to bed with a stomachache."

"Oh, well, never mind." She left and walked over to tell the monarchs.

This was all very surprising. I didn't think he'd ever pick me for something as important as this. Any girl would have died to be in my position.

"So, why me?" I asked sheepishly.

"Well, do you remember last year at your birthday party?"

"Yes," I answered. "Why?"

"Well, do you remember when I said you were easily the prettiest one there?"

I nodded.

"Well, over the last year you've basically become even prettier."

I blushed and so did he.

My family members kept watchful eyes on me. They still seemed to be in shock, but they never approached me.

We danced for about an hour more and then we went to revive ourselves with some drinks. Everyone whispered as we walked by. I ignored them, but I saw my family members asking those who whispered what they thought about it all.

At one-thirty I told Henry that I was expected home in thirty minutes and really had to go, but I assured him that I would see him soon. We both smiled and waved as I walked over to Grandfather and Grandmere.

"Amy, I'm impressed. The prince hardly danced with anyone but you," Grandfather commented.

"Sweetie, is the prince as nice as he seems?" Grandmere asked.

"Yes, Grandmere," I told her. Just then, Aunt Grace caught up to us.

"Amy, Amy, Amy, do you know what everyone is saying?" she asked playfully.

"No, but I'm positive it's nothing good."

"You know you're right. They're saying that the prince is going to defy his betrothal and insist on a betrothal to the serving maid he danced with all night.

Some even said that it's your ambition to get him to defy the betrothal to bring wealth to your family." Aunt Grace laughed.

"They're all very bored people if they had time to come up with that. Princess Hellena went to bed early with a stomachache, and he just decided to dance with me, nothing more," I explained.

"Try telling that to all of them." Aunt Grace pointed to the crowd still dancing and talking.

As we walked out, I decided to convince Jo that she should do this next time. She would love it.

On the anniversary of Mama's death, I wasn't allowed the day off, so I skipped and went to her grave, only stopping when I looked at her tombstone and wished that she hadn't died three years ago. I sat down there and cried.

"Mama, I'm so confused. I know you're with me, but there are times I feel like you're so far away. 'I'll be there always' makes sense most of the time, but this time I wonder how that ever could make any sense."

I cried as I played with the opened locket, which no longer resided on my neck. I felt a hand on my shoulder and I assumed it was just another invisible hand to comfort me: with love, Mama. I went up, as I always did to try and feel my mother's soft, long fingers, which I remembered I loved to grab as we walked into town when I was little. I figured my hand would drop to my shoulder, but it didn't; Papa had one of his huge, comforting hands right there.

"Papa," I wept, "I miss her."

"Amy, we all miss her. But, honey, nothing I can ever do will bring her back," he told me as I saw tears in his own eyes. He grabbed me into a big, warm hug, a hug that was desperately needed. As we hugged, I saw a familiar face, and I smiled and waved at him.

"Papa, I know. I just want her and Will…the two things I can't have."

Henry then decided to turn and leave after returning my wave. Papa released me and then we walked home.

I was grateful for my father; he made me feel like the most important person in Delynelle. I figured I could be and maybe I deserved the treatment. But then I remembered I was simply a scullery maid, and it only seemed that way to Papa.

A week later when I met Henry at the willow, he quickly began to comfort me until I told him I was fine.

We spent most of our time talking about his birthday banquet, which I was serving at. I tried to convince Jo that she should, too, and that she would love it, but she didn't think it was worth it.

"Amy, I know you could go as a serving maid, but what if I dressed you up and said you were the daughter of a duke from Sorret, and you could sit next to me and dine like you were born to do?"

I was speechless. "Henry, who would replace me?" I asked, knowing they wouldn't let me out of an already confirmed job; it was against policy.

"Don't you have a friend about your age?" he asked as his eyebrows lifted, which told me he had an idea.

"Johannah, but I doubt she'll do it." I squinted.

"Even if I asked her?" he asked slyly.

"No, if you asked her, she'd say yes before she even thought it through…Oh, she's in the kitchen right now, if you want to talk to her."

We both ran to the kitchen at the castle. Once we were just outside, we stopped to get some air. I walked in and went to do the dishes. Henry walked in looking regal, as all princes should. I wanted to laugh at him as he strode straight over to Dove.

"I hear there's a girl named Johannah who works here," he told her simply, as my boss curtsied.

Mary, who would only be working until May when she would marry the blacksmith, almost dropped the roast beef for King Sencraugh's dinner as she heard what Prince Henry said.

"Yes, Your Highness, we do. Johannah," she beckoned from across the room.

Jo, who had been listening the whole time, of course, left her bread and walked over to Dove and the prince with big eyes.

"Yes, Dovendella," she responded without taking her eyes off Henry.

"His Grace wants to talk to you." Dove curtsied and walked over to her daughter.

"Prince Henry, how may I help you?" Jo curtsied as she blushed. No one this important had ever spoken to her before.

"For my birthday banquet we're short a serving maid, and I thought you deserved a day off and a day when you could feel like royalty."

Aggie looked up. "Your Highness, if she doesn't want to, I'm more than willing," she yelled from across the room.

Jo looked right at Aggie and told the prince, "I'd love to."

Aggie's face went from its normal peachiness to a blotchy red with anger.

I quickly stuck out my tongue at Aggie.

Henry saw and started to laugh, but Jo looked at him curiously and he immediately stopped.

"I'll give you your dress tomorrow, and you'll have the day off," he told Jo, but winked at me to let me know he would also bring mine.

The next day Henry brought me a very beautiful, dark amethyst dress.

"Henry, it's gorgeous, but if someone asks who I am, what am to tell them?" I looked at him seriously.

"Your name will be Delilah, if anyone asks," he told me.

"Where did you get that?" I asked, laughing because the name really didn't sound very…me.

"That's the name of Duke Hande's daughter, the one you will pretend to be."

"Clever, but what if the real Delilah decides to be there?" I asked impatiently.

"She won't. You see, Duke Isaac Hande is known for how protective he is of his daughter. He never lets her out of his sight. Lord Isaac is scared to death of boats, ships, and anything that floats on water. He has never shown his face in Frindeline and never will because Quane is no longer Quane, if you get my drift," he reassured me.

"Yes, that may all be true, Your Cleverness, but still, how will I explain that I'm her? Hmm, Clever One?"

He smiled as I smiled and looked intently to him for answers.

"Well you see, oh faithful subject." He started playing my game. "You will simply say your mother begged, you received the chance to meet the Frindeline royal family, and that you are not a baby. Tell everyone that only your mother, Lady Gertrude, could convince him to let you come."

I looked at him slyly. "Our next king has a very devious mind, did you know? You remind me a lot of him. You should meet him sometime," I chided.

"Well, if you can arrange the meeting, I think I could do nothing but oblige." He played along as we held in our laughter. Finally, I couldn't hold it in any longer and we both laughed for a while, finding it difficult to stop.

As he was leaving I asked, "So, what does it feel like to be fifteen?" I smiled.

"Like this could be one of the best years of my life."

I looked at him puzzled as he walked away. I wondered what that was supposed to mean.

That night I had a lot to look forward to. I told Aunt Grace what was really going on, because I needed help with my hair. I made her promise that she wouldn't tell anyone, and that not even Papa could know. She agreed, she said, against her better judgment, as if that would make me feel guilty or something. It did, but I didn't change my mind.

She put my hair into a very elegant bun and curled a few lose strands before setting them on my face. I looked at my invitation. It read that I would be sitting next to Prince Henry and my server's name would be Johannah. I thought it was a good thing that I couldn't recognize myself, because I didn't want Johannah to recognize me. I only hoped she wouldn't get a good look at my locket.

Once at the castle, I handed my invitation to the man at the door. He looked at it and let me in. I walked over to my spot, as I counted the relatives in my vicinity. Too many to pull this off, I thought. Once at my seat, I sat down.

"Hello, your name, Lady?" Henry asked with a mischievous smile playing across his lips.

"Delilah, Your Highness, the daughter of Duke Hande in Sorret," I replied as I tipped my head instead of curtsying. I smiled as I held in my laughter, not sure how I would contain myself.

We ate, and I was surprised at how the food that I helped prepare every day tasted. We never were allowed to taste the food. I loved this food, and I hadn't understood why we weren't allowed these leftovers, but now I knew—this food was too good for the undeserving peasants.

The cake that I knew Henry loved, which I baked for him almost constantly for teas, and when he felt like cake and when he was entertaining, was being served tonight. I couldn't wait to try this cake that the prince found irresistible. I knew it had to taste wonderful, but like everything else we made and baked for the royals, I had never tasted it before. I was the only one allowed to bake this cake for the prince. Ever since I was six, I was the only one who could make it exactly how he wanted it. Others had tried, but he finally ordered that only I do it. I don't think he ever asked who baked his cake, but knowing that it was mine always made me feel special.

I put my fork into the piece of chocolate cake with raspberry filling and vanilla frosting. I was amazed with my own cooking skills. I had tasted the batter before but never an actual piece. I wished they gave us more than one piece each. I also wondered how many people felt this way about my cake.

"Do you like the cake, Amy?" he whispered.

"I love it. I never knew this cake tasted so good, almost heavenly." I was shocked with my own ability. I never realized how good of a cook I had actually become.

"Do you know who bakes this cake? When I was eight, I told Dove that I would only eat this cake when it was made by a certain person, but I never found out who it was."

I blushed because I could answer his question no problem while he, without even realizing it, was making me feel very important.

"I bake this cake," I whispered, not sure if he could hear me, but I knew my cheeks had to be very red by now.

His eyes became the size of walnuts and his jaw seemed to drop to the ground. "Really," he finally managed to say. "You bake this cake? That means you were six when I asked that only you make it. I just assumed it was a very experienced cook. Wow—well, thank you. It's delicious. My compliments to the chef," he said as I blushed again.

I was happy that Hellena wouldn't be back until just before the wedding, so she could surprise Henry with the beauty she had become over the years. I couldn't see how that was ever going to happen, but I didn't have to deal with her, and I was glad.

When the bell rang for the serving maids to come and collect the cake dishes, Jo picked up my plate as I turned around. She gasped as I looked at her and realized that she had been looking at my locket. The bell rang before we had the chance to even start a conversation.

As always, Prince Henry had the first dance of the night, being that it was his birthday and all. He picked me, but unlike on New Year's Eve, I expected it.

"Delilah, tell your father hello for me," King Sencraugh told me as Henry and I headed toward the dance floor.

I nodded in agreement, to show that I would.

The serving maids weren't allowed to dance this time. I figured that was the reason he wanted me to pretend to be Lady Delilah was so that he could dance with me. "Would you like to go out to the courtyard, Delilah?"

I laughed. "Yes," I said normally, but added in a whisper, "so you can call me by my real name."

I loved this courtyard. It was a beautifully cobbled stone square with plenty of space, enough space for about four people to spar in with swords. I couldn't imagine it being used for something like that, though, because it was too beautiful. Plants rested in corners and other spots. Benches made of marble and granite were on the edges of it. One fountain resided in the middle; it took the shape of a swan starting to fly away with all its beauty. The aroma of the area captured me and took me away to places I could never even dream of going.

"Henry, this has to be the prettiest courtyard in all Delynelle." I smiled as I sat down on a bench where I could see the whole thing.

"You think so? I've heard that Lavenlee's is very pretty."

"Is that a good thing or a bad thing?" I asked as I started to feel jealous.

"Oh, I'm sure that's a bad thing, and of course this is much prettier—even beautiful."

I smiled. He was trying to please me. "You know, you've done a lot of really nice things for me and you never want or ask for anything in return. I don't quite understand it."

He frowned at me before speaking. "You don't? Well, let me tell you something. If I could change one thing, I wouldn't be a prince or I'd abdicate from the throne. But, then Daff would become queen. As much as I love her, I don't think she could handle a whole a country."

I gasped. "But, why would…why do you want to abdicate? You would make such a good king." I asked, not wanting him to ever do what he just told me he had considered.

"Well, one reason is that then King Gelgar would no longer want his daughter to marry me, so there would be no betrothal. Also, if I weren't next in line to be king, I could go around and do whatever I wanted with you and not have to keep it a secret."

I laughed at his response. "Really, that's sweet." I kissed him on the cheek.

"What was that for?" he asked as his cheeks became a rosy color and a smile started to appear on his face.

"For being so nice to me," I said as we walked back inside to dance.

It was getting close to eleven o'clock, and we were still dancing when Princess Daffodil cut in.

"May I dance with my brother?" she asked as I walked over to the girls waiting for someone to dance with. As I waited, I danced with the son of a duke and an heir to the title; he was rather stuffy and full of himself, and I was glad when Henry came over asked me to dance again.

"Delilah, would you like to dance?"

I smiled. "How could I refuse a prince?" We danced until midnight, when I told him I had to go. He agreed that it was getting late and I shouldn't worry Papa.

Chapter Twenty

When I got home, Papa was asleep. I kissed his cheek, put on my bedclothes, and went to bed with a feeling that I hadn't done something I was supposed to do. I felt like I had ignored something I had said I would do to someone I really cared about, but I couldn't put my finger on it.

I finally fell asleep, but it was fitful, and then my dream started. I hadn't had my dream in at least a year—maybe even two. But now I was having it again, and the voice that tended to repeat itself in my head was one I hadn't heard since before Mama died.

How could I not have noticed it before? Mama was the one telling me to save my family; her voice was the one doing it. Everything that always happened in my dream did, but I didn't see the "I did it" at the end, and I woke up right after Mama died, with perspiration all over my face.

"Amy, are you all right?"

I opened my eyes to see Papa's face in front of mine. He looked scared. "I'm fine I just had my dream again."

"What dream...that dream? But that dream stopped," he half-asked, half-told me.

"I thought so, too."

He looked at me, and I knew he didn't want me to have that dream. I know he felt that I shouldn't have to see all the horrible things that had happened to my family over and over again. I tried to smile at him to show him that I was fine, and I wanted to reassure him that I was.

"Papa, the voice that says 'Save your family' is Mama's." I gulped, and so did he.

"Your mother's?" He looked shocked.

"Yes, Papa, Mama's." I knew now what had been bothering me the night before, and I knew I had to tell Papa.

"Papa, Mama made me promise to do it. I have to at least try and save you and the rest of the Jonestones. This is really important. I have to do it—not just for me, but for Mama." Tears were coming down my face. I wanted him to understand that I didn't want anyone else to suffer because of the injustice inflicted upon our family. I looked into his eyes and I saw a tear trickle from his right eye as he nodded.

"Ames, I'm going to help." He understood. I smiled.

"I love you, Papa!" I hugged him.

"Ames, now listen: I don't know if it's possible anymore, but we'll try and keep on trying until we die if we have to."

I was so happy as I saw the determination on his face.

"So, Amy, I thought you were serving last night. I didn't know I'd be serving you!" Jo's face was turning red, her eyebrows were bunching, and her lips were a single line.

"Jo, you didn't serve Amy. She wouldn't be allowed to feast at a royal ball." Rob looked between the two of us, confused.

"Yes, Rob, that's true, but Delilah Hande would be." I looked at them both, hoping they wouldn't be too mad. They opened their mouths and shook their heads as if they were disappointed.

"It was the prince's idea!" I told them defensively.

"What!" Rob shouted.

"Shhh," Johannah told him. "But I agree with Rob," she told me coldly before turning and walking in the other direction.

"I'm sorry, I really am. I wouldn't have done it if I'd known it would make you mad!" I yelled after Jo. I wanted them to see that I just wanted to be where I felt I belonged. I didn't want them upset with me, but at the same time I didn't regret what I did.

"Well, Amy, when you stop spending all your time with your prince, find me." Rob's face was scrunched and his hands were in fists at his side as I walked away mumbling.

"I thought he was betrothed," Johannah said under her breath as I walked by on the way to the sink.

I went from being really happy to really upset and angry. They didn't have a good reason to be mad at me. Sure, I didn't tell them that I was going to impersonate a noble, but that wasn't even my idea. I knew the consequences if I were caught and I didn't care. They knew I talked to the prince, but they didn't really know how good of friends we were. Jo and Rob both immediately assumed the wrong conclusion. Henry was just my friend and nothing more.

I felt lonely most of the day. I wished I could talk to Mama, but I knew that my running off today might just make Rob and Jo annoyed, and I didn't need that. So I stayed at the kitchen and talked to Mary most of the day. This was her last week at the kitchen before she became Mrs. Cornelius Smith. She was sad to leave all her friends at the kitchen, but she told me she was glad she didn't have to work, and someday neither would her children. I didn't blame Mary; I was sure I would feel the same way.

I guess it was kind of obvious that I wasn't having a very good day and that my friends were mad at me, because at around two-thirty, Aggie decided to come over for a chat.

"So, Amy, where are your little friends?" She asked curtly.

"Working. How about yours?" It wasn't a very nice response, but it got rid of her.

"Mine, too," she replied in a very small voice.

She left. I knew my friends would get over this, and I wasn't going to make things worse for them and or me by telling her that they were angry with me. I knew that if she picked on them, I would stick up for them, even though they were mad.

Lessons with Charlie didn't start out well that night. Rob was about twenty minutes late and I knew it was because he wasn't sure if he even wanted to come. He wasn't helping our situation; he was only making me more upset with him.

"So, how's Charlie doing?" he asked when he came in, as if nothing was wrong between us, but didn't make eye contact.

"Same as usual. You try," I said in the same tone he asked the question.

He scowled and said something under his breath—about me, no doubt. He grabbed a picture of Prissy, Philip, and Charlie then asked, "Who's that?" He pointed to Charlie in his mother's lap and then dropped the frame.

"Rob!" Charlie screamed.

"No, Charlie, I was pointing at you!" He answered, frustrated with the prospect of paying for a new frame.

I was speechless. I jumped and pointed at Charlie, then at the picture, then opened and shut my mouth, covered my mouth, and even screamed. Rob looked at me as if I were insane.

"Amy, what's wrong?" He was still looking at me as if I'd lost my mind.

"Charlie, did you just say 'Rob'?" I asked frantically.

"Yes," he answered simply, as if he talked all the time.

"What? Oh my gosh, he spoke!"

I grabbed Rob's hands and jumped up and down—I couldn't help myself. Charlie had finally spoken. Rob pulled me down and hugged me and then initiated the jumping himself before yelling.

"Charlie, you're talking! Ames, stop it! Charlie, you said my name," Rob said as he grabbed Charlie and pinned him down as a way of congratulations.

"Yes, I said your name," Charlie responded as he laughed while trying to set himself free from Rob's grasps.

"You can talk!" I screamed as I knocked my water glass to the ground. It broke but I was too excited to care. I jumped over my mess and helped Charlie up before hugging him. "Oh, Charlie, oh Charlie, oh Charlie!"

Rob just stood there shaking his head as he stared at his broken picture frame, at my broken glass, and then at Charlie. "Prissy!" he yelled. "Prissy, Charlie talked. He talked!" Rob was just as excited as I was.

"What did you say?" came Prissy's voice, as if she weren't sure she'd heard him correctly.

"Prissy, Charlie talked!" I yelled, before jumping again.

"Charlie, baby, what did you say? You talked!" Prissy grabbed her one and only son into a huge hug and started to cry.

"Mama, stop it!" Charlie told her, which only mde her cry more and hug him tighter.

I looked at the sight of Prissy hugging and kissing her little boy, and wished my mama were still around to fuss over me. I felt as if the wind were wrapping its arms around me, and I knew she was still there with me.

Rob and I were there for hours that night. When Philip came home he joined in the hugging and kissing, and I even saw a single tear come down his cheek. I was happy for them, and I was glad for once that Rob broke something, because it had actually been useful.

After Charlie started to talk, Rob and I could no longer be mad at each other. We were both too happy with what we had accomplished. We both thought it was hilarious that Charlie had a huge vocabulary for anyone his age, let alone someone who had never said even a single word before.

"I'm sorry, Ames. I know the prince isn't courting you, but just tell me I'm still your best friend."

I thought that was a ridiculous question. "The best."

We walked home together until we had to go our separate ways.

"Papa!" I yelled as I ran into the house. "Guess what?"

"What?"

"Charlie can talk—and in full sentences!" I was smiling one of my biggest.

"Amy, I'm glad, I'm really glad," he said, but I could tell he was thinking of other things that he wasn't letting on to.

"Papa, what is it?" I looked him in the eye, not sure what to think of his facial expressions.

"Amy, I don't know if it's possible to prove our family's innocence anymore."

I looked confused. I wasn't sure what to think about his comment.

"Ames, we can look, but I think the last of the evidence was burned in that wooden box."

I thought that was my fault because I'd told them where it was. Was that really our last hope? "Papa, we have to try," I said.

It seemed like things today kept happening that were either really good or really bad. First, I was excited because we were going to prove we were innocent, but then Rob and Jo were mad at me, and then Charlie talked, and then I found out that I might not be able to free my family. My day was now officially an emotional bumpy ride in a carriage, where nothing seemed to be consistent enough to be comfortable anymore.

I made the decision to spend almost all my spare time in the library in town. Papa was always there with me, and Rob came at least once a week. Jo finally helped after we sorted through everything and were friends again. We searched for anything related to the war, but all we could find was that we lost and the Jonestones were blamed. I found it funny that, technically, they told the truth in these books about war and about us, but the "truth" was written in such away that people would all assume we were guilty.

I quote from *Frindelian Wars, Wins, and Losses*:

"Betrayal was the reason for our loss against Lanski. The Jonestones were among the culprits and they were blamed. To this day they are still being punished for this act of treachery against our dear Frindeline. The Jonestones will forever continue to be punished unless they can prove the unlikely hood that they were framed or other words falsely accused."

My family name made its way into history books—not for any reason I was proud of—but it made me wonder why things happened the way they did, and if for some reason my family was supposed to be brought down to this level in order to accomplish a greater good. I had heard of stories where this was the case—the whole story of Sorret was just that.

The story went that once there was a very poor, young archbishop who was poor only because of his father who used to be a very prosperous and widely know archbishop in Aldreen. He'd lost everything they owned in a bet, when his third eldest child, Darren Albert Sorret, was only five. Archbishop Tuan Odo Milton Sorret was considered intelligent and extremely wealthy, third heir to the king in Aldreen. We all know what too much wine can do to the mind of even the smartest and wealthiest of men, though. Lord Sorret was drinking with his friend, who just happened to be second to King Caedom in wealth. The bet was simple enough, and most men with some kind of money bet on it: it was an unspoken custom to bet whether the child of the king would be born prince or princess.

Some say that a Gubolin (a human size fairy with the power to manipulate for the good of Delynelle) was there and witnessed the event. Some even say that was the reason it happened. Lord Sorret found himself drinking wine, when his very rich friend decided to up the ante, because it was this particular king's firstborn. If Tuan hadn't been so drunk—or as some say, manipulated for the greater good of Delynelle—he would have realized he did not own enough to pay off that debt even if he gave him everything he owned and worked for him for the next twenty years. He bet that King Caedom would have a son, but instead he had a daughter whom he named Princess Colette Cara Anima Aldreen.

Lord Sorret lost everything that day, but he was allowed to keep his title only because it was the only thing that couldn't be taken from him. He had to give up his land and everything he owned except for the clothes on the back of his wife and six children. Their oldest was fourteen and a beautiful girl. She was quickly married off at fifteen, and because she married well, she was able to help her family in small ways. Through her connections, Giselle, Lord Sorret's eldest, got her mother a job at the castle doing laundry. As time went by, all of Giselle's younger siblings ended up working at the castle in some capacity. Most as laundresses, but some worked in the kitchen. Lord Tuan became a messenger for the nobles and for the king himself. Everyone felt sorry for the Sorrets, but in due time things would get better.

When Darren was twenty, Princess Colette found Darren in the courtyard daydreaming. She thought he looked too important to be sitting around idly, instead of doing something productive.

"Hello there, sir," she greeted him.

"Your Highness!" Darren said, surprised, as he quickly stopped daydreaming and bowed.

"Don't you have something better to do than just sit there?" the princess asked.

"I wish doing your dishes was worthwhile, but dreaming of changing things seems more profitable. I am sorry, Princess, if I have bored you, but I was just thinking of what I would do if I found myself in the position my title entails."

"And that would be?" Colette giggled.

"If I were really in the position of Archbishop Sorret, I'd help those who are in debt to others, as my father is to Lord Pultarch."

"I've heard of your family and I'm sorry it was my birth that led to your family's downfall. If you don't find it prudent, I'd like to apologize. I feel that I must apologize to everyone for my gender."

"I see nothing wrong with your gender. I find it's much more intelligent than my own. You don't need to apologize for my father's ill judgment."

A friendship started, and eventually Darren and the princess became very close. They became such close friends that Colette begged her father to pay off the Sorrets' debt. He couldn't resist his daughter's request, and granted it.

When, a year later, she told her father that she wished to marry Darren and asked if her dowry could be the western part of the kingdom (because she wished she could be some sort of queen), he consented. And Lord Darren Albert Sorret became the very first King of Sorret, with his wife, Princess Colette, as the very first queen.

Some say the fairy forest was never given to King Darren, and others say that the Gubolin that manipulated Lord Tuan's mind showed up at the wedding, and in exchange for his deed asked for the forest to be given to the fairies, and that the request was granted. But no one really knows.

I was told once that an Authorian told one of my ancestors that the greatest queen to ever exist would be in the Jonestone line. Of course, no one is sure if that was just a tale or if it really happened. If it were true, I don't see how our situation would give us anything that might just get us a little closer to that. At least, it didn't look to be true from where I was standing.

Besides thinking of how some good might come of this mess, I didn't do much of anything besides looking for evidence and working in the kitchen. I did hold the story of Archbishop Darren Sorret close to heart, though. I didn't know why but for some reason it gave me hope.

I couldn't miss Mary's wedding, no matter how much I needed to look for evidence. I wouldn't be able to see her much after that.

Their wedding seemed magical. Mary was beautiful in her white satin dress, which I knew I could never afford. I wished her the best and I knew she was happy. I had met Cornelius on many occasions before; he had been courting Mary for almost four years before they decided they should finally go through with a wedding. He was a nice man who had a very different-looking nose. Most people just thought it was oversized, but I noticed that it had its own shape, too. His nose kind of reminded me of fairies' noses and it made him easy to pinpoint, but most fairies had normal noses. I just remembered once seeing a picture of an Authorian with a nose similar to his.

Soon after, the prince visited the kitchen, and I remembered I'd missed three of our meetings in a row and hadn't even noticed.

"My father would like a word with Amythist Jonestone," Henry told Dove.

"Is she in trouble, Your Highness?" Dove asked with wide eyes.

Henry nodded.

"Amy, what did you do this time?" Aggie yelled behind her mother, before laughing.

Rob and Jo gave me questioning looks, and I shrugged. As I walked I looked guilty, because I knew I *was* guilty. We walked out of the kitchen silently, and just as I was about to speak, he spoke first.

"Amy, where have you been lately?"

I wasn't sure what to say. I wasn't even sure I wanted him to know where I had been and why, because I knew what would be the next question. "The library," I said with a blush, knowing that alone didn't sound like a good enough reason.

"Why?"

How did I know that one was coming?

"Well, you see, I need to do something that I promised Mama I would do before she died."

He looked at as if he wanted more, but I wasn't sure if it was a good idea to tell royalty what was going on. But he was my friend I couldn't just ignore his question.

"Well, you know a little bit about my family background, but I must confess, I didn't tell you all of it."

He looked stern and waited for me to explain.

"I told you why my father was sent to prison—that it was because he married my mama—but I left out part of that night's events. You see, my family was never convicted, they were just not proven innocent." I stopped hoping he would comment, and I think he caught on because he asked a question.

"Why would they punish someone if they didn't know for sure they were guilty?"

That was a good question, and I found myself asking the same thing. "Fredrick Jonestone saved your great-whatever…grandfather…from dying a few days after his daughter was born. To reward him, Princess Gittel was engaged to Samuel Jonestone. Well, Her Majesty the Queen did not like the arrangement because she had no say in the matter, so she struck a deal with her husband."

I paused for air.

"What kind of deal?"

"Well, no one knows how she did it, but she made him promise and sign a proclamation just for the McCarthys, Jonestones, and the royals that if no evidence was found, the Jonestones would automatically take the blame and be demoted from duke to peasant and the betrothal would be withdrawn. Just to make sure, she also said that the only way out was for us to prove ourselves innocent in front of the king."

"You're not serious? How can that even be legal for a king? I mean, that just isn't fair! Why hasn't anyone done anything about it?" Henry seemed to think it all ridiculous, just as I did along with the rest of my family. It wasn't what you would expect from a royal.

"We've tried, but the McCarthys are always stopping us. My great-grandfather tried but was threatened by a McCarthy to have his children sent away. Papa tried, and Count James McCarthy threatened to kill Aunt Grace and me if she didn't give him information. If it weren't for that, today the evidence we found wouldn't have been burned, I wouldn't need to pretend to be someone else to get into the balls. I'd be invited to balls, and I would never in my life have washed a dish or baked your cake."

I wasn't looking at him; I couldn't. I didn't want to see his reaction, but I heard it.

"The McCarthys!" he screamed. "I never did like them, but this is just too much. They're cowards and they have my father's complete confidence, but they won't even own up to something their ancestors did more than a hundred years ago!"

I finally found the courage to look up and was surprised by what I saw. Henry looked angry. I had never seen him that mad before. I liked what I saw; he was in a position that could really help us. If no evidence could be found before he became king, at the very least he could listen to my argument when he became king and give us what I felt my family deserved.

"I've been spending my extra time in the library trying to find enough evidence to prove that my family had nothing to do with that crime," I told him, to finish answering his question.

"I still don't know what to think. I trust you, Amy, but I've never heard this side of the story. I didn't even know that a Jonestone was ever betrothed to a member of the Frindlian royal family," he told me.

"Well, it never happened and most people probably didn't want it brought up. The Jonestones were considered outcasts for awhile, and I'm almost positive that people thought it embarrassing that the betrothal was even considered."

"You're probably right—it would have been embarrassing enough, because the king trusted Fredrick Jonestone and admitted that. Everyone forgot about the betrothal issue," Henry added. "I still can't believe that they wouldn't do a thorough search before convicting someone 'just because.'"

"They searched for months before following through with the queen's suggestion, but they never found anything. Betraying your country was, and I believe still is, a big deal. They couldn't go without punishing someone," I explained.

"It still wasn't right! If there is anything I can, do let me know," he told me.

I never thought that something like this could cause someone to act that way. Maybe that was why the royal children hadn't been told all the details.

"Henry, you can meet Papa, Rob, Jo, and me at the library tonight around five if you want. Help look through some books." I smiled.

"Don't you have to teach Charlie tonight around then?" he asked as he stared me down, as if I'd forgotten to tell him something important.

I smiled again. "No, he's talking in full sentences. Rob broke a frame." I laughed as I remembered that day.

Henry smiled. "I'll be there. See you tonight, Amy."

That night we looked and looked, but once again we found nothing.

"Prince...I mean Henry...did you find anything yet?" Rob asked awkwardly.

"Nope. You?"

"Nothing except some straight, raw facts. Ames, there was definitely a war around that time period, and everyone was definitely mad at your family, but that's all I can find."

"Thanks, Rob. Tell me something I don't know," I replied sarcastically.

Jo screamed. "I think I found..." Jo started as Papa and I both stood up. "Never mind, just something more about the queen's idea and how wonderful it was."

I gasped for air, and Papa sighed. "Jo, please. If it's nothing, don't say anything, but especially don't scream," I told her for the millionth time. I knew I should stop paying attention to those shrieks because they came every time Johannah saw the name Jonestone, but I couldn't. What if the one time I ignored her, she'd actually found something?

"Sorry, Ames," Jo told me as she shifted.

"Ames, it's getting late. We can try again tomorrow." Rob looked downcast as he told me this.

"Yeah, tomorrow," I told him after taking a deep breath.

"Amy, I'm sorry. Hope you find something. So I'll see you Wednesday at the willow?" Henry asked as I nodded.

"Thanks, all of you," Papa yelled at my friends as they left the library.

On the way home, Papa and I were both silent and didn't want to talk about the evening we'd had. I hated the silence and I think Papa did, too, because he finally spoke.

"Ames, the prince…I mean Henry…seems to like you a lot."

I looked at him and smiled. "Papa, Henry and I are just friends, and he's fifteen. Papa, you're really silly sometimes." I laughed.

Aunt Grace became frantic and starting breaking things when we told her, Grandfather, and Grandmere that we were looking for evidence again. I didn't see why she was so scared. Shouldn't we be the ones who were frightened? We knew we might not find anything, and we knew that we would be in danger if a McCarthy ever found out, so why was she afraid?

It was now June, and I never forgot another willow meeting. If I was going to miss one, I'd let Henry know in advance. The prince was one of my closest friends, and that Rob and Jo really got to know him that summer was a present to me. Sometimes I couldn't help but think about him all the time. I even wondered at one point if he were a closer friend than Rob, but I realized he wasn't; my feelings for Henry were hard to place. I didn't really know what they were, and I wasn't willing to discover them, either.

Before Rob and Jo knew Henry, they didn't understand why I would want to hang around royalty all day. But now it seemed they completely understood, and Rob seemed to appreciate it. Henry was two years older than the three of us, but that didn't seem to matter.

Jo watched Rob a lot and talked way too much about him when he wasn't around. It was quite annoying. I talked to Henry about it at one of our willow meetings. He told me that Rob did that about Johannah, too. I sighed, wondering what my world would come to.

On Will's birthday (he would have been eight), Grandfather, Grandmere, Aunt Grace, Papa, and I all visited his grave. I twiddled my locket, which never left my neck. I wanted Will to be a carefree little boy who could stand right next to me and look at the graves, instead of being in one. Why did all my wishes, the ones that I never really meant, have to come true? I wanted my baby brother to stand with Papa and me. I also…I began to think, when I felt an invisible hug and knew she was already with me, so I didn't have to wish it.

On my fourteenth birthday, my father told me that I was the "prettiest girl in all Delynelle." I knew Mama had to have been much prettier than me at fourteen. I had never been pretty, but I figured he felt obligated to say that to his daughter.

Beauty wasn't the main thing that bothered me those days. To tell the truth, I never really cared. I could never be comparable to a Lavenleeian, and that was a fact. I did, however, care that Mama's voice kept getting louder in my dream and sounded more urgent. I was sure this meant I had to hurry. I tried to hurry, but I still wasn't finding anything useful. My friends helped at every chance they could. Papa helped all the time, and Aunt Grace seemed convinced that there was more evidence out there.

On the prince's birthday I pretended to be Delilah again, and Johannah served the guest of honor, upon his request. He was now sixteen. The betrothal to Hellena became apparent, and everyone expected that in a year or two the Prince of Frindeline would marry. What they didn't know was that Hellena wasn't ready to be queen yet, so King Sencraugh wouldn't allow them to marry until Hellena was at least eighteen. So the soonest, unless something changed, would be three years. I found this information a relief, because although I knew I had no right to Henry in any way, I already felt that he should be mine and that it would be wonderful if he courted me.

I was very glad that Delilah was allowed to dance with a prince all she wanted. I knew that I could get into a huge amount of trouble if I were caught, but I didn't care. I also knew Henry would take the blame if I were found out. In reality, it was his idea, but I didn't want either of us to get into trouble.

After the food was served, we began to dance. After a while of contemplating whether I really wanted to hear the answer, I asked, "Henry, what do you really think of Hellena?" I knew curiosity killed the cat, but I just hoped that today I wasn't the cat.

"Well, Amy, I don't know. I barely know anything about her, except that she'll be the next Queen of Frindeline." He looked at me as if trying to figure out what I was thinking, and when he couldn't, he asked, "Why?"

"I don't know," I began. "I just wanted to know, that's all—doesn't everybody? When she was here, she didn't seem very nice and, well, you deserve better." I was trying to be natural, but it wasn't working.

"Is that all?"

I nodded.

"Then why are you blushing?"

I didn't realize that's what I'd been doing until that moment. I started to laugh, "I'm not blushing. It's just there are so many people in here, and in these dresses you get hot."

He laughed, too.

I knew he wasn't telling me everything, but I didn't tell him everything, either. I didn't want to bring up the topic again, because I knew he knew I'd been blushing.

Chapter Twenty-One

Spring continued and summer came, and then fall found its way to us just as it always does. It was October 21, and we were on our way home from our annual grave visit on the day my brother died nine years ago.

"Amy, Amy," I heard Mary call as she walked up to us from behind.

I turned and looked. "Mary, what is it?" I asked, seeing how excited she looked. I knew whatever it was had to be grand. What she told me, I never would have guessed.

"Amy, Corneilus and I are going to have a baby!" She hugged me.

I smiled and hugged her back. "What, really? That's wonderful news!" I hugged her again.

"Amy, Cornelius and I talked it through and we were wondering if you would like to be the baby's godmother?"

I couldn't believe my ears—did I hear her correctly? "Mary, why me? Prissy, she's so much older and wiser. Oh, Mary, of course I will."

She smiled as if it were a treat to answer my question. "Well, Amy, Prissy would make a great godmother. It's just that she already has Charlie and, well, if anything ever did happen she would favor her son over my baby. I know she wouldn't mean to, but she already knows how it feels to have her own. You, on the other hand, don't have any children and therefore would consider my baby yours, and even after having your own children wouldn't be biased toward one or the other."

I took a moment and thought what she said made at least a little sense. "Mary, thank you so much. Congratulations again."

By the next day, everyone knew about the baby and about my being its godmother. I still couldn't believe it and neither could anyone else.

"Why you?" Rob asked surprised.

"Well, Rob, Mary figures that the baby will always feel partly mine because I don't have children yet."

"Then, why not Jo?" he asked.

"I don't know. I'm just as shocked as everyone else. Ask Mary or Cornelius—I'm sure one of them could tell you."

Henry thought it was hilarious. He couldn't believe it at all. "Really Amy, you're not even fifteen yet," he pointed out.

"That's true, but I will be when the baby is born," I told him.

He still couldn't believe it and was the first to tell me that I'd better hope that Cornelius didn't die before the birth and Mary didn't die in childbirth. I told him no such thing would happen.

The next few months passed quickly, and then January found its way to us. Mary came over looking healthy, but she waddled a little bit with a belly that wasn't overly huge yet. Cornelius was with her and they were both smiling.

"Amy," Mary started, "for a girl's name I like Emily, but he likes Emma or Ella. What do you think?" At the sound of the "E" names I felt tears well up, because my parents had debated over almost exactly the same names for a girl before Will was born.

"Emily," I told them. "That's the one I'd use."

"Amy, if the name makes you upset, we don't have to use it." Cornelius added.

"No, it just brings back memories. If Will had been a girl, his name would have been Emily."

They looked at me, not quite grasping what I meant. "Then why do you like that name the best?" Cornelius asked, confused.

Mary nodded. "I like to be reminded; I need to be reminded."

Cornelius chimed in. "Then Emily it shall be."

I felt like laughing because he'd been the one against Emily to begin with. "So, have you come up with a name for a boy yet?"

"Edward," Cornelius announced proudly.

"I like them both," I told them as I got up to leave.

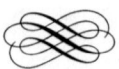

February arrived, and I was extremely happy because I would be fifteen on the nineteenth. I hoped that meant that something important would happen other than that I would be a godmother in June.

I had a small family dinner at Grandfather and Grandmere's. Rob, Jo, and Henry were invited. It was a lot of fun. Johannah and I were each given a beautiful dress. Mine was white satin with pink beaded flowers in the bottom corner, and a pink sash around the middle. Jo wore a pink satin dress with a purple beaded butterfly and a lighter-colored blue sash.

After dinner, Rob and Jo danced, Henry and I danced, Papa and Aunt Grace danced, and Grandfather and Grandmere danced. Because that was everyone who was there, it was easy enough to switch partners, so I danced with Papa a few times, with Rob a couple, and with Grandfather once or twice.

In April, Jo told me that she would be serving Henry again at his birthday banquet. Rob informed me that he was going to be a doorman. He really surprised me; I guess Rob and Henry really were friends. I was again going as Delilah for the third year in a row.

The bells rang as they always did, and my cake was served as usual. We said hello to Rob and Jo, and then we danced. When everyone was assured that the regular birthday routine was going smoothly, he asked me a question.

"Amy, remember last year when you asked me about Hellena?"

I was surprised that he remembered a question I'd asked him a year ago.

"Yes," I answered, not sure where he was going with this.

"Well, I didn't tell you everything."

I smiled at him slyly. "What didn't you tell me?" I asked, trying not to blush or look excited.

"Well, Amy, the reason I don't know much about Hellena is because I don't want to know anything about her." He paused. "Amy, I'd much rather know everything about you. Ever since I saw you...when that herald introduced you at your twelfth birthday, I've wanted to know you more."

I was excited and amazed. What was he saying? Was he saying what I thought he was saying?

We had walked all the way out to the courtyard and I hadn't even noticed. I was so content just to listen to his words. I couldn't believe it—everyone else was inside dancing and here Henry was out in the courtyard telling me that I was all he could think about. If I wasn't blushing before, I was now.

"Really, Henry?" I asked, and then giggled. "Why didn't you tell me last year or the year before or anytime? Why are—"

But I never finished my sentence because he cupped my chin in his hand and kissed me on the lips. At first, my eyes were open, and then I closed them. It was amazing. I'd never imagined this, but I liked it.

He stopped andI laughed.

"Oh, Henry!" I yelled with my arms around his neck. "I've wanted this for awhile."

"Really?" he asked me with a corny smile on his face.

"Yes, why didn't you tell me a long time ago?" I was so happy that I didn't really need an answer. And I kind of already knew, but asked anyway.

"Well, when you were twelve it would have been frowned upon for a fourteen-year-old to be courting you. That's unthinkable. Then I was betrothed against my will, because Father thought it would be the best thing for the kingdom, no matter how many times I told him I didn't want to be forced to marry someone. Did you know he promised Daffodil that he would never do that to her? My father can be so contradictory. Anyway, after that I didn't want to tell you because I thought you would think me horrible for liking someone other than my betrothed. Once we became friends, I didn't want to say anything that might jeopardize that. I mean, what if you didn't feel the same way? How could I even be sure that you felt the—"

I stopped him. "I'm sorry I asked," I told him. "I don't really need to know." I kissed him on the cheek.

He took my hand and led me into the ballroom, and we danced for the rest of the night.

Before it was time for me to leave he asked, "So, Amy, meet me at the willow tomorrow?"

I smiled, looked to see that no one was watching, and blew him a kiss.

"Yes, I'll be there." Then I walked out.

I must have had a dazed look the next morning at the kitchen because Rob was worried, but Jo knew I was just extremely happy.

"So Ames, what happened between dinner and this morning?" she finally asked when she had me all to herself.

I knew I could tell her and she would understand. I didn't know about Rob. "Henry told me that he didn't want to *marry Hellena*, and he would much rather court me…then he kissed me!"

Jo opened her mouth in surprise.

"Amy, he kissed you?!" She looked excited. "Did you like it? Did you even want him to?" She was so full of questions.

"Jo, I've wanted that for awhile," I told her sheepishly.

"Ames, you're so lucky. I mean, I'd love to get what I want in that area."

She paused, and I wanted to ask her what she wanted, but before I could she was asking more questions.

"When are you seeing him again?" She was so eager to know everything.

"Today after lunch. Do you think you could cover for me?"

She smiled. "Because you're going to meet your beloved, the prince, of course." She giggled, and then she screamed.

"Jo, you can't tell anyone. Do you know how much trouble I could get into? How much he could get into?" I told her urgently, trying to quiet her down.

"Oh, yeah, he's betrothed to that brat. Don't worry, my lips are sealed," she told me as she ran to get some flour.

Rob came over not too long after that and demanded more and then asked, "Ames, what's up? There's obviously nothing wrong with you; otherwise, Jo wouldn't have been jumping up and down like she was a few minutes ago."

I blushed.

"So, Ames, what is it?"

"Just something that happened at Henry's party last night," I told him truthfully.

"So what happened?"

Gosh why did he have to ask for details?

"Well, he kind of told me that…Rob, go ask him later. I've never had a problem talking to you before, but I really just don't know how to tell you."

He looked at me as if knowing. "If I guess, will you tell me if I'm right?"

I thought for a second. "Sure, why not?"

"He finally told you, and I'll bet he went further than that—he kissed you, didn't he?"

I was shocked. "What? You knew he wanted to kiss me?" I looked at him, wondering how he had kept this from me for almost three years.

"You know, girls aren't the only ones who talk," he told me before he headed back to work.

The information left me dumbfounded and wondering what else they'd talked about.

After lunch I headed to the willow tree. Henry was waiting right next to it.

"So, Amy, when was the last time you climbed a tree?" he asked, with a smile playing across his face.

"I don't know. How about you?" I smiled back.

"You know, I'm not sure either. What do say about climbing the willow?" He looked excited.

"I'd say let's do it," I told him as my smile grew.

We climbed 'way up high and sat in two chair-like branches across from each other.

It was different, but a good different. I liked it, although I'm not sure why I liked just being there with him and knowing he cared about me and I cared about him. I felt loved, and I loved the feeling. I cared for him a lot. I felt special, and I hoped I made him feel special, too.

We were quiet for most of the first twenty minutes. I didn't care if he ever talked. I just wished we could stay there forever, looking at each other and holding hands. I knew that wish couldn't come true, because eventually we would need to eat, and I would have to work.

"Amy," he finally said, "did I surprise you last night?"

He looked worried, and I didn't want him to worry. "No…kind of…a little." He took his hand out of mine and shook his head.

I didn't like what was happening. "Oh, but it was a good surprise. I really did want you to care for me as more than a friend." I smiled and I think I blushed.

"And you care for me as more than a friend, right?"

I thought the question strange; of course I did. He didn't even have to ask. "Yes, would I want you to like me as more than a friend if I didn't feel that way about you? What do you think I am? Henry, you've known me for three years. Do I seem like a person who goes around pretending to care for someone just for the attention?" I looked at him, hoping I was assuring him.

"No, so I guess everything is good?" he asked as he grabbed my hand again.

"Yes, everything is good," I told him as I squeezed his hand a little.

After we decided to come out of the tree, we walked hand-in-hand to the point where we had to go our separate ways. He had to go to the front of the castle and I had to head toward the back; we couldn't be seen holding hands.

"'Bye, Amy," he told me.

"'Bye," I told him as he kissed me on the cheek before walking away.

I walked the rest of the way back to the kitchen with my hand on my cheek, wondering how this was going to work, but knowing that I wanted badly for it to work. I didn't know what he was going to do about Hellena, but that wasn't a threat yet. He hadn't even seen her for three years. He hadn't talked to her since she'd left. I remember vividly his complaining about her every chance he got when she was around, and I remember that only King Sencraugh and Queen Neeuqa liked her at all. I would have to talk to him about it later.

As soon as I entered the kitchen, Johannah was all over me with questions. I tried, but I couldn't answer them all. I felt overwhelmed; I didn't need to or want to answer all of her questions, anyway. I couldn't see how any of it was her business and I told her so.

"All we did was hold hands and stare at each other, really."

She looked disappointed, but that was seriously all we'd done.

Chapter Twenty-Two

Life after that got a little crazy. Henry didn't tell his parents about me, but he did try to get out of the betrothal by bugging them about it. I didn't tell Papa, Aunt Grace, or anybody besides Rob and Jo about him, either. He didn't kiss me on the lips again. I sometimes wondered why, but I knew he had his reasons; it could simply be because of the betrothal or that he was two years older than me.

Aside from Henry and I becoming a couple, kitchen work became murderous. Dove's hatred for me seemed to become worse. I hated the sight of any kitchen. I liked cooking, especially baking, but a kitchen reminded me of Dove, and that always made everything sour. I couldn't help but wonder what I would do if anyone (and at this point I didn't care who) took Dove's place. No one could ever be worse, and even if they were as bad, it would be a new challenge and a breather from the reality I was in.

Charlie talked like any six-year-old and sometimes better; it was amazing. He loved hanging around Rob and me. His gigantic vocabulary could get quite annoying sometimes, and Rob was always quick to remind me that it was my fault.

"You're the one who dropped the frame," I would remind him.

Then he'd respond, "The only reason I was even there was because you insisted on teaching him. And now we can't ever get him to shut up."

Mary, as far as the world could see, was carrying the healthiest baby in all Delynelle. I didn't care if it was a boy or a girl. I just wished June would hurry up and get here. As you know, it's always when you want time to pass quickly that it seems to slow down and take its sweet, slow time. If I had wished it never to come, it would have hurried its way over and covered me like a storm, but I wanted it to come, and that's all there was to it. Whenever I saw Mary's bulging stomach, I got excited. I wanted Emily or Edward now!

"Amy, the only problem with your being godmother is you're not patient at all," Mary informed me one day.

"I'm sorry, but I don't see how you can be so patient"

"Amy, it's hard, but I know how happy I'll be when it comes, and I know I can wait a few more months for that kind of happiness." Her smile glowed, and I wished I had her patience.

I secretly hoped for a girl because I knew I could really be there for Emily. But I wasn't so sure of a boy. The thought of a baby boy made me nervous. The last baby boy I was able to get to know died a little after a month. I was scared that if Mary had a boy it could share the same fate. I knew that was ridiculous, but it was still a fear that raged inside me. I knew that if I saw a baby boy and it lived, my fear would be gone. I knew that's what would happen, but it didn't stop me from being afraid.

On June 25, 1137, Prissy told me there was a surprise waiting for me at Mary's. I wasn't sure what to do, and by the way Prissy sounded, it seemed that even she was surprised.

I walked, knowing Emily or Edward had been born, wondering which it was and what she or he looked like. When I knocked and they told me to come in, I saw the unexpected: Cornelius held a bundle and Mary held another. Two? Twins? I was shocked.

"They're beautiful," I finally managed to say.

Mary smiled at me. "Amy, I'd like you to meet your godson, Edward Cornelius Smith," she said. She looked at the baby bundle in her arms with a smile and a glow

I knew I would never understand until I had one of my own.

"And I would like you to meet your goddaughter, Emily Mary Smith."

Cornelius was also smiling and seemed the happiest I'd ever seen him. I looked at my godbabies and smiled, not knowing what else to do.

They were beautiful. Emily, I thought, looked mostly like her mother, with her father's eyes; whereas Eddie, as they called Edward, looked exactly like his father (except that the nose wasn't anywhere near as huge), but he had Mary's eyes.

Everything I was supposed to do that day was forgotten. I loved them like I could never explain. I wished I could hold them forever. I felt that they partially belonged to me and that I could never live without them. I guess that proved Mary's point. I have no idea how I would have felt if I were married and had children of my own, but I knew how I felt now and I was the happiest I had ever been in my life.

I was connected to the family with a document which was sent to the records bank at the king's council. I was given a copy, as were Mary and Cornelius. I was now officially "Aunt Amy," as I decided they should call me. Plain "Amy" sounded too informal and "Miss Jonestone" sounded the exact opposite. "Aunt Amy" was simple and gave the sense that I was a part of the family.

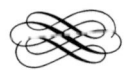

The next day I couldn't stop smiling. Whenever I was asked where I had been the day before, I answered, "To see my godbabies, Emily and Eddie. They were born yesterday."

Everyone would look at me, many commented on the twin factor, and all told me to tell Mary congratulations. Jo wanted to know what they looked liked and Rob really didn't seem to care. I hadn't seen Henry in a couple of days, but I knew that meant I was due for a visit. I just hoped he wouldn't try while I was with my godchildren.

After work that day Rob, Jo, and I went to see the twins. Johannah absolutely loved them.

"Mary, they're the cutest babies in the world," Jo told her as she held Eddie.

Rob just sat there and looked at them, told Mary and Cornelius congratulations, and then whispered in my ear that he wanted to leave.

"Rob, I'm staying, but if you want to go, you can go."

He chose to just sit there and watch Jo and me having a wonderful time holding and watching Emily and Eddie. I completely agreed with Jo about their being the cutest babies in all Delynelle. How could they not be? I didn't ever want to leave, but I realized I had to when it started to get late, and Papa would be worrying.

"Thanks Mary. I'll be back soon. 'Bye, Eddie, 'bye Emily," I told them as I touched their soft baby cheeks before heading out the door.

Rob couldn't believe us. "What is it with girls and babies?" he asked with a disgusted tone in his voice.

"Nothing, Robert," I told him as I kicked him in the shin.

"I thought you liked little children," Jo said sternly. It seemed to me she was hoping he'd answer her question for a reason other than just being curious.

"I do, Jo. It's babies when they're this little—they don't do anything except sit there and cry," he told us deliberately, without looking Jo in the eye.

I walked over to Jo and whispered in her ear, "That's why the women have the babies and not the men. Men can't see the beauty of a baby; they only see its negative qualities."

We laughed.

"What?" Rob asked.

"Oh, nothing you'd find funny," I told him playfully.

He hit me and we hit him back as we broke into fits of laughter.

The next day Henry came down to the kitchen. I pretended I didn't notice him as everyone else turned, amazed. I figured that not noticing would keep everything I held dear about him a secret.

"Dove," he said.

She turned and curtsied. "Yes, Your Highness. What may I do for you today?" She smiled her biggest and evilest.

"I want to meet my cake baker." He already knew who that was, but still it didn't surprise me.

"Well of course; I'll just bring her over here…"

Henry shook his head.

"No? Then how do you wish to meet the minx?" It was obvious Dove didn't want to hand me the privilege of meeting with the prince all by myself.

"Have her bake me a cake and then meet me in my quarters for tea. I'd like to discuss how she bakes such a wonderful treat. Oh, and once she's done baking, let that be her last chore for today."

Dove's face went from a smile, which wasn't the prettiest sight anyway, to a scowl as she muttered angrily, "As you wish, Your Majesty." Then she turned to me. "You heard what he said, start baking." Then she turned and walked over to Aggie.

I smiled at Henry and he smiled back. I looked over to where Dove and Aggie stood. Neither looked too happy, especially Aggie, because it looked as if Dove had given little Agithus all my extra chores. I was thrilled. When I looked back at Henry, he was gone.

It took about an hour to bake the cake and then about forty-five more minutes for it to cool and for me to frost it. It was two hours after Henry's visit that I found myself in his quarters with the cake.

"Amy, you're as beautiful as ever."

I smiled at the compliment.

"So, how'd you come up with that excuse? Thanks."

He smiled back at me.

"I came up with it two days ago, but when I went down to the kitchen, Dove told me that the cake baker never showed up. Then yesterday, I came down about four forty-five, but you must have left early because once again you weren't there. Now I have to ask you, Amy, where have you been lately and what have you been doing?" He smiled and I laughed.

"You didn't answer my question, but I will certainly answer yours. Mary had the babies." I smiled, while he looked at me strangely.

"Babies?"

"Oh, sorry, I forgot you don't know. Henry, she had twins, a boy and a girl, Emily and Eddie."

We both smiled.

"I should have known you wouldn't have skipped kitchen work otherwise," he told me sarcastically. We both smiled, and he kissed me quickly on the lips—something I considered rare.

I grabbed his hand as his face parted from mine. "So, do you want some cake?" I laughed.

"I'd love some. Thanks," he told me as he, too, began to laugh.

That afternoon was one I will never forget. It was the afternoon when I realized something that I hadn't given much thought to. If I had, I doubt I ever would have told him I cared for him as well. I knew it could only cause problems, even if the betrothal were dropped, which I doubted would happen. I never wanted Hellena to return. I never wanted her to be near Henry again. I knew what I wanted more than anything in the world now, but I also knew I couldn't have it.

He sat in front of me as we talked that afternoon, as everything became clear in my mind. We talked and I did my best to make sure that the tears I wanted to come did not, without making me look suspicious. It was against the law; it went against every single stupid rule put before me. I had fallen in love with Prince Henry, the next King of Frindeline, and I could and never would be his queen. It was forbidden—what was I thinking? I didn't even know if he loved me. He cared about me, but how could he love me? I was a speck of dust compared to what he was offered in the world. I was in over my head and I knew he could never find out. If he did, problems would only grow, even if he felt the same. I could never have him, and I felt this was a sad ending to what could have been happy, if it weren't for the curse on my family.

I made many decisions as I talked to Henry about things that didn't seem important anymore. I decided that I would never marry if I couldn't have him. The memory of Henry would have to do. I would never have children, but I could spoil Eddie and Emily and love them as if they were my own.

I decided that I would have to avoid Henry as much as possible, because I couldn't tell him we were through—not when I felt the way I did. I would wait for him to do it, and leave a sliver of hope there for me by keeping him as close as I dared. I wouldn't be able to keep him long, anyway; once he was married to that witch, it would be over and he would belong to her. And I would take myself out of the picture, no matter what he wanted. Hellena had the upper hand, the advantage, unless Henry could convince his father to put an end to the betrothal, which was very unlikely. I hated being helpless as I looked into his eyes, hoping he'd never stop talking and hoping that today could last for forever and he would always be mine.

That night I was silent as I picked at my dinner. Papa looked worried, but I told him I was fine. I was glad he didn't push it, because I really didn't want to talk about it. When he left on his stilts, I went to bed and cried myself to sleep. I wished Henry had never told me how he felt about me, because it didn't matter; he'd have to marry Hellena eventually anyway.

The only thing that was worse than being hopelessly in love with someone you weren't allowed to have was the guilt of being in love with a man who was already spoken for. I felt awful. Even though he barely knew her, he thought she was a pompous pig. I knew I was in for it, and for now, avoiding him was the only thing I was willing to do.

I spent most of my time with the twins that summer and skipped way too much kitchen work. I saw Henry enough but not as much as I wanted. But I really didn't want to end up crying in front of him telling him how

I felt and ruining everything. Henry couldn't know I loved him. So I filled my time and my head with the twins. I was there when Eddie first smiled and when Emily first cooed. I loved them and I knew that at least I would always be able to have them. They were Eddie and Emily, my godbabies, and I was their godmother. I planned on always being there for them.

As I watched them, I often felt my mother's presence. It was a good thing, too, because if she hadn't been there I'm sure I would have melted into an emotional, crying baby myself. She was the only one I could tell everything to, because I knew she wouldn't and couldn't tell anyone else.

One day in late July, Rob, Jo, and I took the twins to a grassy field over by the lake. I was holding Eddie, who had very recently learned to squirm, while Jo held Emily, who sat contently in her arms and sucked her thumb. Rob and Jo seemed to worry about me a lot lately. I knew that very soon they were going to express it. I also knew the two of them had probably rehearsed the whole thing and knew exactly what they were waiting for. I wasn't a fool and never would consider myself one; I knew they worried because I hadn't tried to see Henry and hadn't even mentioned him the last three weeks. I had seen him a week after the cake incident, but not since then, and as much as I wanted to see him I wouldn't unless I absolutely had to.

"Hey, Ames, Henry has been wondering where you've been lately. He's worried he did something wrong," Rob expressed as I set Eddie down on his stomach on the blanket.

"No, he's great. I've just been busy, that's all, with the twins, in the library, and work and everything," I told him.

"Is that all? You know we could help you look for evidence." He paused, "Amy, he wants you to prove your family, too. It'll just make things easier for the both of you."

I smiled as a tear trickled down my cheek. "Rob, tell him I'm sorry, but I've been busy. I'll meet him at the willow a week from today at our usual time."

Rob nodded and left. He was walking toward the lake, and I knew he'd be back after taking a dip. Once he was completely out of earshot, Jo came over.

"Amy, what's up with you? Rob says Henry is worried, too. Amy, something is bothering you. Otherwise, if you were being completely honest, that tear wouldn't have been there, and you know it."

I cried, knowing that telling one person who was actually alive wouldn't kill me, especially when I was sure she would understand.

"Jo, I don't know what to do. In a year or two Henry will marry Hellena and what will happen to me? Jo, I love him, but I can't have him. I don't want to tell him because I can't keep him. Every time I think about him and the last couple of times I've seen him I've wanted to yell, 'I love you,' but I can't." I was crying into my lap with the twins lying on the blanket next to us. I couldn't control my tears.

"Jo," I finally said as I caught my breath, "I'm stuck. Even if he wasn't betrothed, I still could never marry him. It's against the law. Even if the evidence is found, we don't know how long that'll take. And if worse came to worst he could simply fix the problem when he becomes king, but who knows how long that'll take? But then everything would be different, too, and right now that doesn't even matter. He's still betrothed to Princess Hellena."

Jo hugged me and I cried into her shoulder.

As my tears subsided I heard a noise coming from the trees. I wiped my eyes. "Who's there?" I yelled, but no one answered.

"Come out, whoever you are," Jo hollered.

"Ames, any idea who that could have been?"

I shook my head, not really caring but noticing she seemed a little shook up. I wished that my family had never been convicted or that Rob was born the prince and Henry the kitchen boy—anything that would allow Henry and me to work.

When Rob returned from his swim, I informed them that I should be getting back home and asked them to take the twins back to Mary. Rob started to refuse, but Jo answered before he could get a word in.

"Papa," I yelled as I ran through the door into our hovel.

"Yes, Ames, I'm in here," he yelled back as I walked toward the second room we used as a bedroom.

"I need to tell you something, and I hope that it won't come as too big of a shock and you won't get too angry with me."

"Amy, what are you talking about?" He looked at me as if trying to read what I was saying.

"Henry," I told him simply, and then sighed.

Chapter Twenty-Three

Papa obviously didn't have clue what I was talking about. I didn't know how to explain, so I waited for the question he was trying to form.

"What do you mean, 'Henry,' and why does it matter?"

He looked confused, but I had received my question and knew I had to answer it. I was trying to think of the best way to tell him, but as soon as I opened my mouth it all just started to run out, as if doing it quickly would make it easier.

"Papa—I love him and…well, we've kind of been seeing each other since April. Papa, when I realized I loved him I started avoiding him. I know I can't have him…and, well, I wish he'd never told me how he felt about me because now…I really love him. But even if our family was free, I couldn't have him because he's betrothed!"

I stopped for air after not taking a single breath. Then I looked to Papa, who was looking in concentration as if still trying to piece together what I had said.

"All right, Amy, you definitely said something about Henry." He paused and gulped, and his eyes grew big before continuing. "Love, and can't have." He paused again as if trying to digest what I'd told him.

"Papa, I should have told you sooner." I began to sob into my hands as he came over and gave me a hug.

"Amy, does he love you back?" he asked me as he grabbed me into a huge hug.

"I really don't know," I answered as my tears began to cease.

"Have you ever told him?" my father asked, easing me away far enough to look in my eyes.

"I took my gaze away from him. "No, I started avoiding him as soon as I realized, remember?" It was hard enough telling him this without him making me feel worse. I just stared at my feet.

"You said that?" he replied. "Amy, why didn't you ever think about this before? The prince is a decent man but, sweetie, you knew he was betrothed. Why did you even consider it?"

"Papa, I was too excited, and he doesn't want to be betrothed. Whenever Hellena is brought up he shrinks. And if you had ever met the girl you wouldn't want to marry her either. Henry was forced into the betrothal and has been trying to get out of it ever since," I told him.

"Still, Ames, you and I both know that unless he does get out of it, this isn't right. No matter how you justify it—even if you love him and he loves you."

"I know Papa, I just…I don't know what I was thinking…I was being stupid, but what am I supposed to do now?" I looked at him knowing I was in a very messy situation.

"You have to tell him. He has to know, even if he can't have you." He looked at me sternly. I knew this was no laughing matter, but I started laughing, wiping away my tears and nodding as Papa began to laugh with me.

I was scared beyond belief. I was meeting Henry at the willow later that day and I was going to tell him. I wasn't going to make any bigger a fool of myself than I absolutely had to. I wanted him to know and hoped he felt the same way, but what good was is it going to do? I couldn't ever have him. I knew that everything we had should not have happened, even if it was basically nothing. I knew I probably should have thought through it all before ever getting involved. I'd never before made a bigger mistake—kissing a betrothed man! It didn't matter that I loved him. It didn't matter that he didn't want to be betrothed to Hellena or that it was being forced upon him—it was wrong. Still he had to know; he had the right, as Papa had put it. I wished I could just disappear from his life, get out of the way, and not break any more laws. What was it with Papa and me falling for the people who were against the law to fall for? How could I ever do that? I knew what that could do to loved ones. What had I gotten myself into?

When I arrived at the kitchen I decided I was going to be good and stay there the whole day, just in case Henry came looking for me. I needed to be wherever he might be; I knew that if nothing else I would see him at the willow after work, as I'd told Rob to tell him. I had never known this kind of fear before, the fear of rejection that I knew my heart just couldn't take.

At about noon Rob asked if I wanted to go to the wood with him and Jo.

"I'm going after five tonight," I answered, "and I'd really prefer if you and Jo didn't come with me."

"Why aren't you going sooner?" Rob asked simply.

I never was held by time usually. "I have to tell Henry something, and just in case he comes looking for me here…"

"Ames, he gave up on that one a while ago. It was starting to look suspicious. He's waiting for you at the willow, wherever that is. He told me to tell you."

I smiled.

"Go, Amy. I'll cover for you." He practically pushed me out the door.

"Thanks, Rob. You're the best friend a girl could ever have."

He winked at me. "Really?"

"Really."

I ran to the willow that stood in the middle of the Wood of Drell. I hadn't seen Henry ever since a week after having cake in his quarters. I had wanted to see him, but I didn't know how I was going to tell him.

But I had to and I wanted to, while at the same time I was scared to.

When I finally reached the willow, he was sitting there waiting, as if he knew I'd be there sooner than planned.

"Long time no see," he said as I came closer.

"Yeah," I said quietly. I was scared he was mad at me and scared that he wouldn't want anything to do with me. What was I saying? This was Henry! Even if he was mad and just wanted to be friends, he'd never not want to see me again just because I avoided him for a few weeks. I was finally standing right in front of him, and he gestured for me to sit down.

As I sat he said, "Amy, we need to talk."

What was that supposed to mean?

"I think so, too. Henry I'm sorry for avoiding you. It's just that I got scared."

He looked at me and then asked in a concerned sweet voice, "Of what?"

Oh, I loved him, his eyes, his concerned look, his hair, the way his lips moved, everything. I loved everything about him.

"I don't know," I answered, even though I really did. I was still too afraid to tell him.

"Amy, I know you know." He paused. "I need to tell you something."

I looked at him, filled with hope.

"What?" I simply asked, wishing what I wanted to come out of his mouth, and at the same time trying not to get my hopes up.

"Amy, I love you. I've loved you since that one birthday when you served me and I recognized you because of your locket. I've always known you were something special. Even at your twelfth birthday I could sense who you were. You never tried to hide exactly what you are from anyone, and I love that. Your laugh, the way you make me feel, how it feels to love you. Amy, I don't think I could ever go on if I knew I could never see you again."

I began to blush and I knew it. I felt a tear trickle down my cheek. This didn't solve anything, but maybe we could make it work, or fix it.

"Really?" I asked. "Henry, I was scared because I love you too." He smiled.

"I know."

I looked at him, not sure how he could know that, but not caring, because he loved me.

"Amy, I don't know how it's all going to work, but I will do everything in my power to make sure it does. Amy, I won't marry Hellena!" he told me.

"Henry, how can you say that? You certainly can't promise it. I don't have any evidence, and no matter what you do, unless your father does something about the betrothal, you're still betrothed."

He smiled again. "Amy, if I bother my father enough, I'll eventually get out of the betrothal. I'm not going to marry Hellena, I promise…"

"How are you going to convince him to undo it without explaining why, before I find the evidence? Even then, what makes me worthy enough in your father's eyes? I still come from a line people who were despised for over a century." I looked him in the eye.

"The fact that I love you makes you worthy enough in my eyes. Even if we have to get married in secret someday and then let him get used to the idea, I'll do it," Henry told me more seriously than I think I had ever seen him before.

"You just worry about the evidence," he continued, "and I'll help whenever I get the chance and get as many to help as possible. Amy, we are going to find it. I promise."

He held my hand as I put my head on his shoulder, my brown waves of hair flying in the wind behind me. I knew he meant every word.

I was no longer scared that it wouldn't work out—most of the time. All right, I was still scared, but I didn't avoid Henry. We were both working to make everything work the way we felt we needed to in order to survive. I thought about it almost constantly, though. I already knew that if I didn't find the evidence, I wouldn't marry him. I promised myself never to put anyone in the position I grew up in. No child of mine would be put though that. I wouldn't let anything like that happen again.

All that Henry and I seemed to do when we were together that year was look for evidence. We both wanted everything to work. Even after not finding anything, when most people would have given up, we didn't. There was too much at stake now, more than ever before in my mind.

Henry was having a difficult time trying to convince his father that the betrothal was a bad idea. He almost gave too much information. I remember him telling me the story one day as we looked through history books in the library.

"'Father,' I told him, 'I'd rather love the person I marry than marry a person because of the connections Frindeline would and wouldn't have. It would only be fair to let Hellena be loved instead of being forced upon a man who really wants nothing to do with her. Father, she's a handful and a brat.'

"My father simply started to laugh. 'Henry, are you in love with another girl or is this just some sorry attempt to get your way?'

"I looked him in the eye and asked him, 'Does that matter? I just don't want to marry Hellena and I want you to drop the betrothal.'

"'Henry, somehow I get the feeling you're not telling your father everything. I want you to know I'm not going to jeopardize our chances with a connection with the country that has the most jewels unless you are in love and I approve of the family. So stop with this argument. It's getting old. Come back when you have a real argument, but until then you are marrying Hellena, no matter what you think she is!'

"I just stood there looking at him, afraid to speak for fear of what might come out of my mouth. I couldn't tell him I was already in love with someone else, because then he's ask who, and then I'd have to tell him…and, well, I'm scared of what he might do to you, really." Henry sighed.

"Well, I guess that means we really need the evidence," I told him as he nodded. I was thankful my father was more understanding and not as stubborn.

Wintereve was beautiful at Grandfather's and Grandmere's. No one said anything, but it was quite apparent that Grandmere wasn't at all well. This scared me. The last time I'd seen someone I loved get really sick she died before my eyes. I hoped with every ounce of hope that Grandmere would get well.

I must not have seemed my usual self that year because after dinner Aunt Grace came up to me in the corridor and asked me a question.

She had a very concerned look on her face as she pushed one of her red curls behind her ear. "Amy, what's with you lately? You seem, I don't know…distracted."

"I've been searching for three years, Aunt Grace! Three years, and what do I have to show for it? No matter how hard I look or where I look or how often I look, I can't find any evidence! It took Papa only a few months, but when I think I'm about ready to give up I realize everything will be in jeopardy if I do, so I know I have to keep looking. I think I've given up in my head. I know that means I probably won't find anything, simply because I'm not really trying, but I really want to find the evidence, I need to find it, but at the same time it seems almost hopeless."

As I finished my tirade and looked up at her, I knew she had something to say, but I could tell she didn't know how to express herself or explain.

"Aunt Grace, what is it?" I finally asked, unable to wait any longer. If she had a solution, I needed to know what it was.

"Amy, I've been wanting tell you. It's just…I can't really remember."

My confused thoughts must have shown on my face, because Aunt Grace looked at me in the same way Mama used to look at me when she wanted me to understand but knew there was no real explanation.

"They didn't burn the evidence, sweetie."

"Yes, they did. I told them where it was and then watched them pull it out and drop it into the fire. You can't tell me that something I saw with my own two eyes didn't happen," I reassured her, wishing what she said were true.

"Do you remember that someone was missing for awhile on your fifth birthday?" she asked me.

"No. Wait, you were…but, what…wait a second, what did you do?" I began to smile, hoping she did the one good thing that could save me, my family, and my life as I wanted it to be.

"I went to your house and switched the wooden box that had my wedding dress in it with your wooden box that held the evidence, and hid it. I just don't remember where."

"Why your dress? That's your memory. I remember you showed it to me a long time ago. You told me it was what reminded you of Uncle Charles. I don't understand." I looked at her as tears of happiness welled up in my eyes.

"I gave up a very special material item. It was so important to me, because it was the only thing I had left from the short period of my life where I was married to the man I loved. He died and I had my dress, and I kept it to remember the best days of my life. I gave that up because I knew what was planned, and I couldn't warn you because McCarthy had backup plans. I overheard them—they were prepared and expected me to tell your papa, but I didn't because it would have been worse. I explained it to your father, but I wish your mother had listened to me before she died. She would have understood, but that's in the past. I knew your papa was going to be taken away, and that it would be my fault I would cause her just as much pain as I was going through. She would lose her husband, and because it was going to be my fault I gave up the most important material possession I owned, hoping it would be enough. But it wasn't, and I never blamed your mother for being angry with me. I deserved it."

I was impressed as I saw the tears well up in her eyes. I hated my situation in life more and more every day. How could this really be the result of a stupid mistake? It didn't make sense: we weren't guilty and Mama wasn't guilty. Aunt Grace was guilty, but only because we weren't. I knew the consequences of people's choices were huge; I'd already lived through the enormity of these choices, and they can be brutal. Why can't people just think before they do? I knew that every choice had a consequence, but why couldn't the world see that? Why did I have to live like this, and for whose choice was I living it? Not my own choice, but a every selfish king's. Didn't anyone care to even try and think how their choices might affect their future and the future of those they were making choices for? Obviously not, or I wouldn't be sitting here wondering this, as I felt for my aunt, getting more and more upset with the McCarthys every minute.

"Where did you hide it, somewhere in the house?"

"No, I ran for the Wood of Drell and buried the evidence, but it was dark and I don't remember exactly where."

My hope was no longer gone. It was renewed because I knew the evidence could be found. I was also given another reason to hate the McCarthys. They had done so much already, but putting every family member of mine in a state of misery was just another reason to add to my list. I was going to find that box if it was the last thing I ever did.

I jumped up. "Aunt Grace, you've been a big help. I've got to go now."

"Amy, you can't start digging yet. It's cold and there is too much snow. You should wait until at least March," she told me sternly.

I nodded and went to find Papa, who was overjoyed at the news.

"Why didn't you tell us sooner, Grace?" Papa asked joyously.

She cringed. "I thought you might be angry.".

"How could I be angry with you? This only means that we're a step closer to freedom," Papa yelled as he began to skip around the room.

I joined in, along with almost half of my relatives.

On New Year's Eve, I served Henry as usual. After the serving maids were no longer needed, Henry came down to the kitchen, where the music could still be heard, and danced with me where no one could watch and get any ideas.

At midnight he was still there dancing with me. "Aren't you supposed to be upstairs doing the traditional Frindelian New Year's dance?" I asked.

He smiled. "Yes, but if I'm not there, how can they expect me to be a part of it?"

I looked at him as I exaggerated a "Hmm" before answering, "You're not."

He smiled again and we danced.

I loved him so much. When we weren't around everyone else, we could dance close together with my head against his chest listening to his heart beating. If we had been upstairs, I would have been punished. I closed my eyes and listened to the rhythm of his heart as he whispered in my ear. I loved the feeling of that.

"I love you, Amy."

I'd smile and he'd smile. I'd whisper back, "I love you, too."

Then we would dance the rest of the night.

The next day when we met at the willow, he kissed my cheek and I told him how in this very wood one of our problems would be solved. But he also had news, and his could mess up every plan we had.

"Amy, after my eighteenth birthday Hellena is going to come and stay with us. Then on July twentieth, my father wants us to wed."

He looked ready to cry, and I certainly wanted to.

"Do you think we can find the evidence before then?" he asked.

I wasn't sure. All of a sudden, the wood seemed to be ten times its normal size. But we had to; we didn't have a choice.

"Yes, I think we can, but what happened with the nineteen idea?" I was surprised this wasn't King Sencraugh's original plan.

"King Gelgar wants Hellena married before the end of the summer, or there will be no betrothal. When I told my father that wouldn't be so bad, he signed the note that said I'd do it right on the spot—just to prove he still has control over the situation. He's too stubborn for his own good and he's bringing me down with it. I can still get the wedding canceled if we find the evidence before the day I refuse to be married—that is, unless it's to you." He seemed very upset but hopeful.

I understood, but I felt like crying. I was jealous of Hellena. Sure, she didn't have his love, but she was the one who at the moment would get to keep him.

"Why does your father have to be that way? It's not fair to force you into this," I told him as I tried not to sound like I was going to cry.

"I don't have a good enough reason and he doesn't understand. He doesn't want to understand. It's strange, the relationship we have. He's proud of me and tells me all the time, but we have different beliefs. He thinks we should agree on everything, but we don't. I've always had the feeling that he feels he needs to prove he still has control over me, even when he doesn't. It's just kind of the way he functions."

"Still, does he realize that his decisions affect more than just you—that they affect everyone? Me, the kingdom, and in this situation, Lavenlee? It seems dangerous to be messing around with something this huge. What if you did marry Hellena, which you won't, and she found out you never even wanted to marry her, and you spent all those years apart from her trying to get out of it? All of Lavenlee would be angry with Frindeline, especially you and your father. A war could start if she complained enough. Did he think that through? Wars have started over sillier reasons, and in Lavenlee the princesses are considered the most important things of all." I sighed, not liking the situation.

"I doubt it, because his whole reason for me to marry is to prove a point. And because of the connections. If I had a good enough argument that wouldn't get you into trouble, I'd use it and eventually he'd see I was right. The only one I have is that I'm in love with you, but your family is nowhere near optional for a prince."

He sighed, and I saw a tear trickle down his cheek.

"I wish this whole engagement business would be forgotten and we could just…I don't know, tell the world," I told him as I wiped away a tear.

"So do I," Henry said as he grabbed my hand, and I knew he loved me as he pulled me into a hug.

I loved him more than I could ever explain except in those three little words, and that didn't seem to do it justice. I had to find the evidence before the twentieth of July, but even if I found the evidence, the king wouldn't see me as a good enough reason to end the betrothal.

"Henry, even if I do find the evidence, your father still won't consider me a good enough reason for you not to marry Hellena."

I was looking down as he let go of me from the hug.

He lifted my chin and looked me in the eye. "Don't worry. I'll take care of that."

I knew I could trust him, but it seemed the evidence would have to come first, and as long as I found it, everything would be all right.

Chapter Twenty-Four

Everyone searched—Papa, Aunt Grace, Henry, Rob, Johannah, Prissy, Charlie, Phillip, Cornelius, Mary, (when she could get away from the twins), and even Grandfather sometimes. I knew that digging through the snow and the frozen ground was going to be extra work, but time was short. I didn't wait until March, as Aunt Grace had warned, but started in January. I couldn't wait until the snow stopped falling; I had to find the wooden box. We didn't find it in January, but we still had time.

"John, I think this is the area," Aunt Grace would tell us as she jumped up and down with excitement. So we would dig in that area of the wood, only to find that it wasn't where she had buried our precious proof. It wasn't supposed to be more than three feet deep, and she doubted that it was that deep, but we dug four feet just in case. After digging in an area, we'd have to put back all the dirt, which just made everything harder. We couldn't tell if we had already dug somewhere or not.

By February 19, my birthday, we had dug not even a fourth of the wood, and probably not even a half of that. It seemed like we would never find anything.

My sixteenth birthday was unbelievable. Grandfather insisted on throwing me a party. I realized I was now old enough to marry. I hadn't thought about that. My mother was eighteen when she married Papa, but Grandmere was sixteen when she married Grandfather, and Aunt Grace was sixteen when she married Uncle Charles. Most of my aunts were married at sixteen. I was now considered an adult by Frindelian law. I liked that sound—adult. I was an adult with a man I loved, wondering just how many sixteen-year-olds could say that.

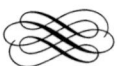

I was wearing a beautiful pink dress that showed my shoulders, and the most perfect amethyst jewels lined the neck of my dress. It was by far the most beautiful gown there. I could have sworn that it was even prettier than the dress Mama wore at her last ball. I found I didn't care anymore; I used to, but it now didn't matter if I wore the ugliest dress at my ball, as long as Henry was near me.

Everything that night went perfectly, unlike most of my memorable events. I danced with Henry almost every dance, and I had to dance with Rob, Papa and Grandfather at least once. All the others were Henry's and mine to cherish. I knew I wouldn't be dancing with him much after that, maybe not ever again after his birthday. I never wanted to leave the dance floor.

Hellena was supposedly aggressive—not a very common princess quality—and clumsy, not to mention snobby and inconsiderate. I hated working for her when she spent all those months at the castle a few years ago, and this time it was going to be pure torture. Hellena didn't deserve Henry. He and the rest of his staff thought of her the same way I did. Even if I hated Henry with every fiber in my body, I wouldn't wish Hellena on him. No one deserved to be married off to someone they didn't want to marry, especially when she would be a bigger handful than five children. I wished she'd die. That would solve most of the problem, but I knew that was wrong and selfish of me.

I felt myself dancing that night with my head against his chest, listening to the rhythm of his heart and his voice as he hummed along with the song being played. I felt as if I were floating; I couldn't feel the ground. I was too busy absorbing everything about him—his face, the way it bent when he smiled, his voice, the way he danced, everything. This made my realizations even harder. I knew I couldn't live without him, but it also made me realize how far away was the likelihood of our ever really being together.

As I thought of this, a tear went down my cheek. How was I ever going to find the evidence and prove my family by July? If I didn't, Henry, my Henry, would be married—not to me, but to the brat princess from Lavenlee. If I married him before I found the evidence, we'd have to hide. And if we were found I'd be sent to prison, just like Papa. I knew the pain that caused, and how it felt to have someone special taken away. I couldn't do that; I couldn't let anyone go through that. Another tear trickled down my cheek.

Henry stopped humming and dancing. I didn't want him to ask questions. I just wanted to dance with him. I wanted him to go on without his knowing. If he proposed before I had the evidence, I'd say no. I couldn't have my childhood relived by someone else. I wouldn't let Papa go through the opposite side of the prison situation. I knew how it felt and wouldn't let anyone go through it—not ever. None of my relatives would have to cry because I was in prison, or feel that they could have done something to prevent it. I didn't want any of them to hurt, as I had every day while Papa was locked up in the cage he didn't deserve.

"Amy, what's wrong?" Henry finally asked, concerned. I felt Mama's hand on my shoulder.

"Nothing, I was thinking of Mama, and I wish she were here," I told him. I could tell he knew I wasn't being completely truthful, but he also knew that I wasn't going to say more, so he didn't ask. I was grateful for that; I didn't want to explain the thoughts that were rushing through my head. Mama never left my side that night.

If only I were really the daughter of a duke and a countess, life would have been so much simpler.

Sure, now I was considered an adult by law, but that didn't mean Dove did. She gave me adult-sized workloads but then treated me like a five-year-old who must have done something wrong. She was driving me insane. I had better things to occupy my time than listening to her reprimanding me. I wanted to shove her in the oven and turn it on as hot as possible! I knew she wouldn't even fit into that oven, which held fifteen chickens at one time but, oh, I would have loved to try.

When I wasn't at the kitchen putting up with Dove and all her commands, I was in the Wood of Drell searching and marking, something I came up with so we wouldn't look in the same spot twice. I did this mostly myself, except on Saturday and Wednesday, when everyone came to help. Every once in awhile, someone came along and helped me on other days, but I didn't do much dilly-dallying on those days.

Chapter Twenty-Five

March went by quickly. We didn't find one single wood chip under the ground, let alone a whole wooden box. April was fast approaching. I wanted to find the evidence before April 22, so I could give it to Henry as a birthday present. We could celebrate that we still had a chance, as well as celebrate his birthday. I gave up on that idea a week before the twenty-second.

We still had half, if not more, of the wood to dig up. I would have to give him something this year, something he could remember me by, just in case we couldn't pull it off. I knew exactly what I would give him. I touched my locket as I thought about it. I knew one item that would send a message and would remind him of me. I just didn't know how I was going to give it up.

Eddie and Emily were now ten months old. Eddie was walking around and Emily, who always seemed to want her brother to take care of her, had him helping her stand up. Everyone knew that as soon as Emily saw Eddie do something, she wanted to do it, as if she could convince him she wanted him to teach her the brand-new tricks he'd learned and no one else could. I knew that soon enough both my godbabies would be walking around and getting into lots of trouble.

Three days before Henry's birthday, as I watched Emily and Eddie by the willow tree, Henry happened to show up.

"Hi," he said as he sat on the blanket I brought with me and then picked up Eddie.

"Hi," I said as I grabbed Emily, who was just about to crawl off the blanket. I looked at the man I was afraid I might soon not be able to call mine.

"Amy, please don't be sad." Was I so obvious? "Be happy we still have a few months. This can be fixed." He pleaded with me and smiled as if hoping I'd do the same.

I could tell he was worried as a twin each tried to get out of our arms.

"Maybe, but what if it doesn't and you have to marry that awful Hellena?" I was desperate; I was about to cry.

"I'm going to do everything I can to prevent that. I promise."

He grabbed my hand, but I still held on to Emily and somehow managed to bury my head in Henry's shoulder as I started to cry.

"Please don't cry, sweetheart. Amy, I won't marry Hellena. I told you that a long time ago and I plan to keep that promise." He held Eddie in one arm and hugged me with the other. Emily was now hugging me, too.

"But how can you promise that? Won't your father make you?" I was very upset, but knew that these questions had to be asked as much as I knew I might hate the answers.

"Amy, he can try, but he can't necessarily force me to if I'm not there."

I looked up, shocked. "Now, you know you can't do that. You'll get into trouble and, besides, where would you go?"

He looked at me blankly and shook his head. "I don't know, but out of Frindeline—and not Lavenlee—but somewhere. I've always wanted to go to the fairy forest, or maybe I'll go visit Princess Aubrey in Quane...I mean, the forbidden forest, but I'd probably go to Lanski because it's the most unlikely place for me go." He was excited, and I cringed.

"That sounds dangerous...I mean, ever since King Yasir died two years ago, that place has kind of been, well, it's sort of gone bad." I looked at him, trying to dissuade him but not doing a very good job.

"I know you're right, but if I can't have you, I won't—"

Emily began to wail, and I looked to her to see what was the matter. "Em, what do you need?" I asked, not wanting to deal with it as I realized I needed to get the twins home.

"I'm sorry, Henry, but it's getting late and I need to get Emily and Eddie back to Mary."

We both stood, each with a twin in our arms. He passed Eddie to me and turned. I picked up the blanket and watched him go. When he was almost out of the wood, he yelled, "I love you. See you at my party." Then he waved and turned.

"I love you, too!" I yelled, but I wasn't sure he heard me, because he was practically out of range by then.

After I dropped off the twins and Mary thanked me, I ran back to the wood. I spent the whole night digging. I fell asleep on the blanket I had brought with me earlier. When I woke up, I decided to skip kitchen work. I walked farther into the forest and began to dig. I had to find the evidence, and at the moment the plan was to keep digging until I did.

Around midday, I was sweating like I had never sweated before. I started to wonder if Papa would worry but didn't stop to think about it.

At around three in the afternoon, I was aching all over from the endless digging and was about to take a dip in the lake before coming back to dig some more, when I heard a voice.

"Amy…Amythist Jonestone, where are you?"

It was Papa. I was right; he was worried.

"Over here," I yelled back as I threw my hands in the air.

"Amy, I was so scared! I thought you were gone. I thought I lost my Amykins," he told me as he practically hugged me to death. "I've been looking for you all day. Where have you been?"

"Here, digging. I spent the night here. I dug until three in the morning," I told him as he hugged me again.

"Amy, come home. We'll dig tomorrow. Okay?"

I could tell he wanted me to get some sleep, so as much as I wanted to stay again all night if I had to, I consented, knowing he was right.

"All right. Just let me mark this area."

As we walked home I was wondering how long I'd live with Papa. Probably forever if Henry married Hellena.

The next day, Saturday, I slept in until noon. Once I woke up, I tried not doing much of anything, because I still ached from the day before. I was in discomfort every time I moved. I didn't know muscles could ache this much.

At three, when I was supposed to meet everyone in the wood, I knew it was only determination and the need to find the evidence that got me there. I dragged myself to the wood, where we all dug in an unmarked area. Everytime I put the shovel in the ground my back and arms ached, but I didn't care; I would keep looking for the evidence even if it cost me my life. We marked two more areas, and then everyone insisted I go home. It was only six o'clock, but I knew they were worried about me. So I consented as long as they kept digging for another hour. They assured me they would. Papa and I left as I yawned.

Henry didn't come that day. He told me he wouldn't be able to. All the same, I wished he had. He couldn't come because he had to help his father get things ready for Hellena's arrival the day after his party.

I wasn't there for this part of the story, but I could imagine it. In my mind this is the way it went and how it sounded when Henry told it to me:

"Father, can't I just go? You really don't need my help; you just keep interrogating me about some kitchen girl, and I have no idea what you're talking about," Henry told his father sternly while clenching his fist.

"Now, son, who was that girl I saw holding your hand in the forest a few weeks ago?" His father had a point, and I know Henry would have had a hard time arguing.

"Father, that girl had twisted her ankle while in the forest and needed help walking." He would smile because he felt clever with the lie he created to protect me.

"Then, Henry, tell me: why did she kiss you on the cheek?" His father would have looked stern.

"Father, it was nothing more than a kiss of gratitude. She was only thanking me." I imagine my prince gulping.

"Son, I hope you have done well to remember that you are betrothed and can't go running off with some kitchen girl just for the fun of it. Remember that, son," the king would scold, as he patted his son on the shoulder, almost as if he knew what was going on behind his back.

"Sencraugh, darling, we need you," Queen Neeuqa called from across the room.

"Now, son, you may run along to your thinking tree, and while you're there you might as well think of something to say to Hellena."

Then his father left for his wife.

I wish I could honestly say that he turned to his father and yelled that he couldn't rub the betrothal in his face, and that he wouldn't think of Hellena. But that would be lying and I couldn't do that to you, now could I?

What I do know is that it was only about six at the time. He thought he'd still find me in the wood, so he ran there.

"Rob, is Amy still here?" he asked, panting.

"No, she just left. She looked really tired, so we made her leave early. If you run toward her house, you might catch her," Rob told him.

Without a response, and before Rob could even think, Henry had turned around and was running out of the wood.

"Papa, will life ever turn out right for me?" I asked, feeling pathetic.

"I can't tell you yes, as I believe it will, Amy. I can't make any promises and I don't know what will happen tomorrow, let alone the rest of your life, but I have faith that it will turn out right in the end." Papa smiled as he opened the door to our hovel.

I looked up and smiled at him.

"Amy, Amy!" I turned to look.

"Henry, is that you? I thought you couldn't come today," I pointed out. I smiled at Papa again and then ran over to where Henry was.

"Well, I had to come and warn you."

I was taken aback as I started to walk closer, and then he grabbed my hand.

"Amy, please come with me to the willow. I'll tell you there." He looked so concerned, so worried, that I had to go.

"Is everything all right? Why do you have to warn me?"

"I can't do it out in the open, so please come with me," he pleaded.

"Wait, Henry, come inside. You can tell Papa and me in there." It was obviously something important, but I couldn't walk all the way back to the wood. I was still sore, but I didn't want him to know that.

"As long as no one will overhear us," he said in agreement.

"We won't be—I promise. Just come inside."

He quickly looked around. "All right, hurry."

So, hand-in-hand we quickly went inside.

Papa, who had overheard parts of the conversation, looked interested and I was curious.

We sat at the table in the first room that was by the fire in the middle and also very close to the stove, under which we once hid the evidence.

"Henry, what's going on?" Papa asked before I could. I could tell Henry was thinking.

"Well, today when Father and I were preparing… well, actually he was preparing and talking and kept telling me to listen…" the prince started, "my father finally stopped badgering me about what I did when I supposedly went to think and, well, about what the word "betrothal" meant." He paused.

"Wait, does he suspect something?" I asked worriedly. If he found out, I would be dead, literally.

"I'm afraid he does." He gulped.

"Did he have any idea who Amy was?" Papa asked quickly.

"No, and I tried to tell him I'd found a maiden in the woods who'd twisted her ankle and I had to hold her hand for support so she could walk."

I looked at him, concerned, and so did Papa.

"Well, did it work? Wait, I didn't kiss you on the cheek that time, did I?" I was now scared. How could he explain that?

"According to Father, you did."

I gasped with fear. Henry saw it and continued. "I told him you kissed me on the cheek to thank me, nothing more, but he still looked as if he didn't believe me. So if he asks questions tomorrow and recognizes you as the girl, just tell him that you twisted your ankle, didn't recognize who I was, and kissed me on the cheek to thank me, just like you would have done to any other gentleman." He stopped.

"Will he recognize me tomorrow night when I pretend to be Delilah?" I was scared, because I didn't want him to get into trouble.

He looked at me. "My father was sure the girl was a peasant. I'm sure Delilah won't have any problems." He smiled at me.

I wasn't so sure, but I wasn't going to disappoint him on his birthday.

The next day I wasn't sure what I was going t o wear. Grandmere was too sick to help me pick out a gown. I decided to wear the same dress I wore on my birthday. I'd be at least as pretty as the daughters of a duke or whatever I was pretending to be.

I wore my hair differently; I put it a tight bun. It didn't quite go with the dress, but I wanted to mostly look like Amy when I gave Henry his gift.

Before I left that night, I looked in the mirror. I looked beautiful, but I felt that something was missing. I touched the place where my locket usually resided. I remembered why but forced myself to ignore it. I was still Amy and I still knew she was there, with or without the locket. I left after Papa gave me a hug.

"'Bye, Delilah," he sniggered and winked at me as I left.

When I arrived at the castle, they sat me next to Henry, as usual. I put the little blue box which contained his present by his plate.

He looked at me, confused. "What's that?"

"Your present," I said, "I insist." I knew he would say I didn't need to give him one, as I pretended with ease that I was Delilah, like I had done so many times before.

"You really didn't have to," he told me as a bell rang in the distance.

"I did. I couldn't help myself," I told him and smiled. "Don't open it until we can go out in the garden, all right?"

He nodded in agreement as we ate. When the dancing started, he took the blue box and put it in his pocket. We both stood up and walked over to the doors that led to the courtyard.

"Amy," he started to say, "why did you get me a pre—"

"Stop asking questions—just open it." I knew I'd start crying as soon as he did, but he had to open it while I was there—so I could explain.

He took off the lid and pulled out my locket by its chain. He looked at it curiously and then at me for an explanation.

"Amy, why are you giving this to me?" A tear trickled down his face.

"Henry, I had to, so if everything doesn't work out, you'll always remember me." Now a tear was trickling down my face.

"Please tell me how I could forget you? I love you, you know that," he told me as he wiped another tear from my nose.

I nodded. "I know it's just that I had to give it to you. I won't take it back. It's yours now, so promise you'll keep it with you at all times, wherever you go." I was still crying, but Henry nodded in agreement. I could tell he was worried. Even if he had a solution, I could see that he had his doubts, and it made me feel better that I wasn't the only one who was worried.

We danced silently for the rest of the night, and I treasured every moment. I knew we wouldn't have very many moments like these again for awhile. I found myself memorizing everything he did. I would never forget this night. We couldn't dance as close to each other as I wanted to, but I still loved dancing with him.

At around midnight we went back out to the courtyard to talk.

"Amy, I promise I'll stay away from Hellena as much as possible," he assured me.

"I know," I said. I wished he didn't have to go near her at all.

"Amy, I also promise I'll help as much as I can and see you as much as possible. It's not going to be easy to get away, but I will whenever I can." Henry was seriously trying to make me feel better, but what he didn't know was I was about to cry.

"I know," I told him tearfully, not being able to form words that were any more profound.

"Amy, I have one more thing to tell you."

I looked up as a tear streamed down my cheek, burning it, and reminding me this could be the end. I looked into his gorgeous green eyes.

"Amy, I'll love you forever."

I smiled through my tears. "I'll love you always," I somehow managed.

We were standing behind two very tall trees where we had decided to sit down. There was so much I wanted to tell him. Just as I was about to start and try to explain how important he was to me, he kissed me square on the lips. I couldn't think. I knew this one lasted longer than the others. He didn't kiss me very often, which made it all the more special when he did. I loved him and no longer felt like I had to tell him anything. It was all explained. He knew how much I cared for him and I knew how much he cared for me, and somehow that was all that mattered.

Chapter Twenty-Six

I was sad when the night was over and it was time for me to go home. I walked with Rob and Jo. Jo had served His Majesty's birthday dinner, while Rob had opened doors and led people to their places at the table. As we walked I cried.

"Ames, I'm sure it'll all work out. Henry keeps saying it will."

I could tell that Rob was trying to reassure me.

"Yeah, Ames, just because Hellena is here doesn't mean anything is going to change," Jo tried.

"Thanks, but what if it doesn't work? What if I'm forced to never see him again? What if—"

"Amythist Jonestone!" Rob stopped me, "worry about something else for a change, and think positive. We are." He smiled as he scolded.

"I'll try," I told him as I opened the door to my house, "'Bye."

They both waved, looking hopeful.

I had no idea how everything was going to work or if it wouldn't. I still didn't know how Henry planned to keep his promise that everything would be all right. I doubted he could because this one depended on me. I had to find the evidence, or none of it could work. I knew it wouldn't be easy, but I had to find the evidence. I promised myself I would find the evidence before the twentieth of July. I had to; there was no other way.

That night I couldn't sleep because Hellena was coming back. We were cooking a huge dinner to welcome her the next day. I decided to put one-fourth cup more salt in the cake; I couldn't help myself. For all I knew, it might make Henry come and find me to ask what was going on. I thought of everything Henry would have to do with Hellena the next night, and dancing came to mind. There was no way he could avoid it. I cried; why did life have to be so cruel? I went for the comfort that my locket often offered, when I remembered I gave away.

"Mama," I whispered into the air as a tear dropped onto my pillow. "Mama, I don't know what I should feel. I feel alone, stuck. I need you now Mama!" This time I yelled her name.

Papa wasn't home yet from lighting the lampposts. Usually he would be, but if a lamp refused to light, or a wick disappeared, he was sometimes gone for hours. I was glad he wasn't home; I didn't want him to hear me. I needed my mother, but she was dead. I could feel her presence, but tonight that wasn't enough.

All I could do was lie there in my bed, crying. I wanted Mama to make me feel better, like she used to. For the first time since she died, I felt as if she was teasing me; she was only partially with me and I wanted more.

It was strange because I felt her leave. I felt abandoned and I didn't know why. I wanted my mother alive and with me, and if her presence knew as much as I thought it did, she knew I needed her now more than ever. I was bewildered and confused, because Mama had never done that before.

"Mama!" I yelled again, hoping it might do something to trigger her spirit into coming back. It was around four o'clock in the morning, and the door opened. I knew Papa would be able to hear me crying from the other room, so I decided to wait for him.

"Amy," said a voice. It didn't belong to Papa, but to Grandfather.

"Grandfather, why are you here?" I asked curiously as I wiped away my tears.

"Amy, your father told me to come and get you. He's been over at our house helping with Grandmere. Amy, she-she's sick." Grandfather had become pale and he looked frightened.

"Can I help?" I wanted to know.

"No, Amy, wait—maybe, come with me."

I was late to work the next day because I was put on comfort duty. I was up all night trying to help my aunts calm down as I tried not to cry. My father was helping Grandfather take care of Grandmere. Papa was doing most of it because Grandfather could barely do anything.

I was scared out of my mind. I didn't want to lose Grandmere along with everything else that was going wrong in my life. I knew no one else wanted her to die, either, but she meant a lot to me—more than someone could ever express on paper, or in words.

That day was hard, and I worked even though I was tired and had to stop and cry every once in awhile. With Henry and Grandmere, I don't know how I made it through the day. When people asked if I was all right, I'd tell them that my grandmother was very sick and they'd nod in a consoling manner.

I didn't want that night to come. I was going to serve dinner as a serving maid, and so was Jo. Rob was once again going to be a doorman. Originally I was going to serve Henry, but at the last minute I was switched, and I now was serving Princess Sophia, eldest of the four Lavenlee princesses. I wasn't at all excited about it.

When the first bell rang that night, I brought Princess Sophia, who was sitting on the opposite side of Henry, her salad.

The bell ringer must not have been paying much attention, because he didn't ring the bell, and Princess Sophia engaged me in conversation.

"How did Hellena get stuck with a good one?" She waited as I noticed she was talking to me.

"I don't know, Your Highness," I replied as I looked two chairs down and was disgusted when I saw Hellena drooling over my prince.

"I'm married to a duke in Aldreen and he's nice and everything, but my understanding is that your Prince Henry is charming—everything my Darren is—but he's handsome, too. You didn't hear it from me, but my sister doesn't deserve him. She's a twit, and I wish my parents disciplined her more or something. Now you know to keep your mouth shut."

She paused and then looked at me, I had no clue as to what she wanted. "Name." she said forcefully.

"Amy, Princess."

"Amy, if I find out you've even breathed a word of how I really feel about my sister, I will send the guards after you and have you locked up," she threatened as the bell rang and I was glad it had.

As I turned around, I saw Hellena try and reach for Henry's hand, but he moved and I saw my locket shift on his wrist.

"Jo, he's wearing it," I told her excitedly as she looked at me in confusion.

"Ames, who's wearing what?"

I touched my bare neck at the spot the locket usually would be sitting. I remembered she didn't know, but it didn't matter anymore. Jo wasn't stupid and realized immediately what I was saying.

"You gave him your locket!" She couldn't believe it.

I nodded.

"And he's wearing it!"

Every time the bell rang, I'd give Sophia her food and she would talk about how Hellena always got her way and how even her sisters, Levina and Malia, agreed with her. I figured Hellena had to be as bad as she seemed, because if she weren't, then her sister had some unspoken reason for hating her.

I couldn't help but think that if the marriage did happen, King Sencraugh would regret it in the long run. No one I had ever talked to had anything good to say about Hellena. Her sister only seemed to be able to talk about how rude and awful she was. I thought she was rude and inconsiderate when I had to deal with her the last time she was here about three or four years ago, but it seemed to me that she must have become even worse over the years. It almost made me feel sorry for her that no one liked her. Then I remembered she wanted my Henry. If anyone more important than Henry had anything to do with it, she'd get her way.

Later in the evening I asked Sophia a very bold question. "Princess, if it isn't too bold to ask, why do most people find Hellena this way?"

She smiled as if she was glad to answer my question. "No, Amy, it's not too bold. My sister Hellena is so unlike the rest of us. She had to have her way and is mean about it. Father spoils her—well, he spoils all of us—but no one should spoil Hellena. It only makes her feel more important. She seems to think it gives her a right to order others around. It's hard to explain it any other say." She paused, and then realized I was still interested.

"Well, I think she is best described as a rat with fangs. Levina and Malia agree with me. All three of us wish

Prince Henry could have someone better—a peasant would be better than our sister. There is no way to convince Father or King Sencraugh, though. They both want an alliance with the biggest country in Delynelle…" She continued to talk, but the bell rang and I had to go. We had just finished serving dessert, and as I turned Henry waved, so I looked around to find no one watching and blew him a kiss.

I spent the rest of the night in the kitchen listening to the music. Jo came down and joined me. Neither of us said much; we just listened and hummed. Finally, after an hour or so, Jo started a conversation.

"So, Amy, I know it's none of my business, but what are you and Henry going to do?"

Great, just what I wanted to talk about. I tried to think of the best way to tell her that I had no clue, and that deep down I felt I was going to have to give him up. Three tears slipped down my cheek. I tried to keep more from coming, but I no longer could count the tears that joined the first three.

"Henry," I started as tears still found their way down my cheeks, "has a plan, but I don't know what it is, Jo. It sounds like it all depends on whether or not I find the evidence before July twentieth, and I won't marry him unless I do." Tears tumbled down my face.

"Amy, I feel like—I'm so sorry—Oh…" She never finished the thought, because she had started to cry, too, maybe even harder than I. We both just sat there crying and crying, for I don't know how long, when we heard footsteps. The kitchen door opened and we both wiped away our tears. I couldn't explain why we were crying, so it was best to look like we hadn't been at all.

Then I saw him without Hellena. I wasn't sure, but I thought I might just be imagining things.

"Hey, what's going on?" he asked both of us.

"Your party, music, you know," Jo answered as if nothing was wrong. I fought back tears, which was difficult.

"You know that I want you upstairs, right?" he asked, looking directly at my tear-stained face.

I nodded as a tear fell down my nose.

He sat next to me. "Amy, please don't do this. You know it's all going to be fine, right? I've promised you that." He hugged me and I felt a tear land on my shoulder. Henry was crying too.

"Stop it," I told him.

I heard a quiver in his voice as he answered. "Stop what?"

"Crying. The last thing I need you to do is cry and tell me everything is going to be all right at the same time." I laughed.

"All right, I've stopped. But listen to me. I won't marry Hellena. I love you, Amy," he told me and then kissed me on the lips quickly and whispered, "I've got to go. I told them I was going to the restroom." He turned and ran toward the exit.

"What did you do to the cake?" he yelled.

I yelled back, "Put some extra salt in it, just for Hellena."

He laughed and was gone. I wanted to yell "wait!" but refrained. I wanted to know how everything was going to be, now that Hellena was back. I guessed I would just figure it out as time went by.

Jo looked at me, and a tear came from her eye as she spoke. "Oh, Amy, you're the luckiest and the unluckiest girl I know all at the same time." She gave me a hug and we sat and listened to the music for the rest of the night.

I didn't know what to do anymore; all I knew was that I had to find the evidence. I started skipping kitchen work again and spent all my time digging. I was there all day, almost every day. Everyone helped on Wednesday and Saturday afternoons, just as they always did. Henry had a hard time getting away because Hellena was always following him around.

I was allowed the privilege to meet Hellena personally: joy! She'd heard Henry loved my cake and happened to taste it sometime after the salt incident and loved it, too. So she pranced her selfish self down to the kitchen and asked Dove where I was. I hated this, the two people I hated most were talking to each other. I decided right there that I'd rather deal with Dove any day than Hellena even once.

"So, you baked the delicious cake?" she asked me in a much-too-perfect kind of voice as she batted her eyelashes and put her hands together, bringing them to her side.

"Yes," I answered grudgingly as I continued with my dishes.

"Well, you're very good," she continued in her annoyingly perfect voice.

I just nodded.

"It's my understanding that the prince absolutely loves it, too. I was wondering if you could stay late and help me bake him one as a surprise?" she asked too politely and perfectly.

I was outraged. I wanted to slap her, even punch her. I hated her beyond belief, and she had my Henry! As I bit my tongue to think of a way to respond, I turned my head and saw Rob and Jo staring open-mouthed in disbelief.

"I'm sorry, Your Highness, but I have dinner plans at a friend's house tonight. Maybe some other time." I smiled because I was pleased that I came up with something workable that quickly, but I'm sure to her it seemed like I was trying to be friendly.

Hellena looked devastated, as if she might start to wail and whine. "Oh…Th…that's…all right…it…it's just that…the…the pr…prince…doesn't like m…me and I…I…I just thought if…if I could make…his…fav…favorite he'd…" she wailed.

"I'm sorry. I really am, but I'm busy the next couple of weeks. If I have a free day, I'd love to help you. It sounds awful the way he doesn't seem to care for you," I said sympathetically, trying not to smile.

Hellena cried that all she wanted was a cake. I left to dig, with her wailing still in the back of my head. I tried to tell myself that this was the way things were supposed to be. No matter how awful she was, I wasn't sure she should be crying like a three-year-old in front of the kitchen staff. She'd better not do that in front of the laundresses or the whole kingdom will think her unworthy. Then again, maybe she should.

Rob and Jo found me quickly. They must have left only moments after I did.

"Ames, can you believe that, and all over a cake?" Rob yelled as he came into view.

"I know, Amy, she's a spoiled brat. If she thinks that just because she's a princess she can have whatever she wants when she wants it, she's daft." Jo told the both of us.

"I know," I started as a smile spread across my face, "and she wonders why Henry doesn't want her."

All three of us laughed. That night I had a lot of fun digging, even though we didn't find anything, because we had Hellena to laugh about.

April and May quickly passed by, and there were lots of things to worry about.

It was a week before Eddie and Emily's birthday, and we had made progress with the evidence search, but the wood was huge and there was still a lot that needed to be dug up. There was only about a month left to search, and

I was starting to feel pressured. We hadn't even found a scrap of wood that could have anything to do with a wooden box full of evidence. I never went to the kitchen anymore. The head laundress, Lavender, actually came to my house to scold and fire me because of how many weeks I'd skipped picking up the laundry.

I had decided to make a dress for Emily and a pinafore for Eddie as birthday gifts. The only problem was that I had less than three days to make them and I was going to meet Henry on the twenty-fourth, the day before the twins' birthday. I was in a rush.

When I went to meet Henry I still wasn't finished with the twins' presents, so I brought them all along with me. Henry wasn't there yet when I arrived, so I tried to finish Emily's pink dress.

"Hey," came a voice.

"Hey," I said, but when I looked up it was Rob instead, and my smile quickly faded.

"What are you doing here?" I asked, not understanding.

"Well." His big eyes swelled as he continued, "Um… Henry told me to tell you that he couldn't—well—you know—come." He gulped.

I stood up and asked with a quiver in my voice, "Why?"

He stood there looking at me, and I knew what he was going to say.

"Hellena." He was nervous.

"How did she stop him? Or did he find that he prefers her?!" I yelled at him something that had been brimming on my mind for quite some time.

He looked at me as if I were insane. "No, Ames, he doesn't prefer her. She just begged for his company and his father made him, promising he could do whatever he wanted tomorrow night." He smiled, hoping this would cheer me up or make everything better.

"Why tomorrow? I'm at Mary's all day because of the twins' birthday." I was quite mad at myself for needing to be somewhere on a day I could see Henry.

"Ames, you are in a situation, aren't you?" he said.

"Thanks for rubbing it in. Wait, tell him to come to Mary's, and before you go anywhere you're going to help me finish Emily's dress. I finished Eddie's pinafore last night."

He stared at me. "Ames, I don't know how to sew."

I smiled. "Well, I guess you'll just have to learn, won't you?" I gestured for him to sit down and take a needle.

"Now Rob, watch. You take the needle, put it through the two pieces of cloth, and pull it in and out," I told him, and away he went.

We talked of many things and I even had a few laughs. Rob didn't find it funny that every other minute or so he yelled "Ow!" but I did. I was surprised he still had all his fingers intact when we were finished.

As we talked, Rob brought up a subject that I never expected him to bring up. Maybe he would have brought it up sooner if I'd spent the time he deserved with him, but lately I hadn't seen much of anyone.

"Ames," he started, "how do you think Jo thinks of me?"

I was startled. Jo was always asking me questions about Rob, but the other way around was strange. I was never really able to give Jo an answer, although I had my guesses, but I wasn't going to go and get her hopes up if I might be wrong. This was new to me, Rob asking me how Jo saw him. I figured he probably would have asked Henry, except that he was kind of hard to reach lately.

"What do you mean?" I asked, knowing perfectly well what he meant but wanting something more specific. I really wasn't expecting what he told me.

"Well, do you think she would act funny if I told her that I think of her as more than a friend, that I think of her as a possible wife?"

I choked on air. I was taken farther aback than I'd ever been taken before. I figured he liked her and wanted to court her, but marry her? How long had he kept his feelings to himself?

"Rob, do you love her?" I asked, wondering what else I could say and knowing that my reaction couldn't have boosted his confidence any.

Chapter Twenty-Seven

"See, Ames sometimes I think I do, but other times I just don't know. I think I'm trying to convince myself I don't, just in case she doesn't have feelings for me. I couldn't tell anyone, but I can trust you. Amy, I do love Johannah!" he exclaimed.

I smiled at him. At one time I knew Jo had a crush on him, but did she now? I ran over and gave him a hug before offering advice. "Robert Garrison, this is so exciting but you have to tell her, whether or not she feels the same. She has a right to know." I stared at him, waiting to see how he would respond.

It took him a minute, but finally he replied. "Ames, you're right, just not now. I'm not ready yet, but I promise before the end of July." He seemed to have a hard time swallowing his own words.

"Rob, that's not exactly what—"

"I know, I'm just not ready, maybe next month, but right now the best I can do is by the end of July. Thanks,

Amy." He still seemed to have a hard time taking it all in. He was smiling like a fool.

The next day was hectic. I was hoping Rob had gotten a chance to talk to Henry about coming to Mary's. I left my hovel, thinking as I walked to my godbabies' house. A dress and a pinafore in one hand and a sewing kit in the other, just in case my measurements were wrong. I was as happy as I ever was those days. I hoped Henry would show up.

The twins, now both walking, walked over to me. I picked them up and hugged them.

"Happy birthday! You two are getting so big." I smiled as Mary walked over.

"Amy, I'm so glad you came. Are those for the twins?" she asked as she took the two small articles of clothing out of my already baby-filled hands.

"Yes, and I brought my sewing kit, just in case they need to be altered."

She laughed. "Oh, Amy, how thoughtful, but that won't be necessary. I'll take care of any alterations."

I smiled. "Thanks."

Henry was late, but he came. I knew getting away was hard for him with everything that was going on at the castle right now. We ate dinner, and just as Henry arrived Mary started to cut the cake.

The cake was delicious, but Henry was quick to inform me in my ear that mine was much better, which made me smile.

Mary looked at us with a smirk. I could tell she thought we were wasting our time. It made me a little upset that she thought we shouldn't even try. I didn't care how foolish it seemed, because *I had to try*. I couldn't give up on my chance of being with the man I loved. I'd never give up on us.

After Eddie and Emily fell asleep, Henry and I decided we should go. As we were gathering our things, Mary asked to speak to me privately in the bedroom, and I consented.

"Amy, I know you love that man, but in less than a month he's getting married," she told more sternly than I had ever seen her.

"No, he isn't," I told her just as sternly acting positive more to convince myself than to convince her.

"Really Amy, did he tell you that? And if he did, how does he have any control over the matter? It's an arranged marriage, arranged by the parents, and he doesn't have a say."

Tears were now starting to roll down my face.

"Mary, please, I know all this, but every time he sees me he promises. I don't ask him to, he just does. He keeps telling me that as long as the evidence is found by the twentieth of July, everything will be okay. I'm starting to think that we'll never find it, but I have to keep trying," I said passionately as more tears streamed down my face.

"Sweetie, wouldn't it just be easier to let what's supposed to happen, happen?" she asked as she tucked a strand of hair behind my ear.

"No, Mary. Pretending is much easier, and I need to. If I just give up, I won't accomplish anything. What if it would have worked but I gave up on him? On us? Then I'd never know. I wouldn't be able to live with myself." Tears were tumbling off my nose.

"All right, Amy, but remember, be careful and don't do anything stupid."

"Thanks." I hugged her.

"Now let me wipe those tears away," she told me as she began to dab my eyes.

Once I looked like I hadn't been crying, we left the room. Henry and I said our goodbyes before leaving.

"So, Amy, what did Mary want?" he asked as we walked hand in hand.

"She asked me something about the twin, that's all," I told him. I didn't want him to again promise me a million times over that he wasn't going to marry Hellena. We went to the willow and talked about nothing of importance. We sat there for hours, looking at the forest around us. It was a quiet night. The only thing that mattered was that my prince was sitting next to me, holding my hand. After what felt like no time at all, he told me he had to get back to the castle. He kissed me.

"I'll let you know when I can get away again, I promise, before the twentieth of July. I love you." That's all I heard from him for the next week.

When I did hear from him, it wasn't even his voice, but Rob's.

"Amy, Henry wanted me to tell you that he can meet you by the willow at seven o'clock on the nineteenth."

I didn't see why I would have to wait that long. Two and a half weeks and the day before the wed—

"But, Rob, why then? And why didn't he tell me? How come you talk to him so much lately? Oh, Rob." A tear dripped from my eye to my nose. As it slid off, I put my head on Rob's shoulder and cried tears that I'd held in since that night at Mary's.

"Ames, he tried to run into you at the kitchen, but you're never there these days. You're always in the wood trying to find the answers to all your problems. But remember that not all answers can be found in a wooden box. Right now what you really need to be thinking about is your mother. What happened to her? I can tell that she hasn't been around much lately. Ames, ever since you gave Henry your locket, it's like you gave her away, too. I know you need her—I can see it, and I know she wants you to ask her to come back."

I was confused about how he could know so much. It was more than I knew myself, but when he said it I knew he was right.

"Rob, what are you talking about?" But I knew exactly what he was talking about.

"Amy, isn't it obvious?" he told me as he grabbed my hand.

"No," I lied.

"Amy, you gave your mother away when you needed her the most. Whenever someone would make you feel awful or made you feel out of place, you'd always put your hand on your shoulder or hug yourself and smile your mother's smile."

A tear rolled down my face as I clamped my hand over my mouth to stifle the noise I was making as I tried to stop.

"Amy, you don't have your mama's smile but your own, so when you smiled like your mother used to, I knew she was with you, and everything you told me about her being there was true. Lately, Ames, that smile hasn't been seen once. It's as if you really let her die. What happened to 'I'll always be with you'? Does that not apply now that the locket is gone? You were always saying things like, 'Mama may be dead to the world, but she'll never be dead to me.' You were always telling people that the only way someone ever really leaves you is if you let them. What happened to that, Amy?" He stopped and stared at me as I tried to stop my tears.

"Amy, a wise man once told me that you should never stop tears that you know will only come later. If you need to cry, then do it. Don't bottle up those emotions." Rob smiled as I began to bawl in front of him, knowing he understood.

In between my tears I managed, "Who?"

"Your father told me that when I caught him crying months after your mother's death."

"Thanks." I grabbed his shoulder and cried the hardest I'd cried since I realized Mama was dead. Now I cried because I let her die to me, which was just what I claimed I'd never do.

"Before I forget, Henry wanted me to tell you he has a backup plan, in case you don't find the evidence by the twentieth. He also wanted me to tell you that he loves you."

I looked up at Rob, and my tears immediately ceased.

"A backup plan?" I smiled as I felt Mama's presence.

"Your mama's smile!" He laughed.

I know," I told him. "Now back to this backup plan. Do you know what it is?" I hoped he could give me all the answers.

"No, I'm sorry, Ames. He wouldn't tell me anything. Told me I'd find out if you agreed on the nineteenth. He also wanted you to know that the evidence might not be necessary." He watched me and waited for a reaction.

"Rob, how can the evidence not be necessary? What is that supposed to mean?"

He wriggled his nose in thought as I impatiently waited for his answer.

"I don't really know. Henry wouldn't tell me," he cautiously told as if he thought I would be outraged.

"If you find out, you'll tell me, right?" I asked.

He looked shocked and, instead of answering my question, he stood to leave. As he exited he saluted. I took that to mean he would.

I didn't know what to do. I was emotionally burned out. Papa was over at Grandfather's, helping take care of my sickly grandmother. I was trying to go to sleep but couldn't; there were too many thoughts rushing through my head. Henry had a backup plan, and he said it didn't involve the evidence. I just realized I'd shut my mother out for the past few months, and I wondered how Jo would react when Rob told her. How could anyone sleep with all that swarming through their head?

"Mama," I yelled out into the empty room, "I'm sorry. I never meant to, and I wish I never did. I really do want you to be with me always."

She patted my shoulder. I tried to grip the hand that wasn't physically there and fell asleep in my chair.

I was more relaxed now that Mama was back. I didn't understand why I had ever dismissed her, which is strange because that's exactly what I did.

I dug night and day, hardly ever taking a break. I hadn't put a toe into the kitchen for over a month. Jo kept telling me that Dove wasn't pleased and she almost sent Aggie three times to come and find me. This made me laugh because I didn't care about the kitchen anymore.

I don't recall much of what happened those last few weeks. I can remember little bits of many conversations; for example, father told me how he didn't think he'd ever marry Mama. He was always apologizing, as if he thought he should fix everything or something.

One conversation I can remember perfectly started after I asked him why everything couldn't go as planned and why everything always seemed to get ruined.

"Amy, I don't know. Sometimes I wish we could rule the world and make it turn exactly as we choose, but we can't.

"When your mother and I were first married, we were supposed to stay in Aldreen for six months."

I had never heard this part of the story and wondered why my parents had never told it to me.

"Papa, you and Mama lived in Aldreen for over five years. I was almost five when we moved here. Why didn't you come back when you planned to?"

Papa looked as if he were about to cry, as if he really didn't want me to know. But he told me and somehow he managed to do it without a quiver in his voice.

"Sweetheart, that's because our original plan was to get married in Aldreen, come home, find evidence, be remarried, and then have children. But, honey, not everything happened that way."

A tear trickled down my cheek, and I knew why he didn't want to tell me.

"Amy, the plan failed because Rose, your mama, became pregnant only a month or so after we were married."

I felt awful as he said those words. I might as well be a bad omen.

"But, Papa, you still could have come back when you were supposed to," I pleaded.

"Amy, the reason we never told you this was because we didn't want you to feel unwanted or that everything was your fault. I want you to know that your mother and I wouldn't trade you for the world, let alone our family's freedom."

Tears were steadily coming down both our faces, as my brown waves fell from the bun that was meant to keep the hair out of my face.

"Papa, if it weren't for me, everything would have been all right a long time ago. You would never have gone to prison and Mama…She would still be here. Papa I shouldn't exist…" I trembled as I said the words.

"Amythist, don't you ever say those words again. There are a lot of people who would greatly disagree with you there. Henry would be nowhere and miserable if you weren't here. Your mother and I certainly wanted you.

"Amy," he continued, "there is some important reason for your being here, and I would go to prison a million more times if that's what it took for you to accomplish it."

He hugged me tight, and I felt my mama give me an invisible hug from behind.

"But, Papa, what is that purpose, and how am I supposed to know if I'm fulfilling it?"

I left my father's arms. He smiled at me.

"Amy, I think we've known your purpose since you were four years old."

"Papa, I don't know what you mean."

"I think you do," he replied with a simple smile.

I shook my head to tell him I was still clueless.

"Honey, no one else besides you has ever had a dream telling them they had to save our family." He grabbed my hand, as my head began to spin.

"But that's just a dream—you said so yourself." I couldn't believe my father was contradicting himself.

"Sweetie, I knew it was more than a dream, but I just didn't want to believe it was it true. I couldn't stand the thought of your mama being dead."

He paused, touched his shoulder, and smiled, and I was pretty sure I knew why.

"Papa, I know I said I'd do it, and I still want to, but I'm only sixteen and a nobody, a scullery maid who's supposed to fix everything. I have so many faults, yet I'm supposed to save my family all on my own. Papa, I'm not a hero." I was scared now that it was put into this perspective. I was meant for the job. Was this decided by the fairies? Did they have a say? I had heard that pixies had done things like this in the past. Had they sent the dreams?

"Amy, I know you can do it. Your mama knew you could do it when you were four. It scared her half to death, but even when I had set the appointment she was sure that you would do it. Rob and Jo want you to do this. Amy, Henry, wants you to do this—he needs you to do it. If he could, he would do it for you, but he can't. Don't you see that you have the whole family and a large group of friends cheering for you, and every single one of us knows you're capable of it?"

More tears found my cheeks and nose as I kissed my father on the cheek.

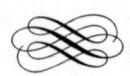

Papa was now working with me every minute he could to find the evidence. One day while digging, we were paid a visit by an unwanted visitor.

"So, John, I hear you're trying to find the evidence all over again. I thought…let's see…" He began to count on his fingers, "one…two…three…four…five years in prison would teach you that your family is doomed forever."

My father's face was reddening as he listened to this vile man.

"McCarthy, I'm surprised you're willing to stand within twenty feet of me, after all your family has done. Your ancestors blame my ancestors, *you threatened my sister-in-law and my daughter, put me in prison, and because of that my wife died!*"

Papa clenched his fists, while I hid behind a tree.

"So now you're going to blame me for the death of your wife. Tut, tut, tut. I would never kill such a lovely creature."

Now he had gone too far. My mother was beautiful, but she certainly wasn't a creature.

"My mother was a beautiful woman, but she was definitely not a creature. Don't you ever talk about my mothr like that again!" I stared straight into his eyes, hoping he would see the venom I had for him there.

"Amy, you stay out of this," Papa yelled at me.

"No, Papa, this involves me, too!"

"Amythist, do as I say," he yelled at me again.

"Now, John, you realize it's too late to get uninvolved. She has a very important role in all of this."

I smiled the cruelest smile I could muster. His evil smile stared right back at me, and I noticed that he was holding something.

"I found this right outside the throne room. I didn't think kitchen maids were allowed in there."

I gulped, because he was holding my locket. He was on to me. How else could he have my locket? I had to think of something quick.

"Please, Lord McCarthy, I only go in there to serve my cake. It's the prince's favorite. He's asked for me personally a few times because he likes it so much. The locket must have fallen off, because I've been looking for it for awhile. May I have it back?" I pleaded.

"Why should I? It looks valuable. Is it worth anything?"

I stood there as Papa looked at me, put a finger to lips to tell me to be quiet, and picked up a shovel.

"No I don't think so, but it's really important to me—please," I begged as his smile grew as he watched me grovel. I tried not to smile as my father inched closer and closer to him from behind with his shovel.

McCarthy laughed as I continued to beg for my locket.

"Please, can I have it back? You don't understand—"

I didn't need to finish my sentence, because Papa had bopped him over the head, and he lay unconscious in the dirt.

I ran over and snatched my locket off the ground. I put it on quickly and felt the wind give me a hug. "Papa, why do some people have to be so evil?" I sobbed into my hands.

"Ames, I wish I had the answer."

We decided to call it a day, taking all of the shovels with us.

Chapter Twenty-Eight

When the nineteenth of July arrived, I decided to go to the kitchen because there was nothing else I could do. I didn't think it was possible to find the evidence before my meeting with Henry that night.

When I showed up at the kitchen, everyone stared—even Rob and Jo.

"Ames, what are doing here?" Jo asked.

"Working, I guess," I answered, as Dove looked my direction, looking disgusted.

"Amy! Well, look who decided to show her face! It's been more than a month! If it weren't for your special situation I'd have you fired a long time ago!" Dove yelled. "Since I can't do that I plan to tell the king of your behavior, as soon as this wedding is over. Here is your list of things to do!"

She huffed off, leaving everyone staring in bewilderment. Dove whispered something in Aggie's ear as she continued in the opposite direction.

As I started my chores, Aggie caught up to me.

"Aggie, go away," I told her, annoyed.

"I can't. I'm supposed to follow you," she told me simply.

"What!" I said a little too loudly.

"Mother wants me to make sure you don't sneak off today. She doesn't trust you."

"Great! Now I have to worry about you, too." I kept walking. I was angry. I busied around all day, and Aggie never ceased to follow me.

"Amy, you seem more stressed than usual today," Aggie commented.

I didn't know what to think of that. Did I always look stressed or something?

"It's just that I've had a lot to worry about lately, and now it doesn't look like I'm going to finish all this by seven, and I'm meeting someone." I stomped as I walked to the pantry.

"You're meeting the prince, aren't you?"

What? Where did that come from? How could she know?

"Why would you say that?" I asked as I took a deep breath.

"Well, two years ago, I served Delilah at the prince's birthday banquet, but Delilah looked a lot like—and wore the same locket as—you. I quickly caught on. He's been talking to Rob a lot lately," she told me.

"How could you—wait, why…why didn't you tell anyone?" I was far beyond being confused. This didn't make any sense. I was sure Aggie, of all people, would do anything to get me into trouble.

"Well, I'm in a similar situation. I'm in love with a betrothed count, and we've been meeting secretly, too."

That was unexpected. This was getting stranger by the second. "So?" I answered.

"Amy, I know how you feel and, personally, I want to torture Hellena. I know that if the wedding gets canceled, that will do it. You're the only way I can do that, so I'm going to help you. Promise you'll do everything you can to stop this wedding."

I nodded. This seemed much more like Agathus, but I still couldn't believe she wanted to help me.

"Aggie, I think I've misunderstood you all these years."

"I'll cover for you. You'd better get going, because you need to look your best."

It was only four o'clock; I still had three hours. I didn't need three hours, but I didn't refuse her offer.

"Aggie, it's all right. Rob and Jo will cover for me."

"Amy, Mother doesn't listen to them anymore. Let me do it. She trusts me more than anyone."

I took off at a run and yelled "Thank you."

I ran home. I had time to make myself look perfect. I was going to wear a different necklace and re-give Henry my locket, since I knew he had dropped it.

When I walked in the door, Papa was there. "Hi, Papa," I said as I walked toward the bedroom.

"Amy, honey, come here." Papa waved me in his direction and smiled.

"Yes, Papa?"

"I want to give you something."

I didn't think he needed to give me anything, but I walked toward him to see what it was.

"All right," I said as he handed me a silver handbag.

"Papa, how did you afford this? We don't have this kind of money." I gasped as I looked at the bag my father had given me. Tiny crystals were embedded in it.

"Open it," he told me.

"More?" I asked, "Papa, this bag is enough."

He laughed. "Not for my angel."

I opened it and inside was a necklace with diamonds and pearls, along with matching earrings.

Papa cried.

"Papa, why did you buy these for me? I don't need them."

"Someday you might. They are my wedding present to you."

I looked at him and I knew what he thinking.

"Amy, you know very well that I don't want you to get your hopes up about Henry, but someday you will get married and then you can wear these. If it does somehow work out between you Henry, then at least you'll have some jewels fit for a princess."

I cried as I looked into my father's eyes.

"Take them back! Take them back!"

He just looked at my tear-covered face. "Amy, I can't do that."

"Papa, if I don't marry Henry, then I don't plan on getting married at all," I told him. "Even if I did, I'd wear my locket, not these. They're beautiful, but…" I tried to explain.

"Amy, right now you don't think you'll ever get married but someday, eventually, you might have to."

"Papa, I wouldn't, just like Aunt Grace won't marry again. I won't ever get married. Papa, I couldn't ever marry anyone but Henry."

I turned and ran into the bedroom, where I proceeded to cry on a pillow.

Papa walked in and hugged me. "Amy, keep these anyway. They'll look ravishing on my young daughter." He set the necklace and earrings down on the pillow and left.

At around six, I finally stopped crying. I couldn't help it, and I doubted anything would work at this point. I would become an old spinster someday. No one seemed to be able to understand that.

I put my locket in the pocket of one of my nice but casual dresses. As I walked to the willow I saw him, already sitting there on a blanket he had brought. Just seeing him made me want to cry over what I couldn't have. I couldn't do that, though, at least not yet.

"Hi." I smiled as I sat on the blanket.

"Hi, how are you?" he asked as he took my hand.

"I'm good, now," I told him as I rested my head on his shoulder.

"Did you find the evidence?" he asked only a few minutes later.

I didn't answer. I just looked at his face and tried to figure out how to tell him.

As I was about to open my mouth, he asked another question. "Amy, will you marry me?"

I was shocked and wanted to say yes, but how could I?

"Henry, how would it work? What's the backup plan?" I knew that wasn't what he wanted to hear. It wasn't how I imagined answering that question, but I couldn't just say yes. I kept my gaze on him to show I was serious.

"Well, I figured we could go away and get married, and then when the others found the evidence they could send us a letter. We could come back and you could prove your family's innocence. Then we'll announce to the world that we're married. All's well that ends well," he told me.

I couldn't believe that was the backup plan. It could go wrong in so many ways.

"Henry, that wouldn't work and you know it. I love you and I want to marry you, but I can't if we don't have the evidence. I promised myself months ago I wouldn't marry you unless we found it."

"Why would you make a promise like that?" he yelled as he scrunched up his face in an effort to look strong and hold in his tears. I knew I had hurt him, but I could explain.

"More people are affected by this than just us. I know what it feels like to live with this curse. I do it every day. I know what it did to me as a child, how much it hurt. It made my mother so sad, so hurt, when Papa was taken away for this exact reason. I don't want anyone to go through that because of me. I won't let it happen. I'm sorry, I just can't, no matter how much I want you, no matter how much I might regret it later, and I can't.

"Go marry Hellena like you're supposed to. It's your responsibility, and all of Frindeline is looking forward to it. I know that sounds awful, but I can't marry you, and you deserve for someone to love you." Tears were streaming so fast down my face that I could barely speak.

"Amy, I already have someone who loves me, and no matter what, I won't marry anyone but her. You know that."

I gasped for air between sobs as he tucked some of my hair behind my ear.

"But, how can you be sure?" I asked as tears continued to pour from my eyes.

"Is it really that hard to tell? I don't want anyone but you. Amy, if I can't have you, then I won't ever get married. I love you too much. It wouldn't be fair to the other girl." He was crying, too. For once I wiped a tear off his cheek.

"I'll look for you once the evidence is found. Where should I look?" I asked as I stopped my tears, thinking that one of us had to be strong to get us through this.

Henry continued to cry. I couldn't help starting to bawl all over again.

Finally he stopped and soothed me. When I had finished crying he said, "Amy, you should go. I have to go home and pack."

"Pack—where are you going?" My eyes were red and puffy from the tears I had shed as I asked him this.

"Amy, if I can't marry you, I won't marry anyone." He looked me straight in the eye as he started to get up.

I held his hand. "But, where are you going?" I asked more urgently.

"Amy, love, I'm going somewhere they won't look for me—not even you."

He tried to leave, but I gripped his hand tighter.

"Please don't go into the forbidden forest or Dragon Forest, or…please don't hide in a forest. Henry, don't go to Lanski. Promise me."

He pulled his hand out of mine. "Amy, I promise nothing will happen to me. Just promise me you'll have the evidence in a year's time."

A year.

"So you'll be back in a year?" I choked as I thought of what a year would be like without him. I wouldn't know where he was that whole time, or anything that happened to him. What if he did go to one those troubled places and I never saw him again?

"You know I'd rather have you live than die because you were attacked by goblins." I knew this had to be hard for him, too.

He just looked me in the eye, saying it all.

"I know, I love you." He pulled me up and held me close in a hug. Then he kissed me like he had never kissed me before. I felt like I was floating—it was perfect. I never knew he could kiss like that. It's true, we had only kissed a few times before, but I wished—never mind, this made this special.

He stopped and so I did. "That was nice," I told him simply.

"I know. I thought I'd save that for tonight." Tears were streaming down both of our faces again.

"'Bye," I yelled as I turned and walked away, unable to look at anything, not wanting to even think about what lay ahead.

As I walked, I realized that I still had my locket. I'd forgotten to give it to him. I didn't want to take it home with me; I wanted him to have it. Unable to will myself to go back to him, I dropped it as I left the wood, hoping he'd find it. But knowing it wasn't probable, I sobbed quietly all the way home.

Papa was there when I got home, but he was about to leave.

"Amy, you knew this would happen," he told me bluntly.

"Papa, no I didn't. I didn't know it wouldn't work out. Everything happened so fast—he wasn't supposed to get married for a couple more years, and then King Gelgar changed it. We rushed to find the evidence, and didn't. Now he's supposed to get married tomorrow, but he's running away to who-knows-where instead! Papa, I had not even the littlest hint that anything like this was going to happen. So, leave me alone." Somehow I managed to say all that and cry at the same time.

Papa looked at me sympathetically. "Amy, Henry is going be fine," he said and wrapped his arms around me.

"But, Papa, how can you know? How can anybody know? For all I know, I could never see him again." I cried into his shoulder, but it was now dark and he couldn't stay any longer.

"Sweetie, you know I'd like to stay and tell you everything is going to be fine, because it is. But if I don't leave now, there'll be no food on our table."

So he got up, grabbed his stilts, and left.

I decided to try to sleep, but instead of sleeping I found myself wondering what Papa was up to. I looked out the window and noticed the wind was blowing, and that meant it was probably taking longer to light the lamps. I hoped he didn't fall off his stilts again. Last time he was knocked out for hours before anyone found him.

Papa wasn't home at eleven. I wasn't worried as I thought of my papa. I found myself in a new state of mind. I was in a lose-lose situation. If Henry married Hellena, I'd be miserable. If he ran off to someplace dangerous, as he was planning to, I'd be miserable, I hated lose-lose situations.

It was now midnight, and Papa still wasn't home. He'd been out later than this before, so I didn't worry. I was now pacing in our first room, when there was a tap on the window. I turned around and couldn't believe what I saw. It was Henry. What was he doing here? If he thought that tapping on my window would help our situation, he was wrong.

"Go around—I'll let you in," I mouthed.

He nodded and then turned to walk around to the door, where I stood waiting.

"Henry, what are you doing here?" I asked.

"Have you been crying all night?" He looked at me, worried.

"Maybe, but you cannot tell me that you wouldn't cry if someone you cared more about than yourself were running off somewhere known to no one except him. For all I know, this will be the last time I will see you." I was sure I looked serious, but for some reason he started to laugh.

"Forget all that. Come with me."

"I told you, I can't go. We don't have the evidence."

He just smiled, but I continued, "What is the matter with you?" I couldn't see any reason to be smiling.

"Amy, are you sure we don't have the evidence?" He couldn't stop smiling.

"Yes, I'm sure, are you drun—"

I gasped as he pulled a dirty wooden box from behind his back.

"Where did you find that?" I jumped up, I kissed him, I twirled, and he laughed. "We did—you did it! Henry, I love you. Where will we go?" I was more excited than I'd ever been in my whole life.

"Sorret," he answered simply.

"Henry, shouldn't I prove my family first?"

He shook his head, his freckles glowing.

"Why not?"

"Because there isn't time. The carriage leaves for Aldreen at five."

It was now two in the morning.

"But that's only three hours away." I didn't think I could be ready that fast.

"Amy, I had to leave before six because according to my schedule I'm supposed to wake up at six this morning. Pack. I'll help you."

As we packed we talked about our future and what we wanted it to hold. When we were finished I wanted to wait a little longer for Papa, who should have been home any minute.

"Amy, let's go." Henry opened the door.

"Wait, I have to leave Papa a note." So I wrote to him all that could:

Dear Papa,
I know last night I told you I wasn't going anywhere and that I rejected Henry's proposal. But maybe something happened and I changed my mind. You know I love him very much and that I cried over my decision, because I wasn't going to let anyone get hurt like I was growing up. I also

told you that the only reason I didn't accept was because we hadn't found the evidence.

Papa I'm very pleased to tell you that that has changed! After Henry proposed last night, he found the box with the evidence in it. I'm leaving with him tonight, and we're going to get married. Papa, I love you so much more than you will ever know.

I'll always be your Amykins in mine and your heart.

Take care of Grandmere for me so that she can stay home. Tell Rob and Jo that I already miss them. Tell Emily and Eddie that Aunt Amy misses and loves them. Thank everyone who helped to find the evidence for me. I'll write as soon as I can. See you soon.

Love, your baby girl,
Amy

I set the letter on the table, where I was sure Papa would find it. I walked out the door hoping that of all people he would understand. As we reached the corner, I saw my father walking into the house. I wondered what he would think of my letter. I wouldn't find that out now, because now there was no turning back.

Chapter Twenty-Nine

As I lay down, I imagined Henry was there and I began to wonder how Mama and Papa handled everything those five long years. I played with my locket, which Henry found after finding the evidence, giving it to me as a wedding present. Mama touched my shoulder. Then I heard the wind whistle a tune that, even to this day, I swear sounded like my mother's voice. I went to sleep listening to the wind, as I had done so many times when I was growing up and listening to Mama.

Sleep couldn't seem to claim me that night. I slept restlessly, almost nervously. After I finally fell asleep, I woke up at an extremely early hour to find myself unable to fall back to sleep. I sat up and looked out the window; it was still much too dark to be awake.

I found myself wishing Henry were here, so I could confide in him about what I felt was unnecessary fear that they wouldn't allow me to see the king. After some time, I felt myself unable to stay in bed any longer, so I got up and tried to put all my fears away with a single breath.

Henry was happy enough to tell me what happened with him the next morning.

"My son, wake up. You're home!" King Sencraugh lifted his sleeping son into a huge hug that could have strangled.

"Father, I'm here—stop, please. You're choking me."

"Yes, of course," the king said as he cleared his throat and ruffed up his voice. "Where were you?"

"In Sorret," Henry told his father gingerly.

"I don't think I quite understand. Henry, you left on the eve of your wedding. Furthermore, you had the whole kingdom worried. Everyone thought you'd been murdered or taken prisoner—you never know these days. Those gubolins, goblins, whatever they're called—could be after us next." The king began to shout, the relief of his son being home safe washing away as the anger began to rise.

"Father, I couldn't marry Hellena. I didn't love her," the prince tried to explain.

"Henry, you should have just told me that a long time ago. I would have canceled the wedding." The king was getting annoyed.

"I did try, but you always interrupted and started talking about how much our foreign relations with Lavenlee would improve once I married one of their princesses."

King Sencraugh looked a little ashamed, and Henry couldn't decide if it was with him or at himself.

"Your mother and sister are waiting on me for breakfast, and we should join them."

Henry nodded at his father to show he agreed.

One thing I have always disliked about Henry's father was his one-sided way of thinking.

About an hour after I had awakened, I was ready to go, so I grabbed the evidence and a cloak, put it on, and was off.

I was nervous as I walked to the castle. I was shaking, and my hands felt like they'd never be still again. I wasn't even paying attention to where I was going, so instead of entering through the main entrance, like most people would if they were going to see the king's council, I walked in the back entrance— right into the kitchen. Habit, I guess. I never thought I'd walk in there again.

"Amy!" Jo shrieked as she ran over to hug me.

"Ames, you're back, but what are you doing in here?" Rob asked, confused.

"I'm going to see the council today, and I came in this way by mistake," I said and then smiled. "Mary told me that you two have something you need to tell me."

Jo smiled as I said it, and Rob looked at her.

"Ames," Rob started, "we're getting married in March."

I shrieked and hugged Jo. We screamed a happy scream together. Rob smiled but covered his ears.

I went over and hugged him, too. "It's about time." I whispered in his ear.

Dove heard the racket we were making and walked over to see what all the fuss was about.

"Oh, that explains it, Amy—the answer to why everything goes wrong in *my* kitchen. I thought you moved. Just when you think your problem has moved away, it comes back." Dove sighed as she glared at me.

"Well, I guess you can say I'm back, but I don't want my job back."

"Who told you I was offering?" she huffed and then turned away to mess up the life of a little boy who was working across the room. The three of us laughed at her as she moved away.

"I'm so happy for the both of you. I promise I'll be there. I have to go now—wish me luck," I told them.

"Good luck, Ames," Rob yelled, as I began to move toward the main parts of the castle.

"We're counting on you," Jo screamed as I left.

"Thanks," I said as I closed the door to the kitchen.

I walked up a few storys until I was in the right hall. I knew the castle better than some who lived in it. I thought it was a bit depressing that most of the scullery maids knew their way around the castle better than the king himself. I continued to walk until I came to a sign that read:

King's Council

This was my door, so I took a deep breath, opened it, and entered. My nerves started to come back as I went to the back of a very long line. The line moved slowly, but the fact that I wanted it to move fast made it all the slower. I wished a clock were nearby so I could see how long I'd stood there.

Finally, I was two away from my turn. The head councilman yelled, "Next!" Then I was one away from my turn. I don't think anyone could have been anymore impatient than I was at that moment. I wanted it to be my turn, and whoever was in front of me was taking their sweet time.

"Next," the voice called again.

I walked into the room, which adjoined the room the line was in.

"What brings you here?" one of the lords asked.

"I need a hearing with the king."

All of them looked at me quizzically. "Why?" asked a very fat and funny-looking lord.

I pulled out the necessary document. "I need to prove that my family didn't do this," I told all seven councilmen as I handed them the decree.

They handed it to the herald, who read it out loud:

The king's council has come to their decision that no evidence can be found. So, as the queen requested, we withdraw the betrothal between Samuel Fredrick John Jonestone and Princess Gittel

Amelia Daffodil Frindeline. From now on, or until it is proven they did not betray the beloved country Frindeline in the year 923 during the war against Lanski, the Jonestone family will become peasants and serve in the homes of the nobility. The way out of this eternal fate of servitude is for Queen Alexandra to withdrawal charges, or for a king of Frindeline to be shown proof that Fredrick Jonestone did not indeed commit the crime he was punished for. You are no longer allowed to marry above your status, which has been reduced to peasant. In no circumstances will that ever be altered, no matter your feelings. You showed no love for your country by betraying it, so now your country will show no love toward you.

The King's Council of 924,
Herbert Sorenson John Lawmen Zachariah Keith Jeremiah Golan Micah Mitchell Kevin Lawry Jacob Conner

"So, are you a member of the Jonestone family, which was convicted of betraying the country in the year 923, during the war against Lanski while it was still a country ruled by a ruler?"

I nodded at another lord whom I had never seen or heard of.

"Name," another demanded.

"Amythist Amelia Annette Jonestone," I answered.

"Born to John Samuel Noah Jonestone and Countess Rosemarie Rachel Reality Somner, the two who were married illegally in Aldreen and had a daughter—you, if I'm correct. Your father was in prison for five years until your mother died of an infection." the lord stated.

"Yes, how did you know all that?"

"It's our job to know." another lord told me. He was scary, with a long nose and scrooked teeth.

"Well, I think you could see the king on February the first at noon, if that works?" he told me more than asked me.

"Yes, that's perfect," I told them, as all seven dismissed me. I knew that now all I had to do was study the letters. I thought they were very convincing, but the most convincing of all was the contract signed by both Stuart McCarthy and King Peter of Lanski in the year 923. Stuart McCarthy was a coward who was willing to betray his own country in order not to become a prisoner of war.

All the letters were alike, giving important information to the king about attacks and plans. The ones to McCarthy from the king thanked him, and threatened that if his information were wrong he'd find himself in a Lanskian prison.

If the letters didn't prove anything, then the contract would. It laid it all out and didn't leave any room for disbelief. At the point I was at after I talked to the council, I had no idea how I would present myself. I didn't even know if I could in any way make it look as if I knew what I was talking about. Women were not held in high regard in Frindeline. Trying to show the king that I was serious would be difficult.

I had a month to prepare and study over twenty letters, and figure out which ones to read, if I read any.

The only responsibility I had to worry about was this: No longer did I have to worry about the kitchen, and I was glad.

I spent almost all my time studying so I could talk without even thinking and argue my points on demand without a written note in my hand. After reading and studying all the notes, I knew there was no way they could say we did it. Papa had found more than enough information.

A week before I was to go and see the king, I still didn't know what I was going to do it. I'd written ten or so speeches, only to crumple them, knowing that it wasn't what I wanted to get across. I wished I knew more. I wished I knew what had gone on in Stuart McCarthy's head when he did what he did. I felt like I couldn't come up with anything right. I had the evidence and I knew what I wanted to say in my head, but it just didn't come out right.

I met Henry at the willow three days before Febuary first. He wanted to know my plan just as much as I did.

"Amy, it's good to see your face."

I smiled as I looked at him, even though I had no idea what I was going to tell his father, who most definitely was not going to say anything like that to me in three days.

"Henry, I missed you," I told him as I gave him a hug.

He kissed me, too. "So you're seeing my father in three days?"

"Yes, at noon."

"What do plan to tell him?"

I knew that question was coming, but I didn't know how to answer it. "Well," I started, as the wind whistle, "Follow your heart", "I plan to tell him what's on my heart, say what I know must be said, and try and make him understand. You know that writing speeches really doesn't work for me—"

He stopped me by putting his finger on my lips. "I think that'll work just fine. I love you. Everything is going to be fine," he assured me.

"I know. I love you too," I told him as I smiled. "You had better go home before your parents think you ran off again."

He nodded, kissed me quickly, and left.

On the walk home, a million things flooded my mind—mostly about how Henry and I were going to tell His Majesty that his only son and I were married. I was sure he wouldn't take it too well, but I also knew he had to be told.

In those last few days I did manage to relax. I visited Rob and Jo in the kitchen. I saw the twins and Mary. I even went and saw Prissy and Charlie. Charlie was talking like any seven-year-old. Most people forgot that he hadn't talked until Rob broke that picture frame, but I still remembered it and smiled.

I had been gone for months, and I had a lot of catching up to do. I talked to Jo about when Rob asked her to marry him.

"Ames, he asked as soon as he came back from taking you and Henry to the boat."

I smiled. "I'm glad, because I'd known for some time that he wanted to tell you."

Jo laughed at this. "Really! I wish I had known."

The day before I was to see the king, I met Henry by the willow late in the evening.

"So, how do you feel?" he asked me.

"Nervous, but I'll be okay," I told him as I sat down.

He sat down next to me, and I leaned my head on his shoulder.

"Hey, Amy."

A tear trickled down my cheek. He looked down at me before asking, "What's wrong?"

I turned around and looked him straight in the eye. "I'm scared—what if it doesn't work? What if he won't listen to me? What if your father doesn't want me even after I'm a duke's daughter?"

He kissed me soundly. "Amy, he'll love you, and if he doesn't, he'll learn to. He can't change anything." He kissed me again. "You'll always be my wife."

I heard something coming from the bushes, which sounded like someone running through them.

We turned our heads. Henry jumped up and ran over to the bushes. "Who's there?" he yelled. "Answer me! This is your prince and future king telling you to show yourself!" he yelled as he searched the bushes. He was mad and I knew that, depending on who it was in that bush, all our plans could be ruined. Finally, after searching thoroughly, he came back to me.

"Amy, I think we should go home. I'll be there tomorrow at noon to support you, and I'm sure I won't be the only one." He was playing with my locket as he looked up at me.

"I know. I love you, and Mama will be there."

He smiled and kissed me goodnight.

As I walked home, I prayed that whoever was in the bushes wasn't McCarthy, because if it were him, I knew I was in for it.

I didn't sleep well that night. Everytime I fell asleep I'd wake up less than an hour later, with my hands wrapped around my locket. I kept having my dream. I couldn't understand it. I never got to the part where I said, "I did it." It was as if it tried to warn me about something that I didn't know, but it was unwilling to tell me.

I woke up around five in the morning, much like the day I'd gone to see the council. Today was worse, and I had to keep myself busy. I was so nervous that I couldn't stop pacing. I left at about eight, knowing I didn't need to be there until noon, but needing something to do.

I went to the lake and watched the fish jump out of the newly thawed water. I went to the wood and saw that my markers were still there, and I smiled. I decided to go to the kitchen and help Rob, Jo, and Prissy with their work.

"Hey, Amy," Charlie yelled as I entered the kitchen.

I smiled. "Charlie, how are you?"

"Great! I didn't think we'd see you till later—you know, after you fixed everything."

I smiled. He was smart for seven years old.

"Well, Charlie, I certainly don't have to be here, but I have some extra time. I thought I'd come and help all of you out."

As soon as I said those words, Dove turned around and looked her evilest. "Who do you think you are, Amythist Jonestone? They don't need your help, and I will not allow you to barge in here and help those who are fully capable of doing their chores themselves." Dove screamed at me, and stomped her foot as she pointed to the door.

I was about to leave when Aggie yelled, "Mother, what's wrong with helping people? I would let her help. You're certainly capable of doing all your chores, yet all you ever do is give them off to someone else. Amy, it looks to me like Prissy could use some help with the prince's favorite cake. It needs to be ready by noon."

I smiled at her. "I'd love to help Prissy with that. Thanks, Aggie."

She smiled and winked.

"Amy," Prissy said, "I don't think I believe my ears. Did Aggie just stand up to her mother and defend *you* of all people? Don't take that the wrong way, Ames—it's just…"

"I know, hard to believe," I told her as we began to work on our cake.

"Agithus Dovendella Dartain, how dare you defy me!" Aggie's mother's shrieks could be heard only for a moment, until they were drowned out as everyone talked and went back to work.

About an hour and a half later, I once again had baked the cake I had become famous for. It felt good to bake it, especially when I knew it was for Henry. At noon, Prissy and I left the kitchen. Rob and Jo wished me good luck as I exited. Prissy carried the cake, and I followed behind on our way to the throne room.

Chapter Thirty

As I took a deep breath, Prissy patted my shoulder. I opened the door to the throne room. Prissy went in after me and set the cake down on a table between the king and his son, Henry. She pointed at the cake and then at me. He winked to show he understood that I had baked it.

"Enter," the king cried. "A girl!" The king began to laugh.

"Yes, if you want to call me a girl, go ahead. I have no problem with it. The fact that I'm a girl doesn't mean I don't know what I'm talking about or that I've come to beg." I kept my eyes on him as I curtsied.

He stared at me, obviously trying to hold his laughter. "Well then, miss, what brings you here? And what is your name?" he said directly to me as he sneered.

"Amythist Amelia Annette Jonestone," I started.

"A Jonestone. The name rings a bell, but tell me, why do these Jonestones send a woman to do a man's job?" the king inquired.

"Your Majesty, I wasn't sent; I chose to come. And for the record, I have personal reasons for being here, other than just family related." I was stern, because I needed my king, my father-in-law, to think I was serious and to stop making a joke out of me.

"Oh, Amythist, is it? Let me guess. You want to change your life so it can be like a fairy tale. Let me tell you, being of noble birth is just as bad as not being so."

I stared him straight in the face. "It is? I supposed the right to marry whomever you please is a drawback of being of noble birth, and having the money to take care of a sick mother is horribly devastating for the likes of you. And I'm sure that having parents who fell in love, had you, and didn't have to worry about what their betters would do if they found out is the most terrible thing of all when it comes to being rich? Not to mention that never lifting a finger your whole life must be awfully painful when you know you could be plowing a field or baking bread, or maybe even simply making a bed. Now that I think about it, being of noble birth does have a lot of drawbacks. What could I have been thinking? Oh, right, I'm just a silly girl," I told him sarcastically, as I eyed him up and down and saw him squirm a little.

He became stern and quickly stopped laughing at me. "Calm down, miss, I didn't realize—"

I interrupted, "So, Your Highness, if you think that I'm going to leave here without even trying, just because you're laughing at me, then I am a silly girl. I promise you I'm not." I stared harder at him, just to make sure everything was clear.

"All right, Miss Jonestone, I'll give you a chance to prove—"

He never finished his sentence, because at that moment the doors to the throne room flew open. James McCarthy walked in followed by several guards.

He smiled at me, before yelling, "Arrest her!"

He once again smiled at me, as if to say 'I win.'

I stared at him, shocked. I was so close—how could this be happening?

I hadn't noticed that Henry had jumped up and was now standing next to me. He looked scared, too, and searched my eyes for the answer, which I couldn't give him. I felt like crying.

The king asked, "McCarthy, what is the meaning of this?" King Sencraugh looked at me in amazement; I don't think he thought I could have done anything wrong.

"Well, King Sencraugh, if I could have a word alone with you, your son…" He paused and looked at me, and then snarled, "…and this girl, I'll explain."

"Father, don't listen to him," Henry pleaded.

"Everyone, if you would leave for just a few short minutes. I'll inform you when you shall be admitted back in."

They all got up and left. Henry and I looked at each other, McCarthy glared at us, and the king looked at the three of us in confusion.

When everyone left, the king asked again, "McCarthy, what on all of Delynelle is this about?" His face had turned red, as if he thought this unnecessary.

"King Sencraugh, this girl is married illegally to a man above her status. I call it "daughter like father,'" he told the king as he smiled his evilest.

"McCarthy, you know as well as I do that the charge is against the man she married. Bring him to me and he shall be punished," the king exclaimed

McCarthy laughed. "Of course it is, but before I send for him, let me ask you a question."

"All right." Sencraugh shrugged.

"See that locket on the girl's neck—do you recognize it?" he asked slyly.

I looked at Henry, who was whispering to himself, "No, no, no."

"I recognize it, but I'm not sure where from—Wait, didn't Henry wear one like that around his wrist?"

He was going to figure it out, and I was going to be sent away. I thought I was going to faint, but Mama gave one her hugs. "I can do this," I whispered.

"Henry's wrist thing, her locket—McCarthy, how are they connected?" The king seemed annoyed.

"Did your son not go missing late on the nineteenth of July?" was McCarthy's next question, obviously planned.

"Yes, I do believe he did."

"Well then, Your Majesty, do you think it's a coincidence that this girl did, too?"

The king gaped. "Henry, how could you...My gosh, my son is married!" The king clamped his hand over his mouth as his gaze went to his son's left hand.

"Boy, what did you think you were doing? And to a Jonestone, of all people! Do you know what the law says?! It says that one of you must go to prison! Did you even think?!" the king yelled, his face redder than a tomato.

"Father," Henry said with a quiver in his voice, "*please* take me. Whatever you do, please let Amy go. Listen to her, please, Father," he pleaded.

"Henry, don't do this. We should have waited," I told him as he took my hand.

"Father, I refuse to let you take her," he commanded.

His father had a look of distress in his eyes.

"Henry," I pleaded.

"Son, how would that look? The prince of Frindeline in prison! I'm sorry, Henry, but she'll have to go." At first his father had been white with fury, but eventually it switched over to a sorry-eyed look.

Henry looked at me. I gave him the box and mouthed, "Make sure your father looks at this."

He looked me in the eye and said, "I don't regret marrying you when I did. I only regret the fact that my father is a moron." Then he kissed me quickly.

The king yelled, "Arrest her!"

To my delight it sounded half-hearted. McCarthy grabbed my arm, and led me away.

"Father, I can't believe you. You had no right. I was responsible, and you know it," Henry yelled. "She left this with me, and if you ever expect me to speak to you again, you'll look at it."

He dropped the box and then said more quietly, "I hope you know that I love her." That was all he said before he ran out of the throne room.

I was taken to the same prison my father had been held in, which seemed so long ago. I sat in my cell and cried the rest of the afternoon.

A few hours after I was put in there, I heard the man across the hall say, "Why does she get a room full of visitors?"

I looked up to see about half a dozen smiling faces. "Papa, Aunt Grace, Rob, Jo, Mary, Cornelius, Prissy… Henry, how'd you get away from your father?" I started off simply counting my visitors, when I saw Henry.

"It doesn't matter, I just wanted to tell you that I don't regret that we're already married. I only wish that stupid McCarthy…oh that—"

"It's okay," I interrupted.

"No, it's not! Don't try and tell me this is the way it is supposed to be because, Amy, I refuse to believe that. It should be me behind those bars! That's the way it's supposed to be. You should be talking to my father, who should have freed your family. You don't deserve this."

"Neither do you," I told him assertively. "It doesn't matter. My family is cursed, and it seems that will always win in the end." I sighed.

"Now, Amy, I've never, ever heard you say anything like that in your whole life. Nothing has ever stopped you before, so don't let this," my aunt said sternly.

"Maybe you're right, Amy. Maybe we should have waited. It's my entire fault. You shouldn't be in there." Henry scowled as he shook the bars.

"Henry, stop it. I take back what I said in there. I would never trade anything for the last few months, even if that means I'll be stuck in a cage. I promise I'll be fine—Papa was." I smiled at him.

"Ames, this is hard on all of us. I'm having a hard time not marching up to that throne and strangling the king myself, but I'm sure Henry here has that taken care of." Rob looked as if he were trying not to cry. "How'd he find out?" he asked while his tears betrayed him as he allowed one to trickle down his cheek.

I shrugged because I didn't have an answer. I looked around at my friends and family to see most of them trying not to cry, trying to be strong. They could have cried—I wouldn't have minded. I'd done the same not so long ago. I turned to Mary, who smiled, her lips shaking as she saw me look in her direction.

"Mary, I'm so sorry, I've set such a bad example for the twins." I looked away, not wanting to see her eyes, which I thought must be filled with bitter disappointment.

"No, Amy, on contrary, you've set the best example my children will ever know. You followed your heart and fought for what is right. I can't set a better example for my children," Mary told me as she began to let her tears flow.

"To think only this morning you were as happy as always, baking cakes with me." Prissy sobbed.

Then came a voice I desperately needed to hear the most at that moment. "Amy, I'm going to get you out of there. Sweetheart, I never wanted you to end up like this, in exactly the same place, for the same reason." My papa shook his head. "Never could I have imagined this—my baby girl in a cell."

He was crying just about as hard as he had the day Mama died. I hated to see him like this. Wasn't this what I was trying to prevent?

"Papa, I hated watching you as if you were some goblin that was caught and put in a cage and that everyone gawked at. I know how you feel. I'm sorry I failed you, Mama, Henry, and everyone. I'm sorry," I said as tears once again began to fall off my nose.

"Amy, you have nothing to be sorry about. You didn't do anything wrong. I should be in there…if only my father wasn't so stupid." Henry shook my bars, to let out his frustration.

"Stop it, please! This is hard enough without blaming yourself," I cried, and as Papa touched his shoulder, he stopped gripping my bars.

We all talked for a long time, when a guard finally came over to tell everyone they needed to leave. Henry told them he wasn't going anywhere, and they let him be. Being a prince does have its advantages, I guess.

"Amy, you know I would never have put you in this position if I'd known—"

"Yes, I know," I interrupted.

"I should probably go, but I'll come every day, I promise. I love you."

"I love you, too," I called after him as he waved.

I was the only woman in the entire prison, which made me uncomfortable. I was in prison for something no one but the Jonestones were put in prison for. All the other prisoners in here were thieves and murderers. I cried again. I felt trapped and unable to come up with a way out.

The man in the cell across from me asked, "So, miss, what're you in for?"

I looked up. He was grimy, with long hair and a mouth full of brown, crooked teeth.

I smiled nervously.

"For…nothing. It was a mistake. That's all," I told him

He laughed, not buying a word I said. "I don't believe that. You're Jonestone's daughter. He was in here for getting married. Are in for som'thin' as innocent as that?"

I turned my head toward him. "How'd you know I was his daughter?"

He laughed again. "Well, he had a daughter that was always visiting him, and she looked loads like him. Well, you just happen to look very much like a grown-up version of that little girl. Plus, you look like John." He smiled.

"Well, you're right. I'm his daughter."

"Well, I'm glad my suspicion was correct." He winked at me. "That last one to leave, wasn't he the prince himself and he loves ya."

I smiled. "That's why I'm here. We were married on a boat while the prince was missing."

He looked shocked. "The prince was mis'in'?" He laughed. "Us down here seem to forget what goes on. Eventually we don't even care. Boy, you're a lucky girl—a prince for a husband."

He put his hand through his dirty hair as he drifted off into his own little world. "If I were out, I'd get meself a pretty little lady."

I smiled as I thought about how fortunate I was, even if a everything seemed to be going wrong.

This part of the story was one I was told by many different people. I was extremely curious about this part, considering what it resulted in, and all.

"Father!" Daffodil screamed through the stone halls of the castle. "Father!"

"Yes, Daffy, what is it?" he asked as he wondered what he did this time to make his daughter yell.

"Father, how could you? Henry loves her and you sent her to prison!" she fumed.

"Well now, Daffy, it's a bit more complicated than that." He tried to calm her down.

"Did you even look at the stuff she brought with her? Did you even give her a chance? *Father, do you even care?*" she yelled at him. "Just because you're the king doesn't mean innocent people should be sent away. You have no proof that her family is responsible. How would you have felt if you hadn't been allowed to marry mother?" She stopped to breathe.

"Daffodil, sweetheart, I'm sorry, but the law is the law," he told her sternly.

"But, Father, what if you just looked at the evidence…."

"Why are you two yelling?" the queen asked.

"Neeuqa, please explain to your daughter that sending Henry's Jonestone wife to prison had to be done."

The queen opened her mouth wide with shock. "What, our son married a Jonestone and you sent her to jail? Now, Sencraugh, was she trying to free her family, and if so, did you even look at the proof?"

Daffodil smiled at her mother.

"No, but I don't need to," he said and walked away.

"Oh, Daff, your poor brother must be in agony," the queen told her daughter.

"He is. That's why I confronted Father, but he won't listen to anyone who has anything to say about it."

"Honey, don't you worry about your brother. I'm going to go see him right now and discuss an idea I have with him. Your father doesn't know what he's gotten himself into."

The king would have no choice, now that both his children and his wife were against him.

"Henry, son, may I come in?" Neeuqa asked as she knocked on her son's door.

"As long as Father isn't with you," he answered.

"He's not," the queen said as she came in and sat on her son's bed. "Henry, is this girl's family truly innocent?" she asked sympathetically.

"Yes, Mother, and even if they weren't it was so long ago. It shouldn't matter." He hugged his mother.

"Henry, I have a plan. Does this girl, I mean—"

"Amy," Henry said.

"Does Amy want to prove her family herself?"

Henry nodded at his mother.

"Well then, Henry, I want you to…"

She whispered the whole plan to him, and then he and his sister went out and informed all those who would be needed for it to work.

Chapter Thirty-One

―◈―

Queen Neeuqa charmingly went over to her husband the next day to see if he would like a walk.
"Sencraugh, when was the last time we went to the town square to see how subjects are doing?"

"Neeuqa, I don't like going to town. Everyone always stares at me," he told her, ignoring her charm, as he had come to do now and then.

"I so wish we could go on a walk. Please?" the queen begged.

"Fine, but only a short one." He huffed and as he lethargically stood up, their daughter Daffodil walked in.

"Mother, Father, where are you going?" she asked happily.

"On a walk. Would you like to join us, Daff?" her father asked, annoyed, as if he felt obliged to ask.

From behind him her mother mouthed "right on schedule." The princess winked to show she understood.

"Yes, I'd love to come," Princess Daffodil conceded.

Then the royals walked out of the throne room toward the castle entrance. As they walked through the stone halls, they ran into the prince.

"Son, would you like to join us for a walk?" his father asked without looking him in the eye.

"No, I don't think I will," Henry told his father as he turned around and deliberately stomped his foot.

"Now, Henry, I forgave you for marrying her. The least you can do is forgive me for putting her in prison." Sencraugh yelled after his son, but received no reply.

Once they left, Henry went into his parents' sleeping chamber and looked for the wooden box. It wasn't too hard to find—it was right under the bed in the exact place his mother said it would be.

Meanwhile, in the kitchen Jo was telling Rob, "Go, good luck. I love you. I know you can get her out."

Robert Garrison smiled at the woman he loved.

"Dove, may I have a word?" Jo turned around and asked.

"What is it now, Johannah?" the grouchy old woman asked as she walked over.

"I was wondering if Rob and I could get a week off after our wedding."

"Now don't push it—I'll give you two days," Dove scolded as she shook her finger at her.

"Oh, but Dove…" The argument raged on.

Phillip had just arrived at the square with Charlie, and they stood there waiting to make sure everything was in place.

When they saw that it was, Phillip turned to his son. "Now, you know what you have to do? And after today you are never to do it again." He looked sternly at the young man in front of him.

"Yes, Pa, only today. I promise."

"Good luck, Charlie," his father whispered as his son walked toward the queen, king, and princess who had just entered the town square. I was told that all heads turned when the royal family entered. Everyone watched as they looked around as if nothing was amiss or out of the ordinary.

Charlie walked up to them, and Daffodil gave him a wink.

"Why, Your Highness, I don't think I've seen an outfit as exquisite as yours before," Charlie said and then bowed.

"Why, thank you, young man." The king laughed.

My father and Rob watched from opposite sides of the square. They spotted each other and waved.

"Please, King, Sir; I'm sure you have enough money. If only you could give me enough to buy my mother a cake. It's her birthday. Please, Your Majesty," Charlie begged.

"I'm sorry, son, but I'm not a bag of gold, nor am I able to just give out money." The king looked at the boy as if disgusted, and he tried to turn away.

Charlie stood in the way and began to open his mouth, when the queen spoke. "Please, little boy, my husband has had a hard day. Maybe you should go," she said with a wink.

"Oh, I'm sorry, Queen, Madame, but I promised Pa that I wouldn't come home without a cake. So, if you could give me just five gold coins, I'd be forever grateful." Charlie continued to beg in any way possible. I heard he did a marvelous job.

By this time, Rob had begun to edge closer and closer behind the king. Once he was directly behind, and when King Sencraugh was much too involved in the battle against the beggar boy, Daffodil said, "Father, why don't I run and fetch a guard?"

"Yes, Daff, why don't you do that," the king agreed through clenched teeth.

As this was going on, Rob, without anyone noticing because of all the confusion, slipped the king's set of keys right off his belt.

"Oh, Your Highness," Charlie began, as Rob ran off with the keys and the princess followed quickly behind.

Now, Henry had been waiting by the prison, hoping everything was going as planned. He never thought his mother could come up with something so devious, especially against his father. Nevertheless, he hoped this plan was successful because if it wasn't, it was very likely that Rob, my father, and Charlie would end up in prison with me.

Then Rob waved.

"Rob, did you get them?" Henry asked hurriedly.

"Yes, they're right here. Let's go," Rob answered anxiously.

Henry looked around. "Where's Daff—is she coming?" Henry asked just as anxiously as Rob had answered his last question.

"Yeah, she's coming. She should be here any minute," Rob told him as he pointed in the direction of the prison door, indicating they needed to hurry.

"Please, Your Majesty," Charlie continued to plead.

"Son, is that you? I've been looking all over for you." My father smirked as he walked over to Charlie.

"Pa, the king wouldn't give me any money."

My father looked down at Charlie, shocked. "Your Highness, I'm terribly sorry if my son has been a bother. Believe me, he will be punished," My papa said sternly, looking at Charlie. Supposedly, he gave him the same disappointed face he gave me when I messed things up.

I'll Always Be With You

"Guards, I demand to be let in," Henry yelled.

I could hear him from my cell.

"Of course, Your Highness," one of the guards answered with a bit of a quiver in his voice.

The next thing I knew, I heard footsteps running down the long lines of cells, and then a faint cry.

"Amy, we're here to get you out," said Rob and Henry. This day was just getting better.

"What, but how?" I couldn't help but ask them as their faces came into view. As much as I wanted out, I didn't understand how they could to do it.

"See, miss," the man I had talked to before said, "you at least have friends who'll bail you out of situations like this."

"Yes, I do," I told the man, as Rob unlocked my cage.

"Thanks." I hugged Rob and then gave Henry a kiss. "How'd you do it?" I asked again.

"Long story," Rob said, "and complicated."

We walked quietly through the prison. Henry held my hand as if he thought he would lose me forever if he let me go. When we got close to the entrance I could hear Henry's sister talking urgently to the guards.

"Please hurry. I already told you some boy is begging my father for money and won't stop."

"Princess, your father has dealt with beggars before—"

"As the Princess of Frindeline, I order you to go to the town square and sort this out," Daffodil stubbornly told the guards.

"We're on our way. Let's go," one guard said to the other.

When we could no longer hear their feet in the distance, I asked again, "What's going on?"

"Just follow me," Henry answered with a smile and a sparkle in his eye.

I tightened my grip in his hand to let him know that I would.

Rob stood there and cleared his throat. "Henry, your sister is waiting for us, and we're kind of on a schedule."

We nodded in agreement as we left the prison.

Once outside, the princess stood waiting impatiently for us.

"Oh, so you must be my sister-in-law. I don't think we've been properly introduced," I said.

"No real time for that, but you can call me Daff." She shook my hand and smiled.

"All right, now can someone please explain to me what is going on?" I asked desperately.

"Well, you're supposed to come with Daff and me to the throne room, where our mother is going to make Father listen to you. We're getting this over with today. Your family will be proven innocent this very afternoon." He smiled at me as I jumped and hugged him around the neck.

"I don't know how you did it, but thanks," I whispered in his ear.

"Oh, believe me, we had help. After this I'd thank your father, Jo, my mother, and Prissy and Phillip for letting Charlie beg for money from the king."

I let go of him and opened my mouth, half shocked. "Prissy let Charlie beg?"

Rob nodded in response. "Only so we could get you out of there."

We half-ran to the castle from the prison and entered through the kitchen, just to make sure we didn't run into the king early.

As we entered, Jo was arguing with Dove. "Now we deserve at least a week!" Jo complained.

"I don't care if you were turning into an elephant. Four days is my final offer. I can't spare the two of you any longer than that."

Then Dove looked up and pointed at me. "And where have you been, Robert Garrison? Your fiancé almost got herself fired while you were gone!" Dove yelled, red in the face, her hands on her hips. "And you! Haven't the three of you caused me enough trouble in this kitchen? Amy, I never want to see your sorry face in this kitchen again!" Dove was angry. For once I think she would have let the whole world know it.

"Dovendella, if you don't give Rob and Jo at least two weeks off after their wedding, then you're fired. If you ever say anything like that about Amy again, you'll be sorry," Henry yelled at Dove.

"Yes, of course, Your Highness. Amy, you're welcome to visit anytime, and you two take two weeks off after your wedding," she said in a very fake-sweet voice. Then she crossed her arms and stomped off to the other side of the kitchen, as if she were a three-year-old.

"Well, we know who to call when she gets on our nerves," Rob teased Henry as he laughed and watched Dove go in the other direction.

"Come on. My father and mother could be back any second," Henry told us as we began to run through the castle halls.

"Why are we running?" I asked frantically.

"Well, according to the plan, we are supposed to be in the throne room when they get there."

I still didn't know how everything was supposed to work, but I was glad that everything had so far.

As we were running, it donned on me. "I don't have the evidence," I told them, afraid that was probably important.

"No, you don't. But I do." Henry smiled as he pulled the wooden box from under his coat.

"You know, sometimes I think you're too perfect," I told him before kissing him.

We finally reached the throne room. I took a deep breath and opened both heavy doors.

The king and queen were already there. I didn't know if that was significant or not. Henry did specifically say that we had to get there first.

The king stared at me and I stared back. Finally he spoke. "I thought you were in jail." He didn't look too pleased as his son, Rob, and his daughter entered the room.

"I was until about twenty minutes ago," I replied.

"Really, now how did such a silly girl manage that?"

I stared harder, unable to understand how he and Henry were actually related.

"Father, she isn't silly, but you are."

The king turned from me to his son. "So, you helped her out, along with these two servants."

Princess Daffodil chose then to step next to her brother.

"Oh, please, Daffy, don't tell me that I have two deceitful children."

The princess nodded and was about to speak, when the queen looked her husband in the eye.

"You may be king of a great land, but that doesn't give you the right to call your children deceitful when they were simply obeying their mother.

"Sencraugh," she continued, "I don't know what's happened to your sense of judgment, but I've never before seen you treat a single situation like this in your entire reign. I don't know if you're disappointed with Henry and his love life, or if it was just too shocking that your son chose who he wanted to marry without your even putting in any input. But whatever it is, it messed up your judgment. You can't call your children deceitful without calling me that, also, because I developed the plan."

The king looked at his family in absolute shock. He couldn't believe what he had just heard.

Then the queen continued. "And I will not allow you to leave this room until you hear what Amy has to say." She stared at the king, letting him know he wasn't allowed to complain.

The king seemed to be at a loss for words, when a grin grew upon his face. "Neeuqa, I'd love to hear what the girl has to say, but who has the evidence?" He smirked.

"For one thing, it's Amy. I swear if it weren't for the fact that my husband has your nose and is next in line to be king, by your behavior I never would have guessed you two were related. I have the evidence," I spat back smartly.

"Oh, you do." He seemed defeated. "Well then, go ahead." He seemed nervous.

"Well, Your Highness, my family was convicted but never proven."

The king nodded.

"They couldn't find the evidence all those years ago, and some even believe that it doesn't exist. It took me four years to find it after it was supposedly burned by your order on the night Papa was taken away." I stopped and took a breath, trying to hold back the tears that were about to flow from my eyes. When Papa, Cornelius, Mary, the twins, Phillip, Prissy, Charlie, and Jo entered, the king stood up.

"That boy, he's the beg—"

"No, Father, that's Charlie," Henry interrupted.

"But why are they here?" he asked, bewildered.

"Well, Your Majesty, can't a father and a few friends watch my daughter make a historical moment? And since I missed her wedding, I think I'm entitled," my papa, John Jonestone, told His Royal Highness with a smile and a wink for me.

The king nodded, and I continued. "As I was saying, your royal self, McCarthy thought he burned the evidence on the eve of the day my father was supposed to do this eleven years ago. Did you know that the next day was my birthday? But, of course, you and McCarthy don't care how your subjects feel. McCarthy has great influence over you and I think you're afraid of him." I paused for another breath.

"But, that's not why I'm here. I'm here because that night my aunt's wedding gown was burned instead. Because of that, I stand here before you, telling you that inside this box the truth lies not in my words but in Stuart McCarthy's. In this box are things everyone thought couldn't be found. Everyone at one time knew what my family supposedly did, but none of them have ever known that what they were told was a lie. Read these letters, and you'll see all the proof you need. But just so you know, right here…" I grabbed a very old contract out of the box, "…is the real proof. I'll read it to you:

> *I, Stuart McCarthy, promise to give you, King Peter Percival Lanski, all the information that is needed in order for you to win this war. So that I will not have to become a captive in a land that is not familiar to me, I am willing to give you our strategies, battle plans, and any other information that will allow this to take place. I am willing to do this so that I will not be kept a prisoner of war, which would take away my honor. I also state that I will not betray King Peter, which would result in*

death. I will do everything in my power, using the trust I have with King Jasper, to get all the information King Peter needs. Long live King Peter and the land of Lanski.
<u>*Stuart McCarthy*</u>

I stopped reading. The king looked shocked. "May I see that?" he asked as he grabbed for the contract.

"Yes, here, you can look at all of these, too," I told him as I handed him the box and contract. I stood there, hoping and pleading with all my heart that this had worked. I felt that everyone had gone through too much for this one answer.

"Young lady, that was a marvelous performance. If it were up to me, your family would be free. You can't get much more proof than that." Queen Neeuqa hugged me. "I think you'll do my Henry good. You might even turn out to be the best queen Frindeline will ever have." She smiled at me.

"Thank you, Your Highness," I replied sheepishly, not knowing how else to respond.

"Please, you are part of the family. Call me Neeuqa." She continued to smile.

"Thank you, Neeuqa," I said just as sheepishly as I had when I called her 'Your Highness.'

"Much better. You're welcome, Amy."

I smiled back at her, and I had the feeling that my mother-in-law and I would get along just fine.

The king was still thinking. As my father came and stood next to me, I could see where tears had streamed down his face.

He whispered to be, "Ames, you know how much this means to me, that my daughter was the one to do this." He smiled that corny smile of his and hugged me tight.

Just then, James McCarthy and a guard came through the door. "Your Majesty, the Jonestone has escaped," McCarthy yelled.

"I know, James. She's been standing right here in front of me for quite some time now. Why she's there I have no questions about, but I do have one referring to this." He raised the contract in the air. "I never realized how cowardly your family really was and still is. You've been trying to cover your backs for generations. So that your family wouldn't be disgraced, you'd let a completely innocent family go through more hardship than anyone deserves. James, that's wrong. I didn't see it until it was put together in front of my eyes. I had to see letters and contracts to believe my ancestors were wrong. I didn't think it was possible. Guards, arrest James McCarthy. And you, Amythist Amelia Annette Jonestone Frindeline, have done your family a great deed. I'm sorry I judged you so quickly and poorly. Not many women would be willing to do what you did today. I'm glad to tell you you're family is proven innocent. Welcome to the family, Princess Amy. You and your father are welcome to come here and live at the palace. I hope you can find it somewhere in your heart to forgive me for putting you in prison. I regret ever doing it."

The king apologized as he came down from his throne and gave me a hug. I could hear Henry laughing in the background and my friends cheering.

I knew I finally could say, "I did it." I couldn't speak because I was having a hard time believing what I had just heard.

I said to myself again, "I did it!" I said it out loud as a tear trickled down my face when what he said hit me.

"Princess, no—I'm just the daughter of a duke and a countess."

He laughed, and I smiled as Henry picked me up and twirled me around.

"Amy, you did it," he yelled as he kissed me squarely on the mouth. When he set me down, everyone stood around me and shared in the joy.

I couldn't believe what was happening. I remembered my dream...my mama's wish that I would do this...I felt her give me a hug—she was there with me now. If it weren't for her, I—

"Ames, I'm so proud of you. I knew you could do it, sweetheart." Papa hugged me and kissed me on the cheek.

"Papa, please come and live here. It'd make me really happy."

"You can count on it," was all he said.

That day, many things changed in Frindeline. Everything was set right in most people's minds. I knew what it was like to live in both worlds—that of the peasants and that of the nobles—and I planned on using it to make everyone's life better. And that's just what I did.

To order additional copies of this title call:
1-877-421-READ (7323)
or please visit our web site at
www.pleasantwordbooks.com

If you enjoyed this quality custom published book,
drop by our web site for more books and information.

www.winepressgroup.com
"Your partner in custom publishing."

Printed in the United States
65293LVS00001B/1-60